Story title	Page

His wife, his one and only love is dead. Bank manager William Travis has gone off on his own to think about the past and to consider his own future. How soon would they catch up with him?

Willie's Place

William H Travis pulls down the peak of his baseball cap, re-positions his forearms on the esplanade railings, sees the age mottled backs of his hands as a mapped-out archipelago of islands. He looks up at the moving sea, blurred now by tears. Oh Tina … Tina … Tina He thinks about the years of marriage and mortgage and moderation in all things and about Tina changing from girl-friend into mistress into wife into mother into grand-mother. Now, this minute, he asks himself, how do you live without her? Well, you just do, William Travis, he answers himself. Or you just don't.

He looked around. They'd missed all this, Tina almost but perhaps not quite as much as himself. The open road and the free of charge freedom, ever-shifting seas and skies and this iodine air, this calling of the seabirds. The folk clubs and jazz festivals of their early life together.

Oh yes, and the singing and the songs. He tried to remember when and why the two of them had walked out on all that; sold out, really. Security, they'd told each other, for once not looking into each other's eyes. Might they really have fallen off the edge of the world or something if their feet and their minds hadn't become so firmly fixed on the so-called property ladder? If they'd managed without the nine to five career, without all that stuff? 'You've a lovely voice, Bill, everyone knows that, like waves on the shingle,' she'd told him, straight faced. 'Pity about the way you look. With better looks and a few more muscles – yes,

1

you could have been a contender!' Cheeky monkey. He smiles, feels the cold drying of the tears in the creases around his mouth and in his moustache.

But the music. Oh, the music! The gift of hearing it, not just listening to it. Really hearing it, storing it in your head, bringing it out anytime you wanted - even if only in the bathroom like everybody does but perfect, note perfect. He shakes his head... bankers don't sing Hank Williams or early Elvis or Willie Nelson, not in public anyway. William Travis's right foot takes up the rhythm that comes uninvited to his head. He hums the intro, sings that one of Willie's, soft and slow; *Well, hello there... My, it's been a long, long time... How'm I doin'? ... Oh, I guess I'm doin' fine ...'* He stops, blinking behind his glasses, somehow aware he's no longer on his own. He puts up his hand to remove any vestiges of tears, turns around. She's pretty, the girl with the baby buggy. Perhaps about his daughter Deb's age, mid twenties? Bit taut around the eyes and dressed by no means well although neat and tidy enough. In her buggy looking up at him there's a round faced, round eyed baby, alongside it a six string guitar. The girl takes up where he's left off, begins to sing; *It's been so long now ... But it seems now ... It was only yesterday ... Gee, ain't it funny ... How time slips away.'*

William touches his cap, claps his hands.

She says, 'Thank you, sir. I think, maybe we should sing together, no?' Strong accent, probably eastern European. Her laugh is tentative and without affectation. The long blonde hair unfurls in the breeze, enwrapping the pale triangle of her face. She turns into the wind, strokes back errant strands. 'Sir, you know *Whiskey River*?'

William Travis strikes a Willie Nelson pose, holds an imaginary microphone close to his mouth, tilts up the brim of his imaginary Stetson, sings *Whiskey river don't run dry ...don't let her memory talk to me ...'* As in all the bathrooms of his life, in his head he's listening to the audience reaction, the yelling and cheering subsiding now so that they can hear the words as clearly as he sees them in his mind… good, simple country words to drown out any bad memories; to tell them, each one of them that they are not alone, help to explain the sorrows of the world

The sea front café is nice and warm and heavy with the odours of fried food. Their plastic seats are not un-comfortable. By the time they've finished their second cups of coffee it's raining outside and by then the baby whose name is Hugo has let it be known that it's time for him also to have something. By then, too, William has learned that the girl is 'legal' - a legal refugee, a young, recently widowed nurse who'd not that long ago come here from Croatia carrying a foetus, a thing that had had nothing to do with her and everything to do with the war in the Balkans even though, right now, she'd grown to love it, her burden, very much. *It*, of course, had become *him*, Hugo. And William has learned that her name is something unpronounceable beginning with a P that she's changed to Patsy out of deference to 'my best lady singer, Patsy Cline.' In exchange the girl, P whatever, has learned about his retirement and his ambitious, successful, adult children and his now not so small grandchildren. Also about the life and the death and the recent funeral of his wife, slightly delayed for the autopsy though he hasn't said that. And naturally he hasn't told her anything about the circumstances of Tina's death, nor what could very likely be the eventual outcome, nor about why he's here in Hastings waiting for the knock on his hotel room door or the closing of the waters of the English channel above his head;   whichever might now come first.

P whatever picks up her baby, opens her coat, lifts up her sweater and applies an eager Hugo to a darkly swollen nipple. William blinks, feels the hot skin-flooding of his face, looks out across the road, across a now rain-ringed esplanade at the white topped waves and wind-weaving gulls. Noticing his embarrassment this Patsy says, 'You not like? Oh, I am sorry, I should go out to ladies.'

He coughs. 'No, please, it's not a problem. I mean, after my lot, you'd think…' he coughs again. 'I have to move on now, anyway.'

'Listen, you will come to our club, please?' she says, changing the subject in the way that she does. 'Tonight? You like. It is good. Good country and western, yes?' She leans forward, her hand shielding the back of Hugo's head against any possible contact with the edge of the table. 'Sometime I sing. This place, it is like for you, because called Willie's Place.' She laughs delightedly. 'Willie's Place in South Street.'

William Travis hasn't wanted any of this. It isn't why he's here. Now he wants to leave. He hesitates, feeling awkward, looking away. 'We'll have to see but I don't really know. Perhaps I'm a bit too old for that kind of thing.'

'Old? No, not old, William. Many old and many young. Willie Nelson is old I think. And Johnny Cash. And Dolly, even. But it is OK, William.' Her face now settles into a kind of sadness. 'I think maybe you do not feel so good to have us here in your country; this I understand.' The baby's tiny fist closes about her forefinger.

Not like 'us' being 'here'? Oh God, he thinks, she's probably right. Well, up to today she might have been, but now does it matter how William Travis feels about immigrants? He pushes back his chair, gets up, takes out a twenty pound note and puts it on to the table, says, 'Look, Patsy, please take this; you know, in case I can't make it tonight? I'd like to buy a drink or two for yourself and your friends. And welcome to England, Patsy. In time you'll find us …' He stops himself, tells himself to forget the homilies. No more bloody homilies. Please. All his life he's been dishing them out: at the bank, to neighbours, to friends, to relatives. Not now, not any more.

She shrugs, unsmiling, nods her thanks as a down-covered cannonball of a head thrusts itself forward, again and then again, settles down to the next slow pull. And whilst William H Travis stands there his new ex-friend sings quietly the opening lines to Patsy Cline's *Leavin' On Your Mind*, her English a perfect Alabama American. Reverting to her usual voice she says, 'You stay good, William. It will be OK ... for your wife, I am sorry ... I know this already. Listen, you sing good, very good.' By then every one of the few in the place has heard her music and seems to be doing their best to listen to what the young girl with the baby at her breast might be saying to that old man.

They've tracked him down. Well, going on holiday without leaving a forwarding address or a mobile on live is not the same as running away, is it? All he'd wanted was a few days of time and space. He'd told Debbie and George as much, hadn't he? Bless them, no doubt they'd been happy for the chance to slot themselves back into their own ludicrously over-busy lives. But now the police have located him, probably through the hotel's credit card verification and he's been quite pleasantly surprised by the care in their approach. No uniforms knocking on hotel doors after all, just the phone call to his room early in the evening, the very minimum degree of coercion in the suggestion that he might perhaps like to help by coming down to the station? It's a woman's voice; 'Sergeant Palmer', she introduces herself as. 'Just a few questions, Mr Travis,' she tells him. 'Something about the recent tragedy... actually ... and actually, Inspector Bellicom from Wood Green's waiting here. And, oh, there's an unmarked police car outside the hotel, the weather having turned so foul and all. Please look out for the white Mondeo, sir, is that all right?'

Inspector Bellicom is dressed in a well-cut civilian suit. He is male, black and friendly. The one who'd telephoned, the uniformed Sergeant Palmer is very female, young, white and just as friendly. Would he like a cup of tea and a biscuit? Yes, thank you, he tells them; that would be most welcome. The sergeant picks up the phone to organise it.

Introductions over now, the Inspector says; 'We're sorry to bother you on your holiday, Mr Travis. Just a few questions. Would you mind if we record our chat?'

'I've no objection, Inspector.'

'Thank you.' He switches on, then: 'Time, eighteen ten; date, Thursday October twenty third; place, Hastings police station interview room two. In attendance Sergeant Palmer and myself, Inspector Victor Bellicom of Wood Green. And Mister William Travis. Just for the record sir, you are Mr William Travis of 16 Muntjak Gardens, Wood Green in London?'

'Yes, I am.'

'You are sixty one years of age and a retired bank executive?'

'That's right.' He smiles. 'They used to call us 'managers', Inspector.'

Sergeant Palmer: 'Please help yourself to milk and sugar, Mister Travis.'

'Thank you.'

Inspector Bellicom says, 'Tea? No thanks, sergeant. Now, Mister Travis, you are of course aware that the coroner's report stated that your wife's death was caused by barbiturate poisoning, self administered whilst the balance of her mind was disturbed?'

'Yes.'

'We have received certain new information that could contradict the coroner's self administration comment, Mister Travis. Would this surprise you?'

'Inspector, I am not young and I am a bit tired and no, nothing would surprise me. However I should perhaps point out that elderly people suffering Alzheimer's dementia often have periods of lucidity during which they may wonder about the logic of their continuing lives.'

'Yes, sir. May I ask you to answer my question, please?'

'Certainly. No, it would not surprise me.'

'Then my next question is simply this; did you yourself administer barbiturates to your wife?'

'Yes, indirectly I did, Inspector.'

Pause, clearing of throat; 'Please repeat that, sir.'

'Yes, I did administer them. I handed the barbiturate pills to my wife and my wife put them into her mouth.'

'And you did not think to inform anybody of this, previous to today?'

'Nobody asked me, Inspector, not directly anyway. And I would point out that I acted under instruction, even if quite willingly.'

'Instruction? Who's instruction would that be, then, Mister Travis?'

'My wife's instruction, Inspector. Remember that this was a matter that until now has been private, only between the two of us. I was acutely aware of how controversial - and how damaging to the happiness of our children and their children my actions could be. I suspect that, in her own fashion Tina also was conscious of this.'

'Yes. Mister Travis. At this point I have to caution you that anything you say may be taken down and used in evidence. You do understand - I mean, you understand the seriousness of your admission?'

'Yes, of course. I believe I just said as much.'

Another, more lengthy pause, sounds of fingers drumming on table top, then; 'I am not prepared to carry on with this matter pending advice. For the record I am terminating this interview at eighteen thirty four hours.' He switches off, sits back, shaking his head. 'Sergeant, I think I'll have some of that tea now, please.'

'Yes sir.' She picks up the telephone.

'Sergeant?'

'Yes, sir?'

'There's no special hurry.'

'Right, sir.' She nods her understanding, puts down the telephone, goes out, closes the door behind her.

'Mister Travis - '

'Please, Inspector, I'm 'William.' 'Mister Travis' was your bank manager. Remember those, Inspector?'

'Yes? Never go in my bank these days.' The Inspector is smiling. 'Never need to. Do all my banking stuff through the Net or someone on the phone in Outer Mongolia or wherever.' The inspector leans forward to speak, but more quietly now. 'I wish you'd not made that admission, sir - I mean, William. We know the pills were prescribed for you. 'Information received', as we put it. But we were hoping you'd just deny everything so I could get back to town in time to get some sleep and you could get on with your holiday. You know, you aren't the first to be faced with a problem like the one you had. Nor the first to come up with that answer. You'd be very surprised. Its just they don't normally own up to it, not straight out like that.' He sighed. 'It's the ones who find that kind of so-called 'remedy' when there's no real problem. It's finding the vital difference, that's what counts to me - actually to most of us.'

'You asked me and I answered with the truth. Funny old word, 'truth', these days, eh? You know, it may be regrettable but even if I had something to lose I'd still feel obliged to tell the truth.'

The policeman shakes his head. 'Something to lose, you say? Of course you have something to lose. I doubt the DPP'd dare not recommend proceedings. Not now, not after this.' He nods towards the recording machine.

'Inspector, I have to accept what you say. Anyway, will it be all right if I finish my holiday here?' He wondered why Bellicom hadn't asked why he had himself been prescribed the pain killers. He must have known. 'Information received'. From the pharmacy, no doubt. If he had asked he'd have had to tell the truth about that as well; he'd have had to tell him about his very own very bad companion, the pancreatic cancer that had already reached out to get its roots into, well, just about everything. And then, after him, who on earth would have looked after Tina? Not George in between his transatlantic shuttling and extreme surgical operations on his patients' brains. No way. And certainly not Debs, God bless her; Debs with her eyes and her heart set on some kind of conquest of the City of London. Nursing home? Tina had extracted his promise; definitely no nursing homes.

The Inspector shakes his head, stands up, paces around with his hands behind his back. He stops, looks down on him, says, 'You still have not mentioned the obvious mitigating circumstances, William. I'll tell you, personally I have to say I'm very sorry because you seem like a good man. But a bloody cool one, I will say that much.' He jabs a finger at a button on the recording machine. A compartment opens and the inspector removes the tape, puts it into his pocket.

Untypically, the words come out before he has really considered them. 'It's a bit late for you to be going back to town now, Inspector. Why don't you stay down here? Look, I met a very nice young lady earlier today. She invited me to a country and western club of some kind this evening. You could come with me if you like.'

'Country and western? My God, man, you've just admitted to one of the most serious crimes - and now you tell me you picked up with some girl and want me to - I ...' he shakes his head but the smile has started and has spread and white teeth have appeared in the good looking face and then come the chuckles and the Inspector's laughter and his own as well, louder and louder, and when Sergeant Palmer arrives with the tray and the Inspector tells her about it she starts in laughing, too, specially when the

Inspector says he wouldn't care but black men aren't into country & western anyway and William says oh yes they are, haven't you ever heard of the great Charlie Pride? But finally they've straightened up enough for Inspector Bellicom to tell him to get off, report to Wood Green police station Monday morning. Please. He and the sergeant would now need to test run the tape.

You know how it is when you're walking into something by your own choice and suddenly come to know it's such a big mistake but you can't easily retreat? Well, that's how it is with this Willie's Place. It's almost empty for a start and you only find out later that you arrived far too early. By that time you should be feeling very conspicuous in your holiday-smart chinos and linen jacket, being surrounded by more and more of the cowboy boots and silver buckled belts and well-fringed wash leather dresses and those big, wide brimmed cowboy hats.

There's a dancing area with chairs and tables all around it in a horseshoe and there's a stage, and there's a DJ with a microphone prancing and banging around in high heels and tasselled, worn leather chaps, silver spurs jingle-jangling. But you like it here by then and you know most of the country standards the man puts on for the line dancing and there's groups from four up to everyone in the place except you when he plays Achey Breakey Heart. They're all linked up at the shoulders, heads down to watch the careful placement of feet, side to side, step forward and back, hands free to clap and twirl. Heels on floorboards; bang, tap, bang, slide. Tina would have loved it.

By ten o clock you've forgotten how tired you thought you were. The third pint's going down exceptionally well and you can feel the alcohol but you've never been a let-it-all-out type drinker and you're not going to become one now, are you? So you empty your glass and ask the substantial cowgirl with the white Stetson serving behind the bar for a bottle of the fizzy, peach flavoured water.

When they play Willie Nelson's version of Georgia On My Mind the lights dim down and the dance lines break up into slow moving couples, shuffling, swaying, hats getting in the way of their wearers' intentions. And then quite suddenly she's here, smiling up at you, pale gold hair shimmering down the sides of her face and neck, cascading over the epaulettes of the red and white shirt, and you cannot help but remember what's there under the shirt. You hope your blushes can't be seen in this lighting. She glances at the dance floor, eyebrows raised in question. You shake your head, ask her what she'd like to drink. You're looking around for her partner and now it's her turn to smile and shake her head.

Georgia finishes. The DJ returns to centre stage, announces in his nearly convincing Southern States drawl, 'OK, it's karaoke time, folks, and tonight we got our own Patsy Cline, right here..... Come on up, Patsy ... Crazy'

Patsy waves to acknowledge the cheers, turns to him, says, 'Please do not you go away, William.' She climbs on to the stage.

She's good, really good. It's not just the voice, it's the depth of meaning she manages to inject into the words of Willie Nelson as long since immortalised by Patsy Cline; *I'm crazy...crazy for feeling so lonely ... I'm crazy for feeling so blue ...I knew that you'd love me so long as you wanted ... and then someday you'd leave me for somebody new ...* Well, you did, Tina, you did. Please, God, I hope you're looking after her. He has to take a long, deep breath, eyes hard shut.

It's not just himself. He can see the effect the singer and the song are having on everyone else, most of them not dancing any more, lining the stage front, looking up at her, swaying ... *Worry, why do I -* The words are on a big screen, the karaoke ball bouncing across it syllable to syllable even though Patsy's the only one singing the words and she doesn't need to look.

In the middle of the song she stops, holds up her hand, turns to the DJ. The music stops, too, and the screen goes blank. She speaks into the microphone to re-assure them all. 'It is no problem. I go on, OK? But you know this song, Crazy? You know it is a song written by the great Willie Nelson, no?' More of the silence. The DJ looks baffled, not amused, obviously wanting to intervene.

William Travis knows what's coming now, looks around for the means of escape.

She goes on, 'Well, back there by the bar? This is Willie. He should sing this song with me, for you. You come up here, William, yes?'

Faces are turned to him and he can see there all the doubts and the reflection of his own embarrassment. Then somebody claps and then some others and the cowgirl-bargirl has reached across to place her Stetson on his head. He leaves the safety of the bar. The alcohol's at work, he knows that, but sing? With more than the usual necessity to concentrate he walks to the stage. How the hell is he going to sing with a throat so dry he can't even swallow?

Patsy's eyes sparkle blue in the brilliance of the stage lighting. She reaches up, tweaks down the brim of his cowboy hat, turns to the DJ. 'OK, Johnnie. Now we go again with *Crazy*, yes?'

The intro starts and he looks out and down on the faces, the smoke, the backlit bar and sees there the expectancy and hope and he sees or senses something else, something undefinable. He swallows, feels quite suddenly that this is going to be all right, knows exactly where and when he's going to come in on this. He looks at the pretty, upturned face of an age to be his daughter and this Patsy smiles back at him and William Travis sings the song *Crazy* to her, and for her, and for Tina, too, knowing his voice sounds rich and deep and true, like - like waves on shingle? And the girl/woman Patsy comes in at times and sings it back to him and somehow the two of them know when it's best for them to do it together. And by the time they've finished the song, William H Travis has become the great Willie Nelson and the music has stopped and he barely notices the silence or the first accolade from Johnny the DJ, nor then clapping and the cheering and the rebel yells. He raises the hat, winks across all the heads through wreaths of cigarette smoke at the big cowgirl jumping up and down behind the bar, hands clapping above her head.

The people don't want to let go of the two of them and he knows what it is now because he doesn't want to let go of them, either. It's a here and now love affair, isn't it? A love affair without touching, the two of them in love with the hundred and the hundred with the two of them.

By himself he goes on to sing them the so very well remembered *Jambalaya*, Hank Williams' epic, his foot tapping to the driving rhythm of the song. She follows on from there with Patsy Cline's *I Fall To Pieces*, the amazing purity of her voice a silver stream by moonlight.

Halfway through his next song William Travis notices Inspector Bellicom and a Sergeant Palmer now in jeans and a check shirt, gazing at him from their position with backs to the bar. They're wearing the same rapt expressions as the others. William lifts his hand in salute, *'I've been dreaming like a child … since the cradle broke the bough … and there's nothing I can do about it now* The two of them wave back at him and he can see Bellicom holding something up - a tape? Yes, a tape. *The* tape? Bellicom's free hand points to it, his finger describing a cross and then a circle. No more? William understands. He nods, lowers his head, looks down and sideways at Patsy, sings on, *'I could cry for the time I've wasted … but that's a waste of time and tears … and I know just what I'd change … if I went back in time somehow … but there's nothing I can do about it now …'*

He comes to the finish and when the applause starts to die down holds up his hand for silence, speaks into the microphone. He thanks Patsy and Johnny the DJ and thanks all of them here for listening to them or rather, to the songs that he and Patsy have sung for them. He says there will be more songs and the cheering breaks out afresh, with Victor and the Sergeant Palmer whose first name he doesn't know, joining in. He tells everyone, then, that this is the first time he's sung in front of strangers since he was twenty years old and he hopes they will forgive him a little ring rustiness and he hopes they will get used to him being here. He's planning to move down here to Hastings, he says. Patsy squeezes his hand. He finishes with; 'But listen to me, folks; being older is as good as being young, you know. Maybe better. Certainly a whole lot easier. And like Willie says, there's nothing I can do about it now. I've been especially lucky to have found my new friend, here. And through her all of you here at Willie's Place. What the future holds I cannot say, but there are times when you know it can't get any better than right here, right now; just like this is for me.'

He steps back, looks down on she who could have been Tina but who is in reality the timeless stranger he has known all of his life. In her eyes is the shine of stars, of things unknowable.

And still the singing and the songs; all the songs in Willie's Place.

The end

Willie's Place had its genesis in a steamy little karaoke bar in downtown Dubai. It was there that I watched a middle aged gentleman in a dark pinstriped suit and sober tie turn into a convincingly all-out Mick Jagger. People can live more lives than one, right?

Childless Norma and Harry Sikorsky have been growing apart for years. Harry stands at the bottom of their garden looking up at the old chestnut tree. He has taken a lover. He has also come up with an idea to resolve everything once and for all.

The Ending Tree.

The massive horse chestnut seemed to be protesting, as well it might. All those creaks and groans and whisperings to the wind. Hurrying, he finished his ragged destruction of one more root, making it seem a natural break. Feeling like an assassin, like some kind of a traitor, he filled this latest hole and, job done, walked casually back up the vegetable garden pushing the wheelbarrow with its cargo of pick and crowbar, shovel and axe.

Pausing in front of the toolshed he turned to observe the lean of the tree over their cottage. How could anyone living here - two hundred years ago? - have allowed such a monster to take root so close to the cottage? Now it towered close enough to drop its autumnal fruits directly on to their roof, shiny-brown nuts and their spiky yellow-green casings bouncing and splitting and sliding down the slates to block the cottage's gutters. And never mind the sticks thrown up by the village boys to dislodge more of them. The sticks that so angered Norma. He glanced at his watch. She wouldn't be back from her Womens' Institute for a half hour yet. What in hell did the WI find to talk about all the time?

He looked up at the November sky. The forecast this morning had looked pretty evil. More than promising in fact, with a south westerly gale coming in. She'd heard it as

15

well, had asked him again, 'Harry Garveston, just when are you going to get the tree people to see to that awful great thing? I'm fed up with telling you about it. You won't be happy till it's levelled the place and killed us all, will you?' She'd sat there looking at him, waiting for an answer, the proverbial sack of shit, un-made up, hair all over. And just who had she meant by '*us all*'? Him, her and her fat bloody cat - the three members of this happy family? 'Yes, Norma,' he'd said, mildly. 'I mean, no. It's just that a tree surgeon costs so much, dear.'

Driving the four miles to his night shift between rows of small houses with well-lit windows, he thought about the folk enjoying their fire and the telly, getting set for their nice warm beds. He'd chuck in the job right now, tonight, if it wasn't for the thing with Mandy - plus the thought of being stuck at home with Norma's nagging. Mandy! He felt the stirrings of an excitement at the thought of her - at the thought of her body actually. And he thought about the possible insurance money ... about a new freedom.

Turning in, his lights swept around a half empty works car park. Mandy's van was in its usual place, backed up against the fence, the canal behind, the lights of the factory gatehouse a hundred metres away. He parked a discreet distance from her, glanced at his watch. Twenty minutes to clocking in time. He got out of the car, locked up, glanced around. Nobody out yet from the afternoon shift and the bulk of the night people still to appear. He looked up at the night sky, turning to face the wind. It was definitely rising. He hurried across to the van, turned the handle of the rear door. 'Well hello there, sir,' whispered a demure Mandy. The woman, *his* woman, was a palely reclining form in the van's dark interior. He climbed in quickly and as he closed the rear doors behind him caught the scent of her, could sense her animal warmth. And now he could feel her. Demure didn't go too well with being stark naked, did it.

Even above the pounding of the machines, by two in the morning the rise and fall howl of the wind across the factory roof and the rattling and banging of loosening sheets of corrugated dominated everything. The sound distracted him as much as did the sight of Mandy, laughing and flirting her way around her quality assurance routine. Several times he needed to remind himself about safety. Tonight the machine seemed determined to trap him. Mandy! He loved her but why did she have to behave like that? But as always after sex with her he got to worrying about stuff like frying pans and fires. And then thought about the tree, that great old ending tree. He shivered.

At four o clock, with two hours of the shift still to go management decided to stop production. According to the Tannoy message the factory structure was in danger of becoming unsafe. There were follow up warnings about conditions on the roads and as the guys washed up to go home they were all discussing the weather, talking about the possibility of it exceeding even the mighty storm of eighty seven.

He hurried outside, bending into the wind, forced at times, between one step and another, to pause in order to keep his balance. Once in the car he sat still, eyes closed, feeling it rocking on its springs under the power of successive gusts. The warble of his mobile phone shocked his heart into chest hammering action. He took a deep breath, reluctant to answer it, steeling himself. The giant oak must have come down. Oh God, had Norma been hurt? Had she...? Now that push had come to shove he hoped not. Just his fair share of the insurance money, that's all he wanted. Please? Throat dry, he prepared himself to be distraught. How had the police got his mobile number? He really wasn't feeling too good. Finally he cleared his throat, switched on but it was only Mandy. 'What's for afters then? We've a bit of spare time now, Harry, yes?' She laughed her husky, imitation Marilyn of a laugh. He turned his head, seeing her van still in position.

'Great idea sweetheart but I've just had a call,' he lied. 'Problems at home.'

'Yeah? I'm sorry. Oh well, spurned again. Listen, give my love to Norma, won't you.' She giggled into the phone; 'Naughty night.'

'Right; that I will not do.' Illogically he wondered whether she and his wife Norma might even be talking. They'd certainly been at school together. Not that his wife was on his and Mandy's conversational agenda. No more than was the chestnut tree, for that matter. 'So I'll see you soon then,' he finished.

'By-eee,' said Mandy. 'See me in your dreams, yeah.'

He let in the clutch, started to move off. Now he definitely did not feel so good. This tree thing had to be the most stupid ... Christ, what if it had come down, what if it had actually killed her? He felt himself close to panic.

It was a slow ride. Branches and other detritus littered the roads. The radio news bulletins carried stories of destruction, hardship and heroism. One set of lights seemed to be stuck on red. As he inched his way across the junction the car moved sideways on its springs and a whole telephone kiosk that must have broken free from outside the sub post office came wheeling and bouncing by, glass and loose wires flailing and flying.

How could he have done this thing with the tree? Why couldn't the two of them have just spoken in a civilised way like they did on the telly? 'Sorry Norma, sorry it hasn't worked for us. It's got nothing to do with kids, I mean, with not having any. It's just one of those things. Listen, I'm sorry, but I have to leave you, OK?' Oh yes. Oh no. The conversation he would never have dared to have with his embittered wife.

At last he drew up outside his home, a wild rain now impacting the car in great, near-horizontal flurries, he could hardly believe it because the cottage was intact, its windows blind and black. In the car's headlights the old chestnut tree bent impossibly low over the roof, a protective arm thrown around someone's shoulder.

The car door was almost torn from its hinges as he got out. He bent low into the weather, raindrops pinging away at his scalp through plastered hair. Above the sounds of the storm the tree seemed to be shouting at him. He wanted to tell it; 'Sorry, tree, I didn't mean it.' But he had; he had meant it. He fumbled with the keys, pushed inside, switched on the lights, shouted out, 'Norma, for God's sake get yourself up. Come on, let's get out of here, that bloody tree's coming down.' He threw open the bedroom door. No Norma. Bed undisturbed. Not understanding, he rushed into the spare bedroom, the one they had set out as a nursery but still unoccupied all these years later. This was the room that had always made her cry, always made him want to cry. But no Norma. He sat down heavily on the edge of the cot, looking without seeing the Peter Pans and Wendys air-dancing hand in hand across the wallpaper, Tinkerbells in the lead and the Lost Boys bringing up the rear. Then this tearing and crashing and all the darkness and Harry Galveston was somewhere else; somewhere in another place.

Everything hurt. He wanted to go back to sleep but Norma was talking to him. No way would the woman let him sleep. He opened his eyes. This bed was surrounded by curtains. Oh, God! There was the smell of disinfectant and fresh-cut flowers, the taste of metal and blood. Hospital. And Norma. Norma? Yes, and looking better than in a long, long time. All dressed up and smiling. Quite obviously, quite unbelievably, quite unforgivably happy. He tried to move, quickly forgot about it. The pain! When he tried again to speak he could barely hear the murmur of his own voice. It hurt just to try. He could feel the wires with his swollen tongue, see the strange metal geometry at the downwards edge of his vision. Now it all came rushing back. 'Where were you, then, Norma? What the hell has happened?' It was a croak, not a voice.

'What, Harry? What was that?' she asked, leaning over.

He repeated his question but she still couldn't understand him. She said, 'Sorry, Harry.' She didn't sound in any way sorry. 'But hi there. I don't know what it is you're trying to say. Listen, it was that chestnut tree, Harry, just like I said, remember? It came down on the cottage. I'd thought it would so my friend came for me and I stayed with him. I went back when you were due off shift, found the house all smashed up and the car out in front. I called the firemen and police. They found you in there. Harry, that was the day before yesterday.'

Now he really could hear himself ; hear the moaning.

With more softness than she'd had in her voice when speaking to him in a long, long time, she said, 'I'm sorry. They said you were found in the nursery. I am sorry.'

He tried to say she hadn't used that nursery word in a long time, nor the *sorry* for that matter, but it probably came out as just another moan.

'No, I still can't understand you. But listen, I've got some more news for you. I'm pregnant again. Better late than never, isn't it? And maybe better luck this time, eh?'

What? Pregnant? Was this some hellish kind of a dream? Forgetting again, he went to open his mouth and tried to shout out aloud. The pain! His mind was back in top gear now. He tried to tell her, he tried to say, 'I have to tell you … ' but it was just too difficult.

As if this time she really had understood him she said, 'You've got nothing to tell me that I didn't already know. We don't need to speak about that, all right? I've had a word with a certain someone from my class and you needn't worry. That lady always was a bit of a tramp with the boys. For her there's plenty more where my husband came from and by the way I've told them you won't be going back to work in their stupid factory. You have much more important things to think about now.' Norma's whole persona was different, had somehow changed, become more authoritative, less demanding. 'For instance, holidays, where to live and all that.'

'The insurance,' he tried to say but, oh hell, no way.

'No, Harry.' She smiled sweetly. 'I can see what you're thinking. Not me and you on holiday, Harry. Me and my friend. You see, well, I said I'd wait to tell you but I can't. Where the roots of the tree came up out of our ground they found a load of old coins that had broken out of a rotten old box. There were loads, different ones, most of them gold, and a lot of other old stuff, too. Really ancient, so they say. Scattered all over, it was.'

His attempt at a what? came out as just a faint sob.

'Harry, don't you try and speak, all trussed up like a Christmas turkey like you are. It took us hours and hours to pick out all the coins we've got so far and they say there'll likely to be more of them still there. They said that was probably why the chestnut was planted there, to hide the chest under the chestnut, see, Harry.' She giggled.

Treasure? Christ almighty. And Norma, actually making a bloody joke? And who in hell was this bloody *friend* of her's, anyway? The fist on his good arm clenched all by itself. He blinked, furious with her and this - this bastard whoever he was. Self pity now so blurred his vision.

She stood up, smiling down on him, the cruel light of cruel in her eyes. 'The police have a night and day guard on the roots, Harry. It's the coins, you see. There's bound to be more of them than we've found already. And they've got these people in, arbor somethings? Tree experts, anyway. The Inspector wants to find out why it came down. Or how ... what for ... And it's to do with the insurance, too - you not being able to benefit from it - or something. Of course that doesn't apply to me, though. Anyway, I have to go.

Jim's taking me for lunch. Somewhere nice, I hope. Get well soon, Mister Galveston.'

Ends

Shakespeare's Hamlet said 'Thus conscience doth make cowards of us all', and the theme of The Ending Tree *is very much based on that. Furthermore we once lived in rural Hampshire in a very old thatched cottage overhung by a giant elm (not horse chestnut!) tree. When strong winds blew you could feel the earth moving and the flexing of those mighty roots, or imagined you could ...*

Claws

A fisherman's life is hard. And being the son of one is harder still if fishing is not a path the son wishes to tread. Sixteen years old Jamie Alexander knows he is gay, and gay - even in secret - is unacceptable to a widowed father, here in a remote Scottish community. But the sea! The sea can ask the most unexpected of questions and can deliver the most complete of answers. ...

Claws

Lady Rose sank from the top of a swell into its following trough, helping him gain a couple more turns. Blue polyester fishing line vibrated under the strain, jumping off droplets of seawater, biting into the fleshy heel and the fingers of his right hand. He leaned over the side, peering down through the deep, dark green. It wasn't what he'd thought. Not just a bunch of weed. Some long lost, barnacle crusted anchor? He stood up as straight as he could on the wet deck of the pitching, rolling little crabber.

'Come on, Jamie, we've enough bait.' His father had finished stacking the latest chain of pots. 'Cut that line away now. Only this lot to shoot then we're done for today.' He looked up at the dark-bellied cloud then at the violence of white water smashing into the foot of the cliff. 'Just as well, so I'm thinking.'

Jamie gained another metre or two, leaned out again over the gunwhale, knife in his free hand. The thing on the end of his line didn't seem to be moving but ...yes ...he sucked in his breath, suddenly quite sure. 'Hey Dad, it's a damn great lobster! Look at it: just huge it is.'

His father was alongside him now. 'Hey - right enough; it bloody is, so. Easy now; very careful, son. He's the line wrapped around one claw. If you panic him, if he starts to move about he'll likely shake himself free.' He bent lower to see more clearly. 'Holy ... biggest one I ever saw.'

Jamie steadily gained line, ignoring the salty sting of the line cuts. With the giant just below the surface his father leaned overboard, grasped the massive shell in both orange gloved hands, heaved it up and over the gunwhale, placed it down on the deck. They stood there, just staring, in awe of the creature's sheer bulk, at the beauty of its indigo, barnacled-studded form, motionless now but for the twitching of its antennae. A wheel of seagulls were screaming out the news over the thunder of wave on rock and the contented pfut-pfut of *Lady Rose*'s idling diesel.

'He'll go seven kilos if an ounce; maybe eight,' James's father said. 'Right enough, he's the biggest I ever heard of from round here. Maybe anywhere.' He crouched down, with care relieving one giant claw of a turn of line and some strands of seaweed. 'Once they get to half this size they don't get themselves caught. Much too big for any trap.' As if concurring, their captive flexed its carapace, slapped a great tail to the deck, levered itself upwards then crashed down, legs moving quickly in futile unison. Its claws, thick as a man's calf, opened slowly, snapped shut. 'Keep yourself well clear, Jamie. This one, he will have your fingers off if he gets the chance.' He unsheathed his knife, again looked around at the cliff. 'We've drifted well over. I'd Best get her underway now.'

Jamie said, 'What we going to do with him, Dad?'

'Cut his claw muscles first, what else? In the tank he'll kill the others and all the crabs, unless.'

'But we could let the crabs go and take this one back on his own. Couldn't you fix up an aquarium, charge the visitors to come and have a look?' Jamie Alexander wouldn't be around but he tried not to think about that. He turned his head away, for his father must not catch sight of the sudden tears.

'There's best part of fifty kilo of crab in that tank. Let them go? No way, boy. But that's not a bad idea of yours. And sure he'll be too tough for the table, so I'm thinking.' He made up his mind. 'There's the old water tank on the pier for him while we think about a proper aquarium. OK. Use some of that netting to wrap him so he can't do any damage then put him in the tank with the others while I get her clear of the rocks. Listen, son, be careful now.' He disappeared into the wheel house. *Lady Rose* jolted into gear, stern settling, bows lifting as she picked up speed on the turn away from the cliff, digging her bow into the seas. Splats of saltwater flew back, showering the deck. The monster moved a little as if in appreciation. Jamie draped the netting across him, rolled up and tied fast the bundle then dropped the whole thing into the deck tank. 'Good luck, old fellow,' he whispered. He watched as the mass of crabs and the few small lobsters in there scuttled clear, scrambling over each other to get out of the way of such a master carnivore.

Jamie towelled off inside the wheelhouse out of the wind and the spray. His father didn't seem so big these days; he was himself as tall, but he still looked good in that rugged way of his. The face below the salt-stained baseball cap had been tanned and creased by weather, time and troubles; and by a life at sea in small boats. Whilst he'd been at the feathering for bait-fish there'd been his father's fake-casual questions. Questions about school and what he might want to do with his schooling and/or with himself, questions he'd answered as briefly and as indirectly as possible and never in the way that he'd have wanted: *Art, Dad, art; that's what I want to do.* But there would never have been any understanding and it was all academic now anyway. He'd tried to steer the talk around to the forbidden subject - to talk to his father about his mother. But his father would never talk about that she in whose dark recess his son had been formed.

He lit the gas ring, put on the kettle, swilled out two mugs. 'That lobster, you said he was old, Dad. How old do you think - and why the he anyway? Couldn't it be a female?'

'I've told you before, all the really big ones are male. How old? No-one knows what age a lobster can get to. Some say more than sixty.' He chuckled, his eyes moving automatically from around the horizon to the compass and back again. 'He's one hell of a lot older than you, anyway. Me too, probably.' He hesitated, then, 'Look, there's the ceilidh on tonight. Let's the both of us go, OK? Celebrate? Spread the good word, give the girls a treat, what do you say?'

Jamie thought about Kurt sitting in front of his PC in suburban Seattle waiting for him to come on line. The lurch to his stomach. 'Not tonight, Dad,' he said. 'I'm not feeling so good. Anyway, I've got stuff to do.' His thoughts returned to the ancient lobster, about how the beautiful creature had seemed to watch him with those bright, stalk-swivel eyes. He wanted to go back on deck to lift the tank cover, say something to him; something stupid like, 'I'm sorry'. But that would indeed be stupid and this was another and a different kind of sadness.

Jamie typed in the words without looking at the keyboard; *Well what do you reckon happens Kurt if we do it?*

With barely a pause, the reply in white letters, rolling out across the black screen. WHATS THIS PAL? NOTHING!!! JUST YOU AND ME JUST STOP BEING WHERE WE ARE. WERE JUST IN CYBER SPACE U AND ME OK. LOOK YOU'RE NOT GOING TO CHIKKEN ON ME??

No, then on an impulse, *Kurt, hows your mother going to take it?*

This time there was a pause and then OK I GUESS SHE'LL MAYBE TAKE TIME OUT FOR THE

FUNERAL!!! JAMES - YOU SAD YOU DON'T HAVE
ONE ONLY YOUR DADDY?

He knew Kurt had meant 'said', not 'sad'. *Right. I never
knew my mother - she went away.* He thought about the hoary
old village talk of police interviews, about all the innuendos
overheard down the years concerning fruitless searches for
his mother's body. On an impulse he added, *but I think she
just jumped out the window!*

GREAT!! YOU THINK??? Hey wE SAID IT THIS
IS ALL JUST CRAP OK. TAKE ANOTHER LOOK
OUT AT THE SESSPIT tell me if iTS NOT NOTHING
BUT CRAP

He looked up, stared out of the window at the two
groups of yellow pinpricks in all the blackness. The smaller
group would be the coastguard boat anchored down the
loch, the other, the more distant cluster of Glendonnell
village. His fingers moved on the keys; *Right, just crap*, he
typed, *there's the usual traffic backed up Fifth all the way to Central
Park.*

RIGHT THE PARK! THAT'S FOR WHWERE GUYS
LIKE ME AND U GO IN YIOUR GOOD OLD NYC.
THEY COME FOR US IN THERE THE BASTARDS!!

He typed, *Right - good old little old New York City. hows it
with Seattle and you Kurt.*

A few seconds ticked by then; same olD SAME OLD
SHIT.

The shout from downstairs; 'Jamie, come on now. My
pint's getting cold.'

James yelled back, as difficult as it was to sound unwell
whilst yelling, 'I don't think so, Dad. I told you. I'm not
feeling so good.' He stared at Kurt's words, hearing his
father's footsteps on the stairs, typed in, *Tomorrow OK - then
after that bye bye.*

The knock on his door. With his finger on the mouse,
the cursor on 'exit', Jamie read Kurt's final contribution;
RIGHT TOMOROW SAME TIME were gONNA JOIN

UP GET THE FUCK OUT. He tapped at the mouse, watched the screen blank out.

'Come on, son' Another knock, a conspiratorial chuckle. 'Listen, there'll be all the girls there tonight.'

Jamie shivered, got up to open the door on his father. The fisherman Alex Alexander had shaved, put on his new red shirt and his one and only suit. Dark blue, a good bit out of date, now tight across the shoulders. He'd be on the hunt for a stray lady visitor tonight. Well, he and his father might not have got around to talking about - about anything important, but after all this *was* his father, the one who'd tried his best. He fought off all the bad thoughts. 'All right, Dad; let's go. Reckon I'll survive.'

Alex Alexander's eyes flicked to the PC and back again. 'Great.' he said, 'But yourself, you're looking a bit peaky, right enough. Reckon it's all the time you spend on that bloody thing over there. God knows … maybe not good for a lad near sixteen. Still….'

Getting changed, Jamie thought about *I'll survive.* But he wouldn't, would he? Not worth it; not in Glendonnell and perhaps not anywhere. Not for a gay. Gay? He'd looked it up. Gay could mean happy so how come he wasn't? He'd looked up 'queer' as well. 'Strange', it said; or 'odd', which was definitely more like it.

Your lot call them discos, not ceilidhs which is what your Dad and the other oldies call them. This one isn't bad. In fact it's OK so far because you've been left alone which is all you want. You're standing with your bottle of Coke just inside the door. Your Dad's over by the bar with a few of his fishing and crofting pals; the ones who'll talk to him. In other words the ones not bugged by those nasty old rumours about what had happened to your mother. Most of the locals plus all their dressed up females sit with their drinks at the tables lining three sides of the hall. You wonder which of them would have known her, your mother. Would it have been any different if you'd known her yourself? Or if you knew what had happened to her?

In here everyone knows everyone except for the few visitors up nice and early for the spring salmon or a couple of early holidaymakers preferring a bit of rain and cold to the summer midges. Most of the people are talking loudly to beat the volume of music. The old DJ, Donnie Macauley, the one in the baseball hat with 'Dodgers' on it, he's up there playing his mixture of Scottish traditional and pop with the odd bit of stuff like *Now And Then* thrown in to prove how cool he really is, like, underneath. The village hall's smelling like it always does, whisky and cigarette smoke and body perfume and too much heating. There's quite a few of the kids from school hanging out over there near the stage. Oh, no! You'd seen her looking over at you. Now here she comes: Moira Ferguson, tottering a bit on unaccustomed high heels across an otherwise empty wooden dance floor, all swinging black hair and very nice legs and big buckled, low slung mini-skirt, a slice of pale belly showing above it. Donnie's started up with that oldie about Chickie Chikita or something so Moira does a bit of a tap and a twirl in the middle. A few people clap. She comes on, laughing. You know she doesn't mean anything except she's trying to be nice, thinking you need company. But where you're going you can only go to on your own. You know that much … whatever Kurt says.

'Hey, Jamie, how you doing?' Moira says.

'Not bad,' you say. You can see Craig McAllister looking. Everybody knows Moira's his and, well, he's welcome.

'They say you got a big one. Biggest ever.' She giggles. 'Lobster, right?'

'Come on.'

'You want to dance with me, Jamie?'

'You kidding?' You try to arrange your expression to convey - what?

'You don't have to do anything.' She giggles. 'Just move around a little bit while I get the old men drooling.'

'Come on, Moira. What's wrong with him, Craig?'

She reaches out, takes your bottle of Coke without asking. 'Nothing. And there's nothing wrong with you. Best looking boy in the fifth, so you are.' She's studying you, assessing the effect of what she's said. She throws back her head and the full, shiny, cherry painted lips purse up around the neck of your bottle. Now you're fixed on the whiteness, the slow movement of her throat. 'Have a drink, why don't you,' you mutter, for want of any other words.

Moira says nothing but backs away on to the floor, moving slowly, feet and body and Coke in hand beginning to go with the music, her eyes teasing, not leaving yours. You feel yourself reddening, sense the people, watching. Well fuck them. You can dance if nothing else and you do look good, you know that much. Donnie the DJ switches without a break from the Chickie thing to the other Abba about 'I am the Dancing Queen' and Moira is that and you are, too, and for a while the both of you are on your own, moving in your own space, the one that isn't cyber.

The number finishes. Moira says, breathing more quickly, 'Well, thank you, kind sir.' She hands you your Coke, turns away, walks back across the floor to Craig. Everyone seems to be watching including your Dad who winks at you, grinning embarassingly, and there's a good few of them clapping and some cheering. Donnie announces a short break and you know his short break will be a couple or so large drams and a pint of Stella. You wander back to your station by the door. You're dry so you take a drink, taste her lipstick on the neck of the bottle. Musty greasy and, and - and her. God, it's awful. You put the bottle down, slip out to the gents.

Standing at the urinal, ready to pee with your cock out in your fingers you hear them enter behind you. Craig stands up at the stall to your right, Jerry the one to your left. They're looking down at you and for now no piss will come.

Craig says, 'Hi there, James, ma old pal. How you doin' then?'

'OK thanks,' you mutter.

Jerry says, 'Yeah, right. He's his cock in his hand, right enough, Craig, all ready for action but it ain't fuckin' standing to attention. So why's that?'

You zip up, turn to go but they're between you and the door. Craig says, 'You fancying a bit of Moira Ferguson then, boy?'

'No I'm not.' You make to go past but they won't let you. 'Please?' you ask.

'Well, well, well. He don't fancy your Moira,' Jerry says. 'That's not nice for a nice boy. Reckon he's - he's a bit different, Craig?' He laughs. It's the ugly laugh in a half broken boy-man's voice and now you know that, soon, two kinds of pain are coming.

Craig has you against the wall, in his fist your best grey shirt bunched up under your chin. You can't look at him but there's the beer smell of his breath to go with the thudding of your heart. You keep your hands down by your sides, hear the sudden whine, feel a blast of hot air as the automatic hand dryer starts up alongside your ear.

Jerry's saying, 'Not so fucking gay now, gay boy, dancing queen, right?'

Over Craig's shoulder you've seen the door opening and your father coming in and you can see the shock on his face as Craig lets go of you.

'What the bloody hell d'you think you're up to?' your father says.

Craig and Jerry say nothing and for a second or two you really think they might turn on him instead and you know and they also know by the slight dropping of his shoulders that your father knows this, is waiting for them, hoping they will. But they don't. You move away from the wall and the sound of the dryer dies away. You mutter, 'It's nothing, Dad. Don't worry about it.'

Craig says, 'Sorry, Mister Alexander. Yeah, don't worry about it, OK?'

When they've gone your father says, too quietly, 'Well then, are you going to tell me about it?'

Miserably you turn away to wash your hands, say, 'It was only about Moira. It's nothing.'

'Nothing? Young Jerry Lofthouse called you 'gay'. I heard him, son. Don't tell me about 'nothing'.'

You don't say anything to that. Your father has this sick, bewildered look stuck to his face. Donnie the DJ has started up again up with a Highland Reel and there's the sound of many feet pounding wooden floorboarding.

'Jamie, you're not; are you -' His voice dropped; 'Are you gay?'

You don't want to but, 'Yes, Dad, I think so,' you whisper. You fight to keep the tears behind your eyes.

'You think so? You 'think'?'

A man comes in; an English visitor. 'Evening all,' he says, not noticing anything. 'Natives getting restless out there. Wonderful.' He laughs at his own words, stands to the urinal without seeing the sudden murder in your father's eyes.

You turn and you run.

It's cold in the house. The body heat generated by your three mile run-walk from the village hall has worn off. Nine o'clock, just gone; late afternoon in Seattle and Kurt isn't on-line. You type out your last message: *Hi Kurt. Stuff happened ghere tonight   Hey man its been real cool. We will see each other like you said, right   in cyber space sometime Take care OK.* He paused, flexing his fingers, looking out at the black blankness of the sea loch, his eyes blurring. He typed out; *U asked me about my mother and I don't really think she jumped Kurt I thought from what people have said my father did it. He pushed her. Anyway so that's it - bye from NYC.* You unplug the PC, remove its cover, detach the hard drive and put it into your pocket. It takes you only a minute or two.

Your father has left his boat's keys in the ignition, like always. A torch hangs on a peg beside the wheel but except for seeing inside the tank it isn't needed now the moon's up. The great cruciform lobster is sprawled out across the bottom, released from the netting and on his own since they had evacuated the rest of yesterday's catch to be taken off down south on the overnight Vivier truck. In the torchlight the giant lies there silhouetted against white plastic, still and dark and full of menace. A cluster of bubbles rose from the air tube trapped beneath his massive carapace. 'We're going where we want to be, you and me,' you whisper. His antennae move slowly as if in a kind of understanding.

Lady Rose's engine starts first time. You untie the mooring lines and jump back on to her deck, engage reverse and then forward, rotating the wheel to swing her away from the pier and into the night. Once out of shelter you find that the seas have steepened, their crests foaming white in the moonlight. Windscreen wipers have to work hard as you steer the heaving crabber along the cliffs to the place, as near as you can work it out, where you caught the lobster those few long hours ago. You kill the engine, go out on deck, take the hard drive out of your pocket. Over the sounds of wind on sea and and sea on sea and sea on rock you shout, 'Bye, Kurt;' then hurl the drive away into the night. And as it disappears you feel the tears for the unseen boy, the one in a place called Seattle, the one who you thought you might have loved.

Getting the lobster out of the tank and on to the deck is a lot easier than you'd thought because he clamps his mighty claws on the frame of the landing net. Just as well; he's much too big to fit inside its mesh bag. You kneel down on the deck, stroke his back, quite calm again now, your decisions all made. Slowly the beast releases his hold on the alloy net frame, its metal now twisted and torn. 'You're going back, old fellow, and I'm going south,' you whisper. *Lady Rose* heaves and settles and rolls again. You're too close in, the crash of wave on rock really deafening. Well, you'll be sixteen next month. No-one and nothing to stop you: Edinburgh. Get yourself a job. Stay at the YMCA for a while just to get started. You breathe in deep of the smell of hot oil and fish and the sea, always the sea.

A voice above the wind and the sea? Somebody's shouting. You look up to the top of the cliff, spot the tiny, figure in the wind-flung jacket over the moonlit-grey shirt that would be red. Your father's arms are waving. You hear again his voice but not what it is shouting. You take hold of your lobster, lift him over the side and let him go. He wasn't yours anyway, was he? Not your father's either. There's nothing there now, just the waters, darkly heaving. 'And goodbye to you,' you whisper.

How close in the *Lady Rose* has drifted, how close in to the cliff's abstract, black and silver menace, moonlit now into a thing of beauty, falling down the face of which you might have seen your mother? Mother? Or your father? Whatever, what you see bounces off the cliff face once and then again before becoming a part of the maelstrom, going around and around and down and down.

And even so soon you know somehow that a great, wide-clawed thing has sensed this new arrival, is clambering across its territory of dark, weed-bouldered caves and canyons, searching through the coiling kelp; searching and, finally, finding.

Claws

You call out 'Goodbye.' And then again, whispering it; 'Goodbye'.

Ends

Claws *was first published by LA's Carve magazine. This story's starting point had nothing to do with the boy or his father - it was the lobster. Our sons grew up sea fishing in small boats. One day they came home highly excited and carrying a sack, inside it the fourteen pound star of this story. Such a monster lobster would not fit into any of our cooking utensils so we cooked it in our top loader washing machine. Sad to relate in respect of such a venerable old fellow, he was virtually inedible - and the washing machine broke down. Served us right.*

Claws

A story about two lives and when love or lust survives but their marriage hasn't ... and of when, with no spoken word to spoil it all, they can, however fleetingly, unite to create the ultimate in happiness. It is the month of May. For Sir Harold Harrington and his ex-wife, artist Siobhan Kelly, time for all the rites of Spring ... again...

Somewhere to Love

The girl on reception actually seemed pleased to see him. 'Welcome to Edinburgh and the Excelsior hotel, Mister Harold. Your wife told us to expect you about now. Room sixty one. The restaurant's still open if you hurry.'

'Thanks,' said Sir Harold Harrington, 'But I don't think so.'

Again she smiled her empty smile. 'Well, have a good weekend.'

Weekend? Siobhan must have decided to make a little holiday of it. For himself there would be only tonight, just this one night. A one night stand. How he disliked the sound of that - and how much he'd been looking forward to it.

One of those electronic card locks. In and out: click. Inside the room all was darkness. He caught the smell of her perfume, closed the door.

One of the bedside lights came on. Siobhan lay on her side facing him, well arranged on the bedcovers like some gorgeous, ample bodied Titian. Right knee raised, left elbow deep in the pillows, the hand supporting her head lost within that auburn cascade. The hint of a smile played around the blue of her eyes. Her free hand held a sheet of hotel stationery strategically in front of the pelvic vee. On on it, of course with her artistry and apparently with the carmine of her lipstick, a great big; '*HELLO, Sir Harold!*'

Nice one, Siobhan. You must have asked Reception to alert you when *Mister* Harold checked in.

He returned the grin, took his time undressing, located the mini-bar then poured himself a miniature of scotch, went to top it up with water. Catching sight of himself in the full length bathroom mirror he pulled in his stomach, the small one stomach that last year probably hadn't been there at all. Even so, some would say pretty good; very good for thirty six. And most of them did. He nodded to his reflection, walked back to the bedside, wrote on his pad, *So how are you?* She took his pen and his notepad, quickly added; *I'm fine. Don't you think that's how I look any more?* Standing over her he raised his glass and his eyebrows. Siobhan shook her head. She never had been a drinker.

He knelt on the bedside rug, leaned forward to kiss her, put out his hand, gently to touch. Sir Harold Harrington, aka Mister H Harold, asked himself why, now, such disorganisation of feeling. Sex: Just sex, right? Wonderful, marvellous, total, but after all was said and done, just a function of the body.

But thus began once more this night and all their complex rites of spring.

Going down to breakfast, this ex-wife of his looked fresh and vibrant, the proverbial million dollars, as expensively casual as befitted any such successful lady of the arts. They went in silence, of course, as per their agreement. No talk, no questions, no arguments: just looks, notes, peace. Why couldn't it have been like this before all the nastiness, domestic then legal and then final? Without unconsidered words? He listened carefully as she ordered from the waitress. Hers was a beautiful voice, low and so very non-assertive for a female of such spiritual independence. Perhaps that had been the problem? Her iron fist in the velvet glove versus his iron fist in the *iron* glove? Anyway, for him the sex last night had been perfect as always it had been perfect. For her, too, he hoped. She peeked at him over her newspaper. Some of the crinkles might be new since last year. He winked, glanced at his watch. Time to get moving. Taking out his pen he wrote across a napkin, *Hotel Francisco Star: Famagusta, Cyprus.*

She glanced at it, made a small fist, wrote; *another city far away! What's with you and airplanes?* He grinned, got to his feet, kissed her cheek then turned and walked away. He hadn't felt like grinning, hadn't felt like walking, but still he walked away and still did not look back. A deal's a deal and in any case there'd be no, well … affection? *What*, as the song goes, *Has love got to do with it* ?

With his train picking up speed through the suburbs of Edinburgh Sir Harold Harrington opened the secret place in his attaché case, took out the agreement, carefully unfolded it. Bit the worse for wear now, this, their final, pre-divorce letter, the private one that had nothing to do with all the bloody lawyers.

Once more he read it through, pleased with the clever symmetry he'd built into the words, his pleasure yet diluted by its acknowledgement of failure, for failure was an alien thing to the man who'd started a money making business whilst his school friends were knocking back the beers and knocking off the birds in their universities, a man who'd built it to world class and gained his knighthood whilst most of them were still farting around with their cripplingly mortgaged, pettily suburban lives.

This agreement is private and confidential to H and S. It takes no account of the terms of their divorce settlement proper.
1.   Following the Decree Absolute we each undertake never to seek out or in any way intrude upon the other, either directly or through third party, except as per this agreement.

2.   *We agree to meet, in strict privacy, for one night only each year. the date of meeting to be as early as is convenient to S in the month of May. (see point 7)*

3.   *We will take it in turns to be 'chooser', year and year about, the chooser to book both H and S into a hotel in a city in which neither of us is likely to be known .*

4.   *The chosen hotel must have the same initial letter as that of the city. That initial letter must each year be the one following the previous year's, in alphabetical order. (e.g. Hotel and city beginning with letter 'A', April / May 1998, chooser S.)*

5.   *For this one night H and S shall be known as Mr H and Mrs S Harold.*

6.   *Each of us will set up a temporary e-mail address, (sharold 456 and hharold 789 respectively.) These addresses will be valid from 1st to 10th April then cancelled and set up afresh by H on the following April 1st. They will be used solely (a) for S to propose and (b) for H to agree the meeting date in May.*

7.   *Should either one of us not succeed in contacting the other in this way, by April 10th, whatever the reason, then the agreement will be regarded as redundant and there will be no further meetings nor any further communication between H and S.*

8.   *H will cover all associated costs in cash. (Sir Harold remembered how she had baulked at this one, insisting on paying her full share.)*

9.   *During the meetings all necessary communication shall be strictly in writing. NO VERBAL COMMUNICATIONS WHATSOEVER!*

If they couldn't talk without argument, why talk? So much unhappiness caused by the quickness of the spoken word, the tragic differences between that which was meant and what was said and then again between those things and that which was really listened to. Underneath the typed agreement, hand -written, the list to date…

    S – *Alhambra, Aberystwyth, Wales - year 1*
    H - *Berkeley, Baton Rouge, USA - year 2*

S -   *Cristophe, Cambridge, England - year 3*
H - *Desert Inn, Dubai, United Arab Emirates - year 4*
S -   *Excelsior, Edinburgh, Scotland - year 5*

Sir Harold Harrington took out his pen, added, *H - Fiesta Star, Famagusta, Cyprus - year 6,* then put everything away and sat back. That's what was good about trains. Temporary respite from his switched off mobile. Soon he sensed the closing of his eyes.. This was not a comfortable dream. The two of them were at one of Siobhan's arty friend's exhibitions cum parties. She was everything and he very little, just another business suit with money. In his dream he called them all to silence and told them who he was and what he'd accomplished but the people in there seemed unimpressed so he told them what he was worth, shouting out now above the airy-fairy psycho-babble. And still nobody seemed in any way interested so he took his wife by the arm and forced her through the crowd. She was on the verge of tears. People looked at him with unspoken hatred. He twisted and turned under the illogical strength of his anger, woke up as the train approached Kings Cross, sat up, switched on the mobile that was the doorway to his real world. Messages, more messages; some should have interested him, even excited him; none of them did.

'Good morning, sir.' At the ticket barrier his waiting driver touched the shiny peak of his cap, took charge of his overnight bag, 'I hope you had a good trip?'

'Excellent, thanks, Charlie.' He paused, the tough young Chairman of the Board again. 'Couldn't have gone much better, in fact.'

'The office, sir?'

'Hold on a moment, please.' Sir Harry closed the glass partition in the Bentley, made his call. Yes, he was told, Siobhan Kelly pictures were hung mainly by Atkinson Greer, New Bond Street. He gave Charlie the change of destination.

It could only have been painted by her, the one in the window. Standing on the pavement he leaned forward, taking in the semi-abstractions of her picture: the bright angular colours of the town houses, the unmistakably Siobhan seagull shapes that seemed to move through visible air; and the title: *Free over Aberystwyth*.

The immaculate young man inside the gallery introduced himself as Algie Smith-Vandevelte. Quite clearly Algie recognised money when he saw it, was even prepared to descend from whichever place on high that he inhabited to treat his prospect as an equal. Yes, he said, as a matter of fact they were hanging eight Kelly's at the moment, including the one in the window. Most were sold or pro-visionally committed. 'Actually Kellys do move so well these days,' he added. *Now that's not necessary.* Sir Harry resisted the temptation to tell the guy never to declare a scarcity to a sales target, however true, for always it would most surely be disbelieved, to the detriment of the buyer / seller relationship and any potential deal.

Of course he'd always known his wife could paint well, perhaps very well, but these new ones - they were better than very good. It couldn't be merely the echo of last night, colouring his judgement? One picture in particular attracted his closer attention. It was a large picture, seemingly an absolute explosion of colour, of happiness, of … well, life. 'Gauginesque' was the word, though she wouldn't have appreciated it. You were looking from the sea and you could hear the shushing of wavelets on sand, feel the heat of the beach, relish the shade of the palm trees. In front of the palms stood a barefoot woman with her baby and two children, one to each side looking up at her, holding on to her dress. But…oh yes, the woman was definitely Siobhan. He walked closer, the thump of his heart accelerating. He stared at the title and then for a long time at the faces in the picture and then back at the title: *'Abbie, Bee, Dulcie and me.'*

'Lovely, isn't it? I thought you might care for a glass of champagne?' Algie Smith-Vandevelde wore the tie that bound him to Eton or Harrow or perhaps Winchester College, held a silver tray with a tall glass, bubbles rising.

'You have any Westerrn Isles malt? I'd rather that, if you do.'

'Certainly, sir.'

'Good. I'd like to buy all seven of these pictures plus the Aberystwyth one in your window.' He hadn't asked the prices. The conflicting emotions in the young man's face were plain to see.

'As I told you, sir, some of them ...' Harry just looked at him, saying nothing. 'Well, perhaps I can make some telephone calls?' The voice had lost most of its assurance.

'Good. Do your stuff. And give me ten minutes, will you. I need to make a call or two myself.' My God! Abbie for Aberystwyth? Bee for Baton Rouge? These children of hers, could they - could they really also be his? Dulcie ... Dubai? Equipped with his glass of Lagavulin, he found the number, dialled the Excelsior hotel in Edinburgh, asked to be put through to room sixty one. He had absolutely no idea what he was going to say, but one thing was for sure; he was about to break the terms of their deal.

A little voice said, 'Hello. Mummy's feeding Dulcie.' He could hear other small voices in the background. His? His childrens' small voices? Close to panic he said, 'Will you tell her it was Harry who called? Will you tell her I'm coming back?' He hesitated. 'Are you Abbie?'

The voice said, 'No, silly, I'm Beatrice. Do you want my sister, or Nannie?'

'Bee, no. No thank you. Please will you just tell your mummy that Harry's coming back? I'm on my way now.'

'Yes all right, Harry,' said the little girl.

The next train departed Kings Cross at 15.00, arriving Edinburgh Waverley 19.07. On his way out of the gallery the young salesman hurried to intercept him, doing his best to avoid any over-anxious look. 'Ah, hello sir,' he said, 'I've managed to get quite a result. I can definitely promise you seven of the eight Kellys. But I was wondering if we could at this point talk about price?'

Harry took out a card, wrote an extension number on it, asked him to call Mrs Kline on that extension in exactly one half hour. 'But I actually said all eight,' he added, 'My offer's for the whole collection. Or there is no deal.' He could feel the sweat on the palm of Algie's hand.

Whilst being driven back to Kings Cross he alerted Mrs Kline to the paintings situation, told her to get them, all of them and at best possible prices, told her something had come up from last night's discussions. He wouldn't be in for the next day or two. Best thing about being head honcho; nobody to query any of your mysterious errands.

He hurried out of Edinburgh Waverley station, head down through the rain and across the square, nodded at reception on his way to the elevator. His heart was pounding and his throat dry as he knocked on the door of room sixty one. There was no response. 'Mr Harold?' He turned around. The porter must have followed him up from the foyer.

'Yes?'

'I'm afraid your family checked out a couple of hours ago, sir.' He held out an envelope. 'Your wife asked us to give you this.' He coughed politely. 'The kiddies were being a bit of a handful at the time. Lovely 'though, aren't they all? You have a really lovely family, sir.'

'Thank you.' What else to say? He took the envelope. 'My wife may have left something in the room for me. Could you let me in, please?'

'Yes, of course.' The porter fished out his master key, opened the door. 'But I'm certain the room will already have been cleaned and there's been nothing handed in. Can I ask what is it you've lost?'

He wanted to say, 'only my life', but he just shook his head. 'Nothing that important. Look, I'm going to re-occupy the room, just tonight. I believe we actually booked it for the whole weekend.'

'In that case I'm sure it will be all right.' The porter took the offered fiver and reached into the room to turn on the lights then stood aside to let him in. 'Leave it to me to inform reception, sir.'

Harry stood for some while with his back against the closed door, imagining her there, lying on the bed, that bit of a smile in those blue eyes. But in his mind he heard the voices of young children as, finally, he moved to pour two miniatures of scotch into a glass. He added some water, took off his tie and his jacket and lay down on the bed, turning the hotel envelope over and over in his hands, searching her handwriting for clues. 'Mr H Harold,' she'd blocked out in capitals, and that was a minor work of art all by itself. Then, in handwriting, 'Unless claimed by Mr Harold this is to be held at the hotel until I phone you for it's return to an address I shall provide.'

He finished the drink, got himself another, finally opened the envelope. he read its contents quickly and then once more, and once more, more slowly...

Dear H –

This is my 'notice of termination' in lieu of you having to wait another year and finding there's no more April e-mails. So, there will be no f----- - in Famagusta or anywhere else! Sorry! In a way I really am. But a deal's a deal, as you always say, so we won't be 'seeking out or in any way intruding one upon the other,' will we. (Note no question mark)

H, I really hope I've given you what you wanted. I can tell you that you've given me what I wanted. That is, Abbie, Bee, Dulcie and now, if my timing and our joint fertility holds up, Eden (whether boy or girl.) And that's it. (Why no Christopher or Cristabel? Come on, even the great and wonderful Sir H can't hit the bullseye with every arrow!)

Please don't try to find us (I don't really know if you will want to) but I can tell you we're going to live in a place, the whereabouts of which even you can't imagine. Here's another note: I cannot say our place starts with a 'Z' although it might - and perhaps should, this being our ending!

Thanks for buying my pictures but I've told Atkinson Greer not to attempt any further gazump on the ones they'd already sold elsewhere (money's just shit paper at the end of the day, H, right?) They will be sold to you for one pound each but you'll need to pay Algernon his full pound of flesh (notional commission.) And yours will include the Dubai one - in memoriam. I was reserving this one. It's the best of them. The best of it, dear 'husband', is that I can paint myself a second version any time.

As the kids grow up I'll tell them about you and if that's what they want no doubt they will make contact. But not me, not Siobhan, the silly little - if now not so very little - painter, but the still loving ex-wife to her very own prospective master of the universe who she really and truly hopes will win everything there is (except her) and be very very happy.

All love that's left

Sxx

In the bleakness, the blankness, the sterile silence, Sir Harold Harrington turned face down into the bed; the last of somewhere to love in which they had observed, with such dedication, all the final rites of spring.

The end

We have had several friends, some married and some not, who were obviously in love but who could hardly tell each other the time of day without it leading on to a major dispute. Words are after all so very easy, so very dangerous, so often so very unnecessary.

Expatriated business manager Jonathan Seymour, through no fault of his own suffers a car crash and falls foul of Saudi law. Shattered by this experience, Jonathan and his wife take up a lower key way of life in the Scottish Highlands. But in Saudi Arabia he has seen something he should not have seen and so has not escaped the darkness that menaces everything.

Call Me Captain.

He drove past the fourth speed trap at precisely the legal one hundred and twenty kilometres an hour. Mozart filled the inside of the Lexus, the inside of his head. Nothing to see but occasional on-coming headlights over on the other carriageway and the tail-lights of trucks, soon passed, and the rod-straight highway with its camel-wire fencing.

A blue and white sign in Arabic and English appeared and disappeared. *Riyadh 100 Kms*. He glanced up at the outside air temperature gauge, reached for his bottle of water; twenty five degrees C even now, at midnight. The white Mercedes burst through the inter-carriageway fence, came at him bucking and bouncing in a storm of sand and debris, slewing around on two wheels, taking off on a rollover, impacting him almost head on. What he remembered the most, afterwards, before he blacked out, was the cacaphonic violence of metal on metal. That and the ensuing silence; those things and the awful, unfair agony and a glimpse of bloody faces inside the wrecked Mercedes.

*****

Always there were two of them: 'Mister Jonathan, at this point, what was your speed?' The one doing most of the talking was the older.

'Listen, I've told you all this and I've signed my statement,' he said. 'Why do you want to keep asking? I was travelling at a hundred and twenty kilometres an hour; I'd probably got it down to around seventy by the time I was actually hit.' He sighed, moved his backside on the bed so as to lessen the ache from his plastered, up-slung leg. What the hell were their names, these policemen? He couldn't remember, probably didn't want to. Wearily he added, 'And to save us all further time let me say again, my name is Jonathan Seymour. I am a British subject, my age is forty four and I am here in Saudi Arabia as general manager of Al-Shattah Establishment for Engineering Fabrications. Yes, I was travelling to Riyadh on my employer's business and yes, my visa and travel letter and all my driving documentation is in perfect order.'

The older policeman again, unimpressed; 'Mister Jonathan, clearly you do not remember my name, which some might consider a discourtesy. But no matter, you may call me Captain and you will please remember that this is a most serious matter. A man is killed and the Prince, he has himself been injured.'

'Yes. I really am sorry. But I told you, Captain, after the crash I saw the Prince and another man in the back with him and the driver, not just the driver and the Prince. And how can you possibly imply that any of this is down to me?'

'Told? *You* told *me*? But *you* do not tell *me* the truth, Mister Jonathan. Remember this, that you are the one who is out of place. It is an obvious thing and quite clear within our Law that, if you had not been there at that time and at that place nobody would now be hurt.'

Jonathan shook his head. The vice consul, or whoever the guy from the Embassy really was, had confirmed it: 'If you park your car beside a high building and some joker decides to jump from a window, lands on your roof - well, old lad, I'm afraid the death is down to you. It was the impact with your car that killed him and it was you who put the car there. Simple. Their rules, their game, their playing field. None of us actually *has* to be here, none of us *has* to be playing their game, but by being here we have to accept the rules, yes?'

The younger policeman spoke with cold authority; 'There was no third man in the Mercedes.' It was just a statement. 'There were two men only in the Mercedes in collision with your Lexus. There was the driver, who is now dead as a result, and the Prince, who was hurt as a result, who was the passenger.' The black eyes were unreadable. 'It is easy to - how you say - imagine things in such circumstances.'

Jonathan opened his mouth, remembering the scene in spite of himself. One of the headlights must have stayed on, God only knew how in all that twisted metal. He could picture it now, the guy climbing out of the wreck, the calm, good-looking guy with the neat little moustache and the bleeding forehead, his fine brown thobe edged with the patterned gold threading of a high ranking Saudi. And still inside the twisted rear doorframe the big-bearded mullah type, starting up with all his agonised calling out to Allah. And he could not avoid the memory of the driver, flattened over the dashboard, half through the windscreen. Nor all that blood. 'Just two men?' He shrugged. 'All right, if you say so, gentlemen.' He was tired of this; tired beyond words. 'Me, I just want out of here. I just want to go home.'

The younger policeman spoke then in Arabic, the rhythm and the music of the words strangely at odds with something that might even have been pleasure. 'Mister Jonathan Seymour,' translated the older one, the Captain, 'We are charging you with causing the death by dangerous driving of Mister Chandana Virachandanaika, of ...

****

Seven months, twenty days and ten hours later Denise met him at London's Heathrow Airport. He'd worked it out on the plane. Thirteen months since she'd waved him off from this place. 'Good luck, my Jonny,' she'd then whispered; 'Take care of yourself.' He shuddered, not just because of the unaccustomed cold. The prison had held many forgotten men, a very few of them expats like himself. He, now, was the lucky one. Limping past a customs officer his thoughts were confused; expectation mixing with several kinds of fear. The blank faced customs guy was looking at him. One thing he had learned. Never smile at a uniform. Well, bollocks, this was England, wasn't it? He tried a smile but there was no response, England or not.

Outside in Arrivals Denise was trying to smile, too. 'Hi!' she said, brightly. She looked so fresh, so wonderfully female; so much the nervous stranger.

'Hi.' And so ordinary a greeting. The kiss was just a touching of faces, as if she knew about the coterie of man-shaggers he'd had to hold off for so long and with such desperation. She didn't, of course. No-one would know about any of that. No-one. Ever.

She did all the driving and most of the talking, too, hopping from one superficiality to the next: She told him of her journey down from Scotland, of the weather, of her mother with whom she'd stayed last night; of all the contacts with his old friends and family and the state of the country and the world. Neither of them really wanted to talk about Saudi Arabia. Not until they had to. Birmingham, Manchester and then Glasgow all fell behind. The car was a lot less powerful than any they'd had before and a long way from being new, but it was what they could now afford. The dogs were a little cramped but seemed well and happy enough. Well, all four of them together again and they must be going somewhere interesting, right? He turned around. Cleo stared back at him over the rear seat, eyes bright, ears pricked. Jasper was out of sight, probably asleep down on the floor. 'I'll do anything for you, ' Denise had written; 'But the dogs have to stay together and stay with me, no matter what.'

She broke one of the longer silences. 'Jonathan, I don't like to bring it up but did they say anything else about your back pay? I told you in my last letter, things are getting a bit desperate.'

'Al-Shattah's man came to see me just the once. Obviously didn't want to know. He reckoned the legal fees would cancel out most if not all my contract salary. 'Don't hold your breath' seemed to be his only message. That and, 'we wish we'd never heard of you, Mister Jonathan bloody Nuisance.' So I'm sorry, love, but it looks like it's 'start over again' time.'

She shrugged, tried a smile. 'Yes. So, what are we going to do?'

'Well, I plan on getting a job of some sort, any sort so long as it gives me time to write my book, find myself a publisher that's not shit-scared of anything with a sniff of the Salman Rushdie's. But, hey, can we forget about it just for now? Why don't you tell me some more about the new place.'

'All right. I've made it as nice as I could but you mustn't expect too much.'

'Don't worry about that, Den. You've been a bloody marvel, selling up and moving us all by yourself. Listen, so long as the rent's cheap and it's got water and electricity and peace and quiet, after the shit-hole where I've been it's going to be heaven. And it's in the Highlands, for Christ sake. Beautiful it has to be. This place, Rhuadro, it's actually within the Sheilingdale estate, you said?'

'That's right. The Sheilingdale estate seems to cover half the county. But it's open country for walkers, you know, and the dogs love it and we have the whole summer in front of us.' She smiled. 'It is rather wonderful, Jonathan. Nobody locks their houses or cars. I think there's a local bobby based somewhere near but I honestly can't think what he does to keep himself amused.'

'Rhuadro is a village?'

'Well, I would say 'village' but any resemblance between Rhuadro and an English village is just, well, two or three miles of loch-side moorland with a few dozen pretty basic houses chucked around at random ...'

'Yes? Anyway it was a brilliant idea. I mean, to move us up there. Inside that place I kept thinking of our Scottish holidays. Especially that first one?' He glanced across at her but now she was fixed on the road, smiling wven as she flicked her eyes up and back and up again to the rear view mirror.

She spoke softly; 'You mustn't bear a grudge, Jonathan. No bitterness. There was a man dead and they said your tyres were worn.'

'No, my tyres were not worn. Those policemen were lying, OK? And I couldn't say anything, Den, but there was another passenger in that Merc as well as the Prince and his driver. Shit, it was just that kind of thing, all the stupid, unnecessary deception, all the in-your-face lies, the casual denial of our kind of decency or of any outside contact ... I'm sorry love but yes, of course I bear a bloody grudge.'

'You said you never met Prince whatever his name was?'

'Prince Mubarak bin Abdullah bin etcetera, etcetera. No, it wasn't thought necessary for him actually to appear or anything. It was enough to read his deposition to the Court. In Arabic of course, like everything else. But lies are lies whether they're in Arabic or English or bloody Swahili. It wasn't the lashes that got to me, it was the thought of the five more years in that pit with all those -'

'Never mind, darling,' she interrupted; 'You're back here with me now, thanks, finally, to our lovely government. As you say, let's just forget it.' She reached across, touched his hand, and he was for the time able to forget about the Saudi gaol and about his own country's weak-kneed, cow-towing 'diplomats'.

The cottage was just fine and his evening job behind the hotel bar was actually quite a lot of fun. The summer visitors came mostly from all parts of Europe and the States, moaning about the rain and the midges and nothing much happening on Sundays, but going on and on in awed astonishment at the beauty of the place and spending good money on drinks for the locals. The locals were, any time, well set for an impromptu, subsidised ceilidh. Denise was also fully committed, working on her paintings. They'd sold well at the craft fairs all through the season. She'd been bringing in almost as much money as his bar-work. His bad leg was almost a hundred percent again. Their morning walks with the dogs up, on 'the hill,' as the locals put it, had helped. After a couple of false starts the book was taking shape. He'd been backing up on the computer every day since the electricity'd spiked and he'd lost the contents of his hard drive. He'd taken to carrying the floppy in to work with him, exchanging it with the one he'd deposited the day before in its secret place behind the bottle of Special Reserve Aberlour, working with the disc in his portable during slack times. 'I think I'm actually saying something quite important in this book, Den,' he'd told her. 'I think it's going to be more than just a true story.'

And then, one breakfast time in early September she informed him, her eyes shining, searching his face, that she was pregnant. People said that pregnancy brought beauty and it was true, for his wife had never been more beautiful than on that morning. He'd blinked back the tears. He thought that he'd probably never been happier than just then.

Tuesday September the eleventh. After the news from New York broke most of the locals came into the bar. It was as if they needed each other but didn't know quite why. In spite of the numbers gathered in front of the big screen TV the bar was quiet. Time and time again the twin towers collapsed in spectacular, disgusting slow motion and repeated images showed the Boeings' flight tracks into the side of the Pentagon. Commentators speculated continually as to what exactly had happened aboard the other one, the fourth plane that had come down in Pennsylvania.

Denise was sitting up at the bar, watching along with the others, not saying much. The ghillie Murdo MacLaren, sitting next to her, shook his head, muttered darkly about his employers, the folk up at the big house. Bloody foreigners, never wanted to say so much as a hello, did they? Nor wanted to do any shooting when the hill was running alive with deer screaming out to be culled. Wasn't worth him getting his gun licence any more, was it? He didn't know why they kept on paying him. If the owner was this financier fellow, Bransgore, where was he? How come his people were all Indians or something, folk who could but hardly speak the language? Bloody oil. Never in Rhuadro, just to and fro from the big house in their damn great helicopters. But, Jesus, this in America … Everybody in the place heard him but there were no protests nor any arguments. How easily had the man's racism become an OK thing. Jonathan himself had kept quiet of course. It wasn't just that people weren't keen on over-opinionated bar-staff. Nobody here knew of his recent experience and neither he nor Den was about to tell them.

A few mornings afterwards he came upon pictures of the Al-Quaeda and Taliban leadership in the Times. He blinked, looked again, turned to Den, stunned; 'My God, this guy in the paper, it's him you know. He's the one that was shouting his head off in the back of the Merc.'

She frowned; 'You're sure? How can you be sure? Didn't they deny anybody else was there?'

'Of course they did but I'm not in Saudi Arabia any more, thank God. Should I go to the Law – or whoever's involved in this search? It says here the guy's one of the leaders of the whole damned bunch.

'Come on, Jonathan. Nobody at the time believed there was any second passenger so what chance now? It's just history, horrible history. Let's just forget all about it. Please? We're doing all right now, darling. Nobody here knows about any of that so why risk spoiling it all?' When she smiled and took his hand like that and placed it on her steadily expanding stomach he would have forgotten the whole world had that been what she wanted. He folded up and laid aside the newspaper.

They were following a deer track through the bracken and heather, Jasper and Cleo casting around for scent, the river in spate thundering through a ravine cut deep into the hill to their left. When the helicopter came it swooped down over them, very low, its dark plexiglass windows reflecting the afternoon sun like the magnifying eyes of some gigantic insect. Its racket echoed deafeningly from the rock faces, drowning out even the rush of spate-water. Seriously concerned, he pulled Denise down into the heather. Cleo ran back to them, shaking, her tail between her legs, but Jasper remembered his guard duties, stood his ground near the edge of the ravine with hackles raised, barking out futile warnings. When the chopper finally banked and turned away the down draught caught him. For one instant, recognising the danger, the old dog pressed himself down into the bracken, but then he'd been rolled over and had gone and the helicopter had circled once and hovered over the river and flown off, the chatter of its rotor blades fading away, merging with Denise's screams.

He made her stay where she was, with Cleo, whilst he climbed down. The descent wasn't easy. He found Jasper lying on the boulders alongside the thundering water. The dog was pleased to see him but no dog could wag his tail when his back was broken. At any rate he didn't have to die alone now, didn't have to suffer any more agony. Jonathan cradled the old dog's head in his arms, whispered comforting things, things of significance only to the two of them, the tears coursing down his face. Later, after he'd found the right rock and had done what had to be done he tried his best to cover the body with stones and scree. By the time he'd climbed back up it was beginning to get dark.

Den was exactly where he'd left her, cuddling the still trembling Cleo, white faced. He dropped down in front of them, gathered them both into his arms, 'I'm so sorry, love. He's - well, he's gone.' He tried to make it easier; 'He wouldn't have suffered very much.' He could smell Den's lovely, special smell, and Cleo's, and that of the tough, unforgiving heather rasping his knees.

Denise did not cry. She looked at him. There was this kind of deadness. 'I'm sorry, too, Jonathan,' she whispered. 'And our baby's gone as well. Gone with Jasper.' She gasped, the pain now obvious. 'Oh, I don't think I'll be able to walk just yet.'

There was this nightmare in which the more and the faster he tried to run, the more times he fell and the more times he lost the track. But once back in the village he quickly rounded up all the help he needed. By the time they all arrived back at the scene it was well after dark. They found Cleo lying half across her mistress. They had heard the bitch's howls from almost a mile away. Denise was quite cold, quite dead. The doctor said something about exposure, shock, loss of blood.

He didn't tell anybody about the helicopter. What good would that do? What could anyone actually do about a helicopter coming to take a look at people out on the public hill deep inside this wilderness? Put it another way, he thought, what would anyone *want* to try to do against all that money?

At home, his computer had spiked again. Everything was gone, as, of course, was the copy disc in the bar. Even before he looked behind the bottle he'd known it wouldn't be there. And when they read what was on it? What then? Not that it much mattered. Not now.

Denise's mother and father came up to Rhuadro for the funeral. Afterwards, taking them to one side during the wake at the hotel he told them he hadn't yet decided what to do but asked if they'd take Cleo back to England with them, look after her for a while. With some reluctance they agreed. He had to hold himself together as their car pulled away with Cleo staring back at him through the rear window, ears laid well back. He went slowly back inside the house that had been their home, and finally came his tears.

Giving his in-laws a decent start he returned to the hotel. Most of the folk were still there, still holding the wake for Denise that would most likely turn into a sombre kind of a ceilidh. He told them he was going to go down south for a while. Understanding, each of them in turn shook his hand, muttered the genuine inconsequentialities customary on such occasions. He left some money behind the bar. Several of them, Murdo MacLaren included, were already quite drunk. Just as he'd expected Murdo's Landrover was parked out front. He returned to the cottage to get changed, pack his token suitcase. There was a message on the answerphone. He pressed the 'play' button. 'Sorry, Jonathan, it's us.' Denise's father sounded weary, worried, possibly quite angry. 'We're at Inverlochan. It's just, well, Cleo jumped out of the car when we stopped for petrol. She probably saw a deer. We've got people out looking for her. I'm sure we'll find her but - I'll call you again later if we don't.' The hesitation then; 'We'll have to move on, anyway. I've got work tomorrow. I absolutely must be there. Speak soon.'

An hour after dark he approached the hotel car park from along the beach, keeping well down out of sight. Murdo's Landrover was still in its place, unlocked as always, the deer stalker's rifle in its specially built, sheepskin lined case, and that, too, unlocked. He stole back the same way with the gun then drove to the start of that pathway, the one he called Den's track. Parking well off the road he switched on the interior lights, picked up the rifle, taking comfort from the warm, smooth feel of it, the scent of its machine oil smell. It took him back to his days in the Army. He'd been good with a rifle in the Army. He counted out ten rounds, familiarised himself with the gun's action, put the encased scope into his pocket and set off.

Even though there was a half moon and a clear sky the track was almost as difficult to follow as it had been on that more hurried night a week ago. It took him nearly three hours to get to Den and Jasper's final place. He sat down there in the bracken, in total silence and near total darkness, ate half his sandwiches, made his way to the edge of the ravine and dropped down the rest. 'That's for you, Jasper, old son,' he whispered.

Two or at the most three hours more, that should do it. He continued on, following the river upstream. Cutting a way through the eight foot wire fence around the vast grounds of Sheilingdale House was no problem. An hour later he'd found and taken up his rock-bound station. He was perhaps twenty metres above and one hundred or so metres away from the front door of the main building. In the near stygian dark of the now moon-less night he could just make out the bulk of the helicopter. It sat in the centre of the big house's front lawn, right there, right in the centre of his killing field. He found the least uncomfortable position he could. As cold and as exhausted as he was he fell asleep, one hand on the rifle.

There was the sound of a car engine. Daylight. A Landrover was making its way down the drive. The car stopped in front of the house. Jonathan blinked, raised his head, trying to uncramp himself whilst keeping low. He picked up the rifle, put it to his shoulder, peered through the scope and adjusted its focus. The driver of the car was Murdo MacLaren. Two men had come out of the house, one of them a white man he'd never seen before and the other? He stared hard. Blinked to clear his vision. No doubt about it, Prince Mubarak bin Abdullah bin whatever, the man he'd last seen with such a bloody head on the road to Riyadh. The Prince was not a happy man, even from here that much was obvious. Jonathan rubbed at his eyes, watched again through the scope as the white man ran to board the helicopter. This had to be the bastard of a pilot. His finger tightened on the trigger, the voice of his instructor sounding clear down all the years; *Squeeze it, sir, squeeze it. Don't pull the sod.* All he could think was that this was the pilot who'd killed Jasper, had consciously and deliberately done for the old boy; this was the man who'd set off the chain of disasters that had followed. He wondered again whether he could still shoot straight and true, hoped the scope and sights were correctly calibrated. Afterwards? Who bloody cared?

His scope moved back to the Prince, picked up another man now standing alongside. He shook his head, shut his eyes and opened them again, heart pounding, the scope now trembling. This new arrival was the leader, definitely the one that had been pictured in the Times! Almost clean shaven, dressed western style; tall and spare and stooped, the most wanted man on planet Earth. If not him it had to be his twin brother. He seemed to be gesturing at the helicopter, now with it's engine coughing into life, its rotors beginning to turn.

The cross wires in the scope would still not stay still. He felt the point of the knife to the side of his neck just one split second before he heard the murmur of the man's voice. 'Take your finger off that trigger, Seymour. Like, now, OK? I doubt you'd hit the fucking house, anyway, never mind the bastard you're trying for. Keep very quiet.' Jonathan did as he was told, heart thudding against the earth beneath, automatically opening his mouth in response. The knife point moved in, just a fraction. Quietly he laid down the rifle.

The rest of it was like a stop action tragic-comedy. The group of them down there in front of the house, pointing at a very muddy Cleo, unsteady on her feet, nose down and following his last night's trail across the lawn. Then the calm, quiet voice of the man with the knife, 'Go, go,' and the ragged pop pop popping heard faintly over the accelerating helicopter engine. The leader seemed to be sitting down quite slowly, folding forward, face to the gravel drive, jerking sideways under the impact of another fusillade. The Prince almost made it to the door of the house, dancing like a badly handled marionette before also going down. Murdo had his hands up but, sickeningly, that did not save him.

The pilot must have been hit just as his hand manipulated the throttle for the rotor whine grew into a howl and the whole aircraft shook and hopped twice before falling to one side, disintegrating in a great ball of white and orange heat. Hooded, camouflaged figures with guns had appeared all over the place, crashing through doors and windows into the house. More pop-popping from inside.

Then Cleo was standing over him, licking his face. The firing had stopped. Into the relative silence the voice beside and behind him said, quite conversationally; 'That was good, wasn't it? And that's a nice bitch you have there, Seymour. Looks like she's come a long, long way for you. No, don't look around. I'm going to blindfold you. Right, listen up now; none of this actually happened, understand?' Without pausing, 'You're not even here. At this very moment you're actually a few hundred miles south of here and still travelling, just as you told everybody back in the pub. Your treacherous friend, Murdo? Unfortunately he got himself killed along with the pilot in a nasty helicopter crash. Real tragedy, that. Pilot error of course. And the man calling himself Bransgore will have buggered off with his exotic pals and sold up the estate after the shock of it. We don't want to make a bloody martyr out of anyone, do we? And you? Well, you're going to spend a little time with us and then you're going to be just fine. Believe it. Oh yes, your lovely old Cleo here, she'll come along for the ride as well. Understood?'

Jonathan opened his mouth to speak, decided against it.

'Good man, Seymour. Least said, etcetera. But hey, thanks for leading us to the bastard. We knew his unlovely guys would sooner or later have at you. Couldn't afford to have that book of yours in circulation. No more can we, mind. Linkages with our oily Middle Eastern friends and all that. So you'll have to write about something else, won't you? But Christ, we didn't reckon on the Big Man himself. Pretty bloody good! Clever son of a bitch. Everyone combing the Pakistani hills and he's hiding up right here in his private wilderness deep in the heart of bonnie old Scotland. Oh yes, very nice.' The pause, the small cough. 'But ... I'm very sorry ... really sorry - I mean, about your wife, Seymour.'

Men were carrying bodies out of the house, laying them out without ceremony side by side on the lawn, well clear of the still flaming wreck of the helicopter. Sound of more choppers approaching fast. 'So; OK, you can stand up now. MacLaren's rifle goes back where it belongs. Don't bother to ask about me, about my name; nothing at all about us. You'll just be calling me Captain, OK?'

The end

The Saudi road accident happened to a business friend. The rest is fiction. But good fiction has to be truer than the truth and it is true that I have culled other bits and pieces of this story from real life.

The lady should have had - everything. They'd moved to this picture postcard village called Dinling Cross. Great home, wonderful husband, friendly neighbours. But there's so often that pesky little something, isn't there? Some fly that insists of getting into the ointment? Ex ballet dancer Tina Saunders-Mallory likes to ride her horse but there is this swan; he has to be outwitted because he most certainly does not like horses.

Swan Lake at Dinling Cross

There was only going to be one winner and it wouldn't be her. She stood, arms folded, beside the reed fringed pond. She was booted, jodhpured, cravatted, hard-hatted. What was it they used to say? *All jacked up and nowhere to go*? How bloody, bloody ridiculous.

But she had to admit he was a beauty. Strong of eye, yellow of beak, thick, S-curved neck, wings half unfolded ready for instant protective action. He was patrolling close in to the sedge, hissing out his warnings, keeping himself between her and his mate on her massive platform of a nest. What was a female swan called? A *pen*? Yes. She lifted her eyes to the other side, to The Cricketers pub and the village shop next door to it. Had anyone witnessed that performance. Not exactly Swan Lake, but still...

'Dead handsome, ain't he, lady?' She turned around. The old man was standing behind her, leaning on his stick, tabloid newspaper under one arm. So this must be the

63

famous George Perkins. Bit of a war hero and one of the local characters, they'd been told.

'Good morning,' she said. 'Well, handsome he may be but actually he's being a bit of a bloody nuisance.'

'Yes'm. I seen the old boy having a go at you and your horse these last few mornings. If I can say so, lady, that were damned good riding, seein' you didn't come right off, I mean. But I'll be guessing you won't get him past here for love nor money again. Not now you won't.'

Her problem had obviously become common knowledge. She said, 'You may well be right, George. It *is* George, isn't it?'

'Yes, lady, George it is.'

'Any idea as to what one might think to do about it, George? By the way I'm Tina Saunders-Mallory.' With some difficulty she raised a smile.

He lifted his cap, scratched his head with the same hand. 'I knows your name, lady, and I'm pleased to meet you. I seen you moving into the old Manor last month and before that I seen your picture in the press.'

'You have?' The old farm worker must have picked up Country Life, probably in the doctor's surgery or somewhere.

'Yes, that's right, lady, and very nice too. Welcome you be to Dinling Cross. What to do, you say? Ain't nothing to be done. Nature has to take her course, don't she?' He shook his head. 'They pair of swans, they comes here regular as clockwork. They comes soon after Easter time, repairs their nest, has their family then takes off with the young 'uns down the river before first frost. Been coming here about ten years, this pair. And before them there were another couple for more years than ever I remembers. They pairs up for life, you know. But you should see 'em when they're courting. They touches their beaks and they has their necks all arched over, like this, lady...' He traced a heart-sign in the dewy grass with the point of his stick.

'Yes, I know. It's charming, but a pity nobody told me about the swans before we bought the Manor. How am I expected to ride out on the common without coming past here?'

'Yes'm, ain't no way 'ceptin' swimmin' the river out back o' your manor then through old Jamieson's cornfield.' He shook his head. 'Jamie wouldn't like that. 'Tis a pity. But that old cob swan, he don't worry about you and I, lady. It's only horses he worries about. And white cars, he ain't too partial to they, neither. I seen 'im taking' lumps off the paintwork o' they buggers. Must think they'm comin' after 'is mate.' The laugh was a chesty rumble.

'Yes? Well, I must get on, George. Perhaps the RSPCA can offer some advice.' She smiled again. 'But thanks for yours, anyway.' Flicking the whip against her shiny boot she strode back up the Manor house driveway. The air was full of scent from the rhodedendrons. In spite of the swans it really was great to be here, even if it seemed a very long way from Tramps, Quaglino's, first nights at the ballet, the theatre, all the West End shopping.

'Hey, you'll get used to it,' Tom had told her. 'You'll simply love being the Lady of the Manor, darling girl.'

Well, she had got used to it, hadn't she? The sweet smell of moneyed success was such a wonderful introduction, the magic words 'merchant banker' so obviously acceptable a background. And her own, carefully non-specified life within the world of the London ballet, that hadn't hurt too much either, had it?

It took her half an hour on the telephone finally to realise that no matter how hard she played the danger to life and limb card, nobody wanted to know about her problem. The silly little rich bitch undertone of those she'd spoken with came across all too clearly. She shook her head, thinking about her years in cheap, most often shared apartments, spending her every last penny on looking and acting like the ballet star she never had become, always on the lookout for the big chance. Well, the chance *had* come and she *had* taken it but it hadn't been on the stage, had it? Not unless Dinling Cross was the scenario for her very own Swan Lake? Naturally, herself as Princess Odette with Tom her leading man and these real swans and the village people their supporting cast. Sounded OK. She smiled in spite of herself, sighed, set about the wearisome business of boxing up Hector. As she drove out and past the pond she could hear the shuffling and banging of his hooves. Thank God the Landrover wasn't white but the old swan still reared up amidst a spray of water, flapping and clapping those huge wings of his. Damn it, she'd just have to give the pair of them names. Margot and Rudolph? Yes, Margot Fontaine and Rudolph Nureyev; Swan Lake. She shook her head, laughing.

In the morning, after Tom had left for his commuter train she answered the doorbell, still dressed only in her housecoat. A uniformed policeman was standing there, his red and white chequered car behind him on the drive.

She smiled. 'Good morning, officer. Can I help you?'

'Morning, madam.' She realised her smile was not to be returned, could see with what care he was observing her.

'I'm Police Constable Cameron. You will be Mrs Saunders-Mallory?'

'That's right.'

'I'm sorry to disturb you.'

'Oh? It's not a problem. Perhaps you'd better come on in, officer.'

'Thank you, madam, but no. Just a couple of questions' How very young he seemed - and how conventional a sign of getting old was that! He coughed, got out his notebook. 'I have to tell you that last night someone attacked the swans over there on the village pond.' He stopped, glanced up, watching for a reaction.

She frowned, bewildered. 'Attacked the swans? What on earth do you mean?'

He cleared his throat, still unsmiling. 'Do you know anything about this incident, madam? Did you perhaps hear or see anything unusual last night?'

'No, I'm afraid not. But this is awful.'

'It's just that we were informed about your problems with them...?'

'What? With the swans? What on earth are you implying officer. You surely don't really think I might have some connection with ... but this is quite appalling.' She forced herself to stay calm. 'Now look here, I want to know everything about it. Rudolph and I may not exactly have been best of friends but that was a battle fought and won by him, fair and square.'

'Rudolph?' the policeman asked; 'Who might he be then?'

She soon had all the details. Rudolph had obviously tried to defend his nest and his Margot but he'd received neck wounds and what seemed to be an injury to one of his wings in the process. The RSPCA inspector said it was best to leave him on the pond. He would most likely heal naturally. The female was a different matter. She'd fought the aggressor or aggressors to the point of death, receiving a large number of airgun pellet wounds in the process. She'd been taken to a specialist sanctuary in Cambridge somewhere, was not expected to live. The policeman coughed and frowned, doing his obvious best to look severe. 'Trouble is, madam,' he ended, 'some of the folk hereabouts have got the idea you might have something to do with it. Might have paid someone to try to shift the swans, you know?'

'No, Constable,' she said, levelly. 'I can tell you categorically that I did not.' She felt herself close to tears. 'So, that will be all?'

As soon as he'd gone she ran upstairs, dressed, hurried down to the pond. A group of villagers were standing around, talking. They grew silent as she appeared. An almost immobile Rudolph, bedraggled and with one wing trailing floated motionless on the water close to the scattered remains of the nest-pile.

George was coming by with his newspaper. She called out, 'Oh George, this is terrible,' but the old man continued on his way without acknowledgment. In desperation she persisted: 'Please, George, I have to talk to you about this.'

Without interrupting his limp and without looking at her he said, 'Bloody money talks, don't it? Why don't you just bugger off an' talk to all yours, then?'

Tom arrived home mid-evening. He was as tired as always after his day in the City but nevertheless listened carefully, sipping at his whisky whilst she told him the story. 'The worst was in the shop,' she finished. 'It was really awful, Tom. They didn't have any bread or milk. At least that was what they told me but I could actually see there was plenty there. When I pointed it out Cathy just said it was 'reserved for orders.' What on earth am I to do?'

He got to his feet, held out his hand. 'Come on. *You*, dear lady, are to do nothing. But *we* – *we* are going down to the pub.' She loved it when he laughed, the way one side of his mouth went up more than the other.

She'd been well used to a temporary lull in conversation when she walked into a crowded place but this was a different kind of silence. For one awful moment she thought the landlord was going to refuse to serve them but then someone laughed and that was the signal for a general resumption of conversation. Tom ordered a pint and, for her, a half pint of the local bitter. He glanced around then turned back to her, an odd expression on his face. Without words, smiling fixedly, he indicated a yellowed page three of The Sun. Someone had fixed it to a black oak beam where it stood out amongst all the holiday postcards. A youthful, Tina Saunders leaned into the camera, the perfect breasts that had probably come between her and ballet stardom proud and bare. 'That's one you didn't tell me about,' he said. She felt the hot flush of tears at the backs of her eyes. 'But hey, let me tell you something,' her husband went on, 'You had a really great figure then, darling girl, but it's an even better one now if I dare to say so.' Those standing near enough could hear his words.

She lifted her chin, blinked, smiled at him, said, 'Oh, I remember that photograph well enough. It paid my rent for a month. But I wonder what sad kind of person would keep it all this time? I mean, what - about three hundred of those pages each year? And that one of me is what, eight years old?' She bent forward, looking down the bar past the standing drinkers to the old man sitting in his usual place by the wall. 'Good evening, George,' she called out; 'It's very nice to see you.' There was no response. She turned back to her husband; 'Can we go now, Tom?'

'Oh, I shouldn't think so,' he said. 'I've never yet been known to leave a pint un-drunk.' He grinned, took her hand, leading her to a table. 'Good to spread a little happiness, isn't it? These tossers can't take their eyes off my bright and shining little ballet star.'

She'd found out where the swan sanctuary was. The hundred mile trip hadn't taken long. She'd asked the vet what were the bird's chances. He had just shrugged, told her it was doubtful whether Margot would make it. She hadn't eaten for a week. 'I mean, we've got most of the pellets out but swans do make very uncertain patients. They're used to lording it – or ladying it, in her case. When they can't do that it seems to me they're really not too interested in very much at all.' When he'd left she'd knelt down and stroked the dulled feathers, had made up her mind. 'I'm going to take you home, Margot,' she'd whispered. 'It's better you die there with Rudolph if he's still … there. If he isn't, at least that's where you'd prefer to be. Better than here all by yourself.'

The vet had wished both of them good luck, waved them away. She stopped the car by the village green, switched off and got out. It was very dark. There was the smell of warm pondwater and new mown grass. Waves of music, loud voices and singing came from the pub as the doors opened and closed behind departing revellers. With some difficulty she lifted out Margot, laid her on the grassy bank, released the straps and the damp sacking in which she had been wrapped. Should she put her on the water or just leave her here? She knelt down and took the lovely head in both of her hands, lifted it, unresisting, to her lips.

A car's headlights temporarily illuminated them, then extinguished themselves. The sound of the engine faded and died. Doors slammed. A man's voice. 'See, she's 'ere with that bloody swan. I told you I seen her, didn't I? Hey, lady.' She got to her feet, turned around. Two forms confronted her, blacker than the darkness of the night. 'We've just been taking a good look at you. Over in the pub.' His laugh came out as an ugly snigger. 'We was wondering, see, any chance of a private viewing? We'll show you ours if you show us yours, like, OK?'.

To run, to stand and scream or just to fight? She spoke evenly, assessing her options. 'Please, why don't you go away before you get yourselves into serious trouble?'

'You're not scared? No, course you ain't. What you doin' with that old swan anyway. All as we wanted was a couple o' eggs. The buggers goes ragin' mad.'

There was a quick movement in the dark, the brush of a hand against the sleeve of her coat. She turned away, ran for the Landrover, managed to wrench open the door and grab her riding crop before the man had her down on the grass. She slashed wildly, heard his cry of pain and then there was only the male and the tobacco stink of him. Too incredulous to be truly frightened she could hear the buttons being ripped off her shirt. No, this couldn't be happening. Not here. Not to her. The other man seemed to have his knees to either side of her head, had pinioned her arms out in the cruciform.

She heard the sharp thwack a fraction before he'd pitched forward, apparently unconscious on top of her. His friend levered himself out of the melee, jumped up.

It was the old man's voice. 'Come on, matey, why don't you? Cowardly young bastard though you be.' George! There were the sounds of a struggle then George was down here on the grass alongside her and the unconscious man and the principal aggressor was off and running, caught in a car's headlights, above them the fast revolving blue …

She rolled over, raised herself on one elbow. 'George! Oh, Thank God. Are you all right?'

'All right? 'Course I be bloody all right, lady,' George said; 'Once over I've 'ad 'alf a Brigade of Panzers on me back so I don't go worryin' about no buggers like they.'

People from the pub seemed to have joined in the chase, which had ended in several great splashes and a thrashing about in the pond. She helped him to his feet.

He went on 'And I heard what he said to you. About the swans and all? I'll be telling' the Law about it when they've got 'em both dead to rights.' He paused, chuckled, 'And I'll be having my page three back off the pub, too. Best one in me collection. Allus 'as been.'

She realised her shirt was gaping wide open. The whole scene was now well lit by headlights. 'George, you really are quite incorrigible.' It was her turn to laugh as Tom came running across the green.

George said, more seriously, 'And I am - I'm right sorry, lady. You know…'

Constable Cameron was hatless and breathless, appeared to be soaking wet as he handcuffed George's now conscious victim. He brought the man to his feet, turned to her; 'Mrs Saunders-Mallory, what in heaven's name were you doing down here on the green at this time of night?'

Tina turned to indicate Margot but there was just the pile of discarded sacking. 'May I borrow your torch please, officer?' she asked. Out on the pond the powerful beam lit on something pale. She steadied it, holding her breath. The whole village, silent now, could see the pair of them, Margot and Rudolph, battered and tattered but still transfixed as everyone knew they must have been when first they'd met, their high arched necks and touching bills the heart-sign once again. She could hear the lift and swell of Tchaikovsky's wondrous climax, could feel herself dancing, no, flying weightless across the stage.

George whispered. 'Don't you be crying now, lady. They be having some more eggs. Don't you have no worries about that'n.'

'You think so, George?' she whispered back. 'That's good.' She wrapped her desecrated shirt more tightly around herself, linking arms with her husband. 'I have something for you, George. Somewhere in my things there's the original of that picture in The Sun.' She squeezed Tom's arm. 'I'll get it nicely framed for you. My man won't mind, will you Tom?'

The end

Years ago I was poling a punt along the river Cam with my family when we passed close - too close - to a swan's nest. The big old cob came at us with evil intent. We moved on in a hurry and watched from a safe distance as he repeated his behaviour - this time directed against a hard-hatted lady horse rider (or her horse?). Later we heard that the nest had been despoiled and the birds injured by vandals.

'Oh what a tangled web we weave when first we practice to deceive.'
That's what we all are taught in childhood. Anne and William's lives
certainly are tangled up. So much in real adult life is deception, and so
little of deception leads to happiness...

As They Lay Down.

She closed the curtains to kill the sunlight, returned to his
bedside. She could cry, him being brought home like this.
At such times she really, really did not like her husband.

'I was cold, so cold, Anne.' The little boy appeal for
sympathy wasn't much more than a whisper.

'You were drunk,' she said, 'And you still are. You're
lucky you're not sleeping it off in the police station. Why do
you have to let that man get you so absolutely totalled every
time he comes here?'

'Ben's my friend.' Unnaturally slow; the actor's voice;
tired, slurring, hurting. 'He's always been my friend.' There
was a pause, then, 'How about you? You're still my friend?'

She didn't feel like answering that one. 'I suppose he's
gone back, this friend of yours, having left you to fall asleep
in some ditch to get picked up and brought home by the
police. Thank God you weren't trying to drive. I suppose
your car's still at the pub? How I hate all this. You call
yourselves, well, *artists*! There's another word ... my God,
you're fifty two, William!' She only called him William when
she wasn't OK with him, like now. She stood up. 'Anyway
I'm going shopping, remember? Oh, don't worry, I'll be
back in time to cook your dinner.'

'Wait a minute,' he whispered, 'Look, it wasn't Ben's fault; he didn't stay long. A bunch of them in the pub. Old pals. Mike Drayton and those, you know? Quiz night?' He was waiting but she didn't ask. 'We won again. But listen, Ben and me, we're partners. So we do have to talk, the two of us. That's what made us pretty OK, and that's what makes you the Lady of the bloody Manor, Anne. Oh God; my head!' The ordinary features on the balding head seemed to Anne to be too dry, too tight, too pale; unshaven stubble pricking out hair by hair around the greying goatee.

She said, knowing her own cruelty, the cruelty that came from anger, 'Oh do come on! You're just another B List Celeb. And the two of you - you're putting together scripts for East Street soap episodes. When you aren't - aren't like this, that is. Oh, and your old plays that mostly don't get played any more because they're rubbish, probably. Writer! Thank God you managed to get yourself all the acting, that's all I can say.'

She turned away, slammed shut the door to guest bedroom one behind her. Hurrying downstairs she told herself she had every right to be angry. But not with herself, not for the guilt. Why should she be the one to feel guilty? Excited, yes; guilty, no.

Actor-dramatist William Shaftesbury closed his eyes against the pulsating pain and the late winter sunlight. Through a latticework of thin, winter-bare branches he saw again the pre-dawn sky with its cold queen of a moon and her retinue of stars - and the concerned, good humoured faces of the two local policemen, bending over him, lifting him up, one to each arm. 'We'll have to stop meeting you like this, sir,' one of them was saying, 'Folk'll be starting to talk.' And the other one laughed.

Anne Shaftesbury listened to the air-rush whisper of steel on steel. She tried to relax, watched the countryside changing into manicured parkland then less quickly into the dulled nothingness of suburban development and finally, slowly, into the sparkling glass, sky grey concrete and all the garish colours of the inner city. She focussed on her image in the carriage window, instinctively put up a hand to lift and pat her hair into shape. Not too bad; very good really. Well, for nearly sixty. Sixty! She cut off the incipient panic with thoughts of her long time lover, still eager for that which still she was. Would he remember her birthday? He usually did, even if only through a surreptitious telephone call or with a last minute bunch of flowers - always provided Willie was away. And him? She had to admit that her husband - he had always remembered, wherever he might have been at the time. Oh Willie, Willie! He really hadn't looked good this morning, a tattered old nondescript standing at the door propped up between two large uniforms. Perhaps she should have stayed at home with him today? Perhaps, this one time, she should have ignored the lure of Thomas' studiedly casual invitation; 'If you happen to be in Town on Tuesday give me a call, Anne; why don't we have some lunch?' She smiled. The star-bound government officer still spoke like the respectful young tenant who would never dream, when Willie was away working, of leaving his room, would never dream of making his way through the big old darkened house to tap tap on her bedroom door. He'd never then moved on to slip, so late at night and with so much urgent need, into the dark anonymity of his twenty years older landlady's guest-room bed, had he? She swallowed, shifted her hips. 'Lunch'! That was a good word for it. You shouldn't still be having these feelings, she told herself, but the inner voice stuck there, high up in her throat. She swallowed again as her journey jerked and rattled to its close.

Out in the station concourse she switched on her mobile, glanced around, called her ex-lodger at his Government Office. William? To hell with William.

'I'm no alcoholic.' William opened his eyes, realising he'd whispered it aloud. 'Oh my - !' He was feeling truly, truly awful, Food poisoning? Something he'd eaten in the pub? Anne would laugh at him for that but there'd be no joy in the laughter, only scorn. Where was she when he needed her? Bloody shopping, their bank account no doubt going into fast reverse. He groaned, turning himself over despite the protest of his head, taking extra care with the damaged right knee. He pulled the duvet up around his ears to shut out the muted sounds of the garden and the village beyond, re-closed his eyes against all things in here, dimly seen.

And yes, there they all were, his people; the miscellany of those who had come to their lives through his, through the words he had entrusted to paper. The two newest arrivals were here in the foreground talking to each other, of course not realising they were under such close observation. He strained to hear them, to observe their every facet of behaviour. He should get out of bed, switch on his PC, write down their words and his own words. He wanted to make the words sing the line, skip-dance down the page. He could feel the stubbled smile that had visited his face as he listened to his lovers and heard their words: as he was now seeing the words of his own. 'And so to sleep, perchance to dream ...'

She liked this just as much as what had gone before; she liked the feel of herself against his newly spent body, herself unspent and now totally if temporarily in command. She brushed her fingers down the side of his face and on down his neck, as yet so little lined, then moved her right breast into the softest of contacts with his left one. His eyes opened. Without expression he lifted his hand but it was merely to ascertain the time by his wrist watch.

'Christ, I've got to go,' he said, as she'd known he would, hoped he wouldn't.

'No late lunch for us today, Thomas?'

'I told you. I have this meeting. The Minister …'

'Yes, Prime Minister,' she said, giggling. 'Far be it from little old me to interrupt any affairs of State.'

'It's not like that. You know it's not.' He wasn't amused. Thomas Green didn't do amused. With still youthful fluidity he moved away from her, got off the bed, began to dress.

'Yes,' she murmured, 'I know.' But it was. It was indeed just like that.

He closed the bathroom door behind him and she could hear the sounds of his toiletry merging into the rush and bustle of the city outside the double glazing and the rattle of a trolley being pushed past the room. 'A base for my shopping forays,' she'd explained to reception, but lightly, like some of the other ladies up for the day from Hicksville. The receptionist could not have cared any more or any less, whatever the given reason, about the old biddy and her love trysts. Anne drew herself up from beneath the covers, placed her elbow on the pillows to support her head with her hand. Venus reclining, awaiting his return.

Immaculate once more, Under Secretary to the Minister without Portfolio Thomas Green sat himself down on the edge of the bed, searched for and found her free hand. 'Anne, we have to talk,' he said, frowning. 'Trouble is, there's not much time.'

'Oh yes, dear?' So, finally, here it came. Just as she'd known one day it must come.

'Look, we have to call time, don't you think? On us?' He looked at her, employing his most earnest of expressions, reached out with his other hand to brush away a stray lock of her hair.

She blinked, tried to misunderstand, turn it into a joke; 'You mean, until you next …'

'No. Willie's supposed to be retired now. He's home with you, Anne. It was really good when he was away all the time and I had my room at your place, working at the Town Hall. But now?'

'But now you're no longer our or anyone else's tenant and you've climbed most of the way up to the mountain top and you can't afford any 'trouble' at this stage, is that it?' She withdrew her hand, pulled up the duvet to cover herself. 'Or perhaps you've found something more to your taste, perhaps something a bit nearer your own age, Thomas?'

'Anne, please.' He got to his feet, carefully buttoned the pinstriped jacket. 'You know how much you mean to me. But equally we both also know that your husband is terribly well connected and that, well, there'll be no divorce … You understand me, I know you do.'

'Oh yes, I understand you.' She sat up, then, very straight, for he was not looking at her body. 'You're worried about lovely Willie. Let me tell you, he has about as much interest in me - all the years he's been running hither and yon, probably shagging everything he can get his hands on while I've been the little woman at home bringing up the girls and burying his son; burying his son when he couldn't even get home for the funeral!' She wanted to cry and, oh, how she hated herself for the self-pity in that.

'I'm sorry, Anne. Like everyone else I know all about it, him being away and out of reach in one of his godforsaken outposts when - when your little boy died. I know how you felt when the media were telling everybody how sad that was; but really almost understandable - all those adventures for some kind of a genius.'

'Genius!'

'Not that I agree with them. I'm sorry.' He turned away, walked to the door, opened it, looked back at her. 'Anyway, I'm sure we'll be seeing each other.'

'Yes, of course,' she whispered. 'Go on, then. Please? Just don't say it's been good, that's all.'

'Bye, Anne.' Still not looking at her he waved his hand once before closing the door behind him.

She could see herself in the mirror on the wall opposite the foot of the bed. Horribly. She lay back down, drew the covers over her head and let go of the tears. He hadn't even tried to say it, hadn't tried to say that it *had* been good. For him this long time screwing of his ancient landlady - ex-landlady - in the extended absences of her famous husband had simply been some necessary indiscretion. Some very natural if reasonably long-time diversion.

Willie tried to sit up. The clock said it was two. Filtered light told him it had to be two in the afternoon. The number one guest room, was it? Yes. Well, all right. She must have exiled him again into the very best bed. This private joke of their's was getting to be as familiar a territory as their proper, second best, marital bed; the bed that had once been her mother's; the one in which she had taught him, actually, had told him, exactly how he had to love his much more experienced girlfriend, then wife. The second best bed in which they'd gone on to squirm and wriggle and hump and laugh and vocalise their way through all the early married years. The one in which his seed had sought and three times had found her own. 'How nice to have you home, Mister Willie,' she would say and then he would be able to tell everything was all right with them. 'Would you like to join me in our second best bed?' she might go on to say. With Anne, joking always equalled loving, invariably led on to that matching of hands and bodies and minds and everything.

Always he had loved her, that he knew. But ... he had to have a drink of water. His mouth... the bathroom seemed such a very long way away.

By the time she'd slept a little and showered, got herself dressed and made up, tidied the room and paid her dues it was two o clock and too late for a proper lunch. But she was hungry and she was sad and she was more than a little bit angry. Frightened, too. Frightened by the passage of time and with it the passage of her life. And tired because she'd hardly slept last night with Willie still out and with the prospect of this - this assignation.

Anyway she'd get a quick something at the Café Bleu then make her way home, see what she could do for him, her writer, support part actor or whatever. He who, aged eighteen all those years ago when a girl's (woman's) missed period almost always equalled wedding bells, he had managed to impregnate his eight years older first time lover. Accidentally on purpose on her part because she might really have been in love with him. No, she told herself, definitely *had* been in love with him, and with his youth, and yes, with the concept of marriage.

She bought herself a magazine, found a nice bright corner in the still busy café and ordered a quiche and a pot of coffee. Halfway through her second cup and well into a piece intriguingly headlined, 'Big X After The Big M', she became conscious of someone standing over her. She looked up, irritated, into the smiling face of Ben Thompson. 'Good afternoon, Anne,' he said, 'Mind if I join you?'

'Help yourself,' she said, unsmiling.

He pulled out a chair, sat down. 'Not a bad old day for April.'

'No.'

He signalled the waitress. 'How was my partner in crime this morning?'

'How on earth do you think he was?' she said.

'Oh dear: not very good then?'

'No, Ben, not very good.'

'I'm sorry.' He looked up at the young waitress who had recognised him, naturally. 'Cappuccino, please? And for you, Anne?'

'No thanks.'

'Thank you.' In the new silence he drummed the tips of the fingers of his right hand on the glass table top, then; 'I take it you know your fellow is working on something new?'

'Is he?' she said, 'Oh, I'm sorry. I thought he'd come home to retire.'

Ben frowned; 'It's really good, this one. Brilliant in fact, although he says it himself whose original idea it was.'

For the first time it occurred to her that this meeting had not been by accident. She said, 'Come on, Ben, what's happening here? You don't just want to talk theatre and stuff with me. Why *are* you here?'

He sighed. The smile had gone. 'There's no easy way to say - ' He nodded his thanks to the girl delivering his mug of coffee. 'I have to be a little concerned about - well, about the two of you, Anne. Because you are my friends. Both of you.'

'What?'

'Look, I hate this - how was everything at the Holiday Inn?'

She drained her cup, picked up her handbag, glanced towards the door.

'How was Tom Green?'

Desperately she looked around for the waitress, repeated, 'What?'

'Relax, dear lady. I'm here to help, OK?'

'How did you - do you know?'

'Paparazzi. You know, like the little man over there? The one who's job in life it is to pick up on events involving those tainted with the sweet smell of celebrity, especially involving hotels? He followed you here, called the newspaper to ask about how much for the story? 'Top Civil Servant In Sex Romp With Mrs Willie,' that sort of thing, you know?'

She followed his eyes. A nondescript man was looking at her over the brim of his cup. The man lowered the cup, grinned and nodded, moved his hand from side to side, palm out. Something in her chest clenched into a spasm.

'Luckily it seems this call was his first shot at making money out of it so there's no-one else in the bidding. Not yet. The Ed's an old chum of mine, of Will's, too. But this - Anne, I'm afraid it's going to cost.'

'Please?' she whispered, 'Please, Ben, Will you deal with it for me?' Suddenly the strong smells of this place and the babble of talk and the over-animated faces and Ben's face, too, all of it was making her ill. Faintly; 'Whatever it costs me, OK?'

He nodded, spooning his cappuccino.

'Look, I want to take a walk. Over in the park. Can I see you when - afterwards - by the lake?'

'Of course.' He reached over, lightly to touch her hand. Involuntarily she recoiled. He smiled. 'Please. Don't alarm yourself unduly. It's going to be all right.'

Somehow he'd made it to the loo before his stomach finally decided to part with its content, which came up in waves, acid bile stinging the soft membranes inside his throat and his nose. When he thought it might finally be over he got up off his knees, exclaiming against the lash of pain from the leg he'd damaged. He put his mouth to the cold tap, swilled water around and around, expelled it down the waste pipe. His head and the inside of his chest were banging away in some kind of uncomfortable disharmony. It was so hot in here. He wiped his face, threw the towel into the laundry basket, hobbled oh so slowly to the top of the stairs. Tea: a cup of hot tea and a biscuit. And then? Switch on the computer to process words? But his head, good Jesus Christ, his head. He felt his knee giving, his foot slipping, hand ripping away from the banister under the energy of the unchecked fall. His shoulder hit something. He was tumbling, violently out of control, tumbling and hitting things and then it was dark and without any more sensation. William Shaftesbury was back amongst his people.

Grey-bellied cloud scurried low across the trees. Now there was no sun. She felt the cold, shivered, turned up the collar of her coat. Ben presented her with the bread roll he'd brought over from the café. She fed it a bit at a time to the pretty little grey and yellow fluff-balls and the adult ducks, bobbing and scurrying like nicely painted toys across the choppy surface of the water. She let him talk, let him explain how much it had cost her - had cost them, rather, her and William. She didn't worry about the money. So much had come into their bank account and was still piling into it, mostly from his Hollywood years. But Willie would notice. Even now the quite famous Willie could not rid himself of his old penny counting. Oh yes, William Shaftesbury would notice all right.

'You can make out the cheque to one of my overseas accounts,' Ben said, as if reading her mind. 'It will be quite anonymous. You're buying yourself a pension annuity, OK?'

Miserably she looked up at the craggy features of her husband's friend. 'I'm so sorry, Ben. I mean, about putting you through all this. Anyway it's finished, as it happens. Thomas finished it today. Before, you know …' They were never far away, the tears. 'But I feel so, so shabby.'

'Well you could say feeling shabby, that's traditional,' he said. 'Look, there are no perfect people. We all know that, even if most of us don't ever want to acknowledge it.' They strolled on along the lakeside pathway. 'That's what we like about fiction you know, Anne. In fiction we're allowed inside a place where uncomplicated is good and visible and safe and where perfection is allowed - indeed, encouraged - where people seldom take a hard crap or do any of the other very inelegant things, you know?'

'Ben Thompson!'

'It's true. Fiction is for heroes and for the Gods we all know we are not but would like to be. And nobody does fiction better than your old fellow.' He looked down at her. 'Because in his stuff there are no absolutes other than the writing itself. All the shades of grey. I'm telling you, Anne, some of the stuff he does, it's going to live on and on.'

'You think so, Ben?'

'Oh yes. He can take us right out to the stars, my dear Anne Shaftesbury.' He kicked at a paper cup, print-faded and crumpled. 'And take us all inside, as well, into the hearts of all kinds of people including oneself, whatever one may be. That's my view, anyway, and so here endeth the first lesson.'

She stopped, shivered again, looked up into his face. 'Do you think - in all fairness do you think I ought to leave him, Ben?' But she knew they both knew she was looking for the negative. She threw the last of the bread to a bobble of ducklings. A big, multicoloured drake rushed in, scattering all before him.

'No,' Ben said. 'I think you should own up to loving him just as much as he loves you.'

'But, Ben, he's had plenty of lovers if that's what you want to call them, hasn't he? You can be honest with me. God knows, I'm in no position ...'

''Love's spark comes from the nature of our God / the tending of its fire to careless Man', right? Isn't that what he wrote? Sometimes we're not very good with our part, are we? Yes of course he's had lovers. As I said, lady, there can be no perfection in what we are. Only, if we are born very lucky, in what we actually *do.*' He stopped, turned to her, catching hold of both of her hands and grinning his grin. 'Take me, for instance. Or not. You know, I could fancy you myself.' He laughed softly. 'Come on now, cheer up dear heart; reckon we both need to make tracks.'

'Oh, Ben,' she said. A gaggle of ducks or whatever you called a group of them came flighting low over the water, quacking comically. In a series of splashes and wing shakings the birds touched down, but there was no more bread for them.

He could see through the glass in the front door that it was almost dark. Late afternoon then. He tried to move, aiming to reach the hall telephone. No use. Whenever he tried it was like fireworks exploding inside his head. Really remarkable. Had he broken his neck? How very, very stupid of him. But he was not that uncomfortable provided he did not move at all, not one little bit of him, here on the polish-perfumed, hard wood flooring of the hallway.

'Oh, Anne!' he muttered, 'Anne, Anne.'

Seconds or minutes or hours ... a key turned in the door lock. He was forced to shut his eyes against the sudden force of electric light. He heard the small, agonised gasp, the high heels quick-clacking towards him. He could smell her perfume. 'Anne?' His voice was no more than a murmur.

'Willie? Oh my God, Willie, what's happened to you? Don't move now, I'm going to call for an ambulance.'

'Anne?'

'What?'

'Come back please? I want to talk.'

'Oh, Willie,' she said. He thought she might be crying.

After she'd made the call she took off her coat and, very gently as instructed she laid herself down next to her husband. She put her coat over them both and her arm across him to help keep him warm. 'Please don't say anything now, Willie. There'll be bags of time later. Just try to relax. They told me not to move you,' she said. 'They're going to be here very soon.'

'That's good,' he muttered. 'I think I've broken my neck.'

'Yes,' she said.

'Anne?'

'Yes, Willie?'

'It doesn't hurt if I stay still. Not afraid, only of hurting you. Done enough of that. Listen, if I go ... I've taken care of Susan. And Judith. You'll have most.' That almost inaudible sound might have been his attempt at a laugh. 'Including the second best bed.'

She lifted her head to kiss his cheek.

His voice was the merest whisper. 'But my work; the manuscripts in the files. The PC. Destroy them. Burn it. Will you do that for me, wife?'

'Oh, Willie, there's no need - but why?'

'Just pop culture,' he muttered. 'Could have done better. Much better. Could have been a contender.' She knew how he was afraid to laugh.' Doesn't owe us... Enough damage... To us all, our little boy, you know?'

'Shush... I shall do what you want if it ever comes to it but now there'll be no need,' she said. 'The medics will soon be here and then you'll be all right, Willie. They're going to make you all right. You'll soon be home again. Back in that good old second best bed of ours.' She lifted her head to look at him and saw his eyes turn to her. Yes, yes, she could see the laughter there, still there within her husband.

William Shaftesbury heard the dying wail of the arriving ambulance. Anne got up to let them in. He didn't want to see them seeing him like this so he closed his eyes. For a while he could feel and he could hear them fussing and probing around but as soon as they began to move him came the explosion and he could only marvel at this light of purest white and at how easily he now seemed to be able to move.

He turned around and they were there, behind him as he knew they'd be, all his people; the inherently good ones always with something of ungodliness in them and the really bad ones with his or her inbuilt streak of something better. The mean ones and the marvellous ones and those of all between but so very few without that grace, so few without it somewhere. He nodded to his waiting people, smiled; 'Now come along with me,' he told them; 'Because now is the time for us together to go.'

Naturally she'd looked for him in the funeral congregation but Thomas, of course, had not turned up. Ben had done the eulogy. It had been a very fine one, all were agreed on that. 'He was not just for our time but for all time', was one of the more elegant things she remembered him saying about her late husband. Whilst preparing the bonfire at the back of the garden she thought about what Ben had told her afterwards, when she'd told him she was going home to burn everything because that had been her promise to Willie. She thought about how Ben had started to argue but, seeing her expression, had stopped and said how very sorry he was to hear that, but that he understood. She thought about how he'd said it wouldn't matter much because most of the scripts would still be around somewhere and he, Ben, with some of their actor friends would in time be able to get most of it together if that's what they wanted to do..

First the twigs and the branches and the petrol then the whoof as it all went up at her first match, thrown from a distance. She had to move around to dodge the gouts of swirling, wind driven smoke that stung her eyes, excused her tears.

She threw the PC box on to the top of its blazing pyre. One by one all his files followed. She saw his handwriting on many of the thousands of type covered, heat curling pages, blackening then yellow and red and gone. One by one; file after file, batch after batch of pages.

She could feel the heat of the fire on her face and the drying of her tears. Briefly she noticed one of the file titles;

'A Midsummer Night's Dream.' *Oh yes, a midsummer night's dream; as they, together, had lain down.*

Ends

In case you haven't already made the connection, (and unless you've studied the life of the Stratford Bard there's no way you could), this is based on the death of one William Shakespeare in the year 1616. Legend has it that he died of drunken exposure after a night out in a tavern near to Stratford-on-Avon with his old friend Ben Johnson. That is the legend. The fact is that, in his Last Will and Testament, Shakespeare left to his wife, Anne, just their second best bed. Nobody has ever been able to explain that, although many have tried (i.e. have made scholarly guesses). And yes, in her husband's extended absences Mrs Anne Shakespeare did take in a long term lodger ... I have in my later years become intensely interested in the works of one Wm. Shakespeare and in what little is known about his life and times.

Injustice is only the second most bitter of pills - the most bitter is revenge. Revenge that should be ever so sweet but never, never is. David Lockeridge has been unfairly fired by his company's new ownership, has allowed himself to be talked into the most final of reactions.

The Seagull Contract

He couldn't eat his breakfast, shoved away the plate. He forced himself to tell himself; *Today, David, you're going to have a man killed.*

Blin looked at him in her special way. 'What's up? You look really awful.' She dropped the mail on the kitchen table, buckled up her raincoat, not waiting for any answer. 'Look, I'm off. You can open that lot after I've gone.' The top envelope bore the Barclays Bank plc logo. She turned and called out into the hallway, up the stairs. 'Molly, Susan, hurry up and get ready. Your father's getting your breakfast. Don't forget he'll be walking you to school OK?' One of those teenager-in-the-morning silences hung in the air. She added, 'Now he doesn't have a car and I have to get myself to work in mine, right.'

No need for that twist of the knife. He extracted the bank's letter, unfolded it, looked and looked again, chuckled then laughed out aloud. Which must have made a nice change. Anne paused on her way out. 'That's - that's really unfair. You think all this is funny, do you?'

He tried a little light conciliation. 'Actually, Blin, it *is* quite funny. Just have a look at this. They're only sending me a platinum card with a ten grand limit.' He handed her the letter.

'Yes? Well, put the lot on the two thirty at Newmarket, why don't you?' Unsmiling, unforgiving, blondie curls bouncing, she shook her head slowly side to side. 'You'd best remind them we're in it up to here with their credit. You best tell them you've been six months out of work and that you're about to sign on, for God's sake.' She went out into the hallway, called upstairs, more urgently; 'For pity's sake hurry it up, girls, will you?

At last a sign of life; 'Mummy, how can we walk? It's raining.' Good girl, Molly.

'Ask your father.' The front door clicked shut behind her.

He couldn't blame his wife. For her it had been harder. At least he'd recognised the vulnerability of the long term employee, even the fifty year old who'd reached the top of his own now not so little tree but who had not thought he needed any written contract. Johansson, now *he* would have a bloody contract. A damn good one no doubt produced by expensive lawyers with a Group verification stamp and all the L.A. signatures and prettily tied up with red tape and sealing wax. Got to look after their wet behind the ears hatchet man with the film star looks and the Harvard MBA, hadn't they?

Well, today it's David Lockeridge's turn to be judge and jury. And executioner by proxy. No contract, just the verbal one, call it the Seagull Contract. So, Mister bloody Sven-Rolf Johansson, you're guilty as charged. Black Cap time for you, mister. But still he felt bad about it. Or sick. Or both.

Largely in silence he walked the girls to school then struggled on through the weather down to the seafront, pinged open the door of the Seagull Café. Lew was already there, and as usual hard into the propped up Telegraph's appointments section alongside the usual full breakfast. It was warm, well fugged up, smelled as always of fried food and old cigarettes. Behind her servery the girl, Sandy, was already pouring his cup of coffee, all smiles and teeth and shiny long black hair like the girl on the TV adverts. Very nice hair that served also to hide her deaf aid. Mid-thirties? She waved, called out her usual 'Hiya, Dave.'

He waved in return, winked, leaning his dripping umbrella up against the wall, then removed and hung up his old Barbour coat.

Lew looked up, grinning his best salesman's grin. 'And the top of a lovely morning to you, boss.' He nodded towards the counter, chuckled. 'Play your cards right and the lady's yours. Fuck knows why, mind.' The man looked as well polished as ever. *I come out every day looking like I'm on for an interview, old son*, he'd probably say, not needing to add, *and as for you, if you insist on looking like you've started to look, like a broken old bag of shit, that's how you'll bloody feel.*

'Morning, Les. And forget it - about Sandy, OK? You don't think I have enough problems?' He sat down, rubbed a slice of the outside world into the condensation covered window glass. Be casual, he told himself. Over on the other side of the road a splintered sheet of seawater reared up and over the esplanade railings, crashed down, flooded across the pavement and into the guttering. He changed the subject; 'How's Joanna?' he asked.

'No probs. Sorry about that. Jo? Oh, she's good. Off on her travels again.'

Had the man actually told his wife about getting fired? Not necessarily. In any case it couldn't matter as much to them as it did to Blin and himself. They'd no kids, Joanna's big job, top of the range Merc and all that. He thought about Blin clocking away all day at the bags and bottles shuttling by her supermarket check out. Did Lew's wife know her husband knew the kind of people who knew the kind of people who ... who could do to mister Johansson what was to be done today? He shivered.

Lew pointed his knife at an ink-circled box. 'This one here's just right for a slightly mature, well maintained managing director, only one careful user.' He opened his mouth, forked in a heap of beans sausage and egg.

Dave ignored that. 'So, this is it. Shit hitting fan day.' He spoke in a virtual whisper.

Lew said, 'Shits and fans? Don't know what you're on about, old son, do I?'

Sandy was coming across with his coffee. For once Dave forgot about his customary discreet appreciation of her figure, and her contact with his shoulder might have been accidental. He waited until she'd gone. 'Sorry, Lew, but I have to talk about it. Christ, today's the day.'

'So what?' Lew's knife sliced neatly through a sausage. He forked it, glanced around, leaned over the table, whispered, 'Relax. We agreed not to discuss it. It's a done deal, old son. There's damn all we can do about it, right?' He glanced around again and carried on, his voice barely audible above the spatter of rain on the window glass. 'And then after that - end of story.' He re-addressed his plate. 'And the little shit's off the sweet face of mother earth, OK.' His voice may have risen an octave.

Dave kept his voice low but tense; 'Ten grand: for ten grand I should damn well hope so. Half my pathetic pay-off gone on a debt Belinda knows damn all about.' It was his own turn to laugh, if a little shakily. 'When she finds out, I lost it on the horses. She hadn't reckoned on being hitched to a secret gambler - such a crap one at that ... OK my friend, mum is the word from here on.' Diet or no diet, for once he didn't envy Lew the full breakfast. He made an effort to pull himself together. 'Right, let's see about all these jobs for oldies.'

Lew frowned. 'Don't say that.'

'What?'

'Talk like forty odd is old, OK?'

In your case I should have said fifty odd, Dave thought. What the hell, none of the jobs were worth applying for, not without a fairly recent degree in philosophy or English Lit or something else totally necessary to the running of a company fabricating stainless steel. He finished his coffee, stood up. He and Lew donned their coats. On their way out he said, 'I'll catch up with you tomorrow, then. You take care, Lew, right?'

'Yeah, I'll be seeing you. If not here, in court.' Lew grinned, held up his hand, palm out; 'Joke, joke. Where you off to now?' He opened the café door, looked up at the clouds and the rain, shuffled out his umbrella.

'The bank.'

'Yeah? Well, don't worry about it, old son. Remember, you're really only talking to a bloody computer. They're all too bloody busy doling out billions of what they've taken to calling non-performing loans to Eastern Europeans and fast guys in tower blocks who toil not neither do they spin.' He laughed. There was no humour in it. 'So why the hell should you worry, eh?'

'No, it's not like that,' said Dave. 'It's just, Johansson's driver came to pick up my BMW yesterday. I've got to see about buying something maybe a little bit in keeping.'

'Him again, the bastard Swede, late of this parish any time now.' Lew put his finger to his lips, stepped out into the downpour, umbrella snapping into shape over his head. Another massive sea came up against the esplanade, rose high, paused and collapsed in a spectacular crescendo of sound and fury. Dave could taste on his lips the salt of it.

Nearing the bank he changed his mind, turned up Calcutta Road and walked on towards the factory. He just couldn't rid his mind of the man Johansson. The worst of it was, he'd thought their relationship had been OK. On the one hand himself, the long-serving, industry wise managing director. On the other Sven Johansson, bright new Chief Executive emplaced by the company's new owners. He'd thought everything was OK right up to the day of the axe. *This is always the way, David. It has nothing to do with your performance. That has in fact been excellent. This is about business culture. Old must go when the new one comes in, you know? And listen, about your money, the guys back in LA, it is their policy. 'Out*

93

of contract' has to mean the minimum settlement according to the local law. Hey, man, I've tried for you. Still I am trying, but...' Well, well, well; the lying bastard. He hurried past the factory site, head down, now and then stealing a sideways glance. They'd changed everything, even the name of the company. The new sign just about said it all; 'X-Fabriqué plc.' What kind of a bollocks name was that for a world class engineering shop? Sounded more like a designer of brassieres or something. Pictures of the café girl Sandy unreeled through his mind, then the look on Johannson's face. He shivered. How was it going to happen? How did they know the man wouldn't be away in Chicago or Lausanne or Basingstoke or somewhere? Lew's assurance: *They'll get him on the day for us. No problem, Dave. Doesn't matter where the hell in the world he is. These people are pro's, old son. We just get to enjoy the results of their work, OK?* Trouble was, he was not enjoying this. Quite the opposite. He could hear the big train coming, felt himself close to the edge of panic. What happens if Lew's hit men balls things up? What then? The Costa del whatsit in a hell of a hurry? No extradition treaty there? Shit, he had to be joking. But maybe not. What would he use for long term money? And what about Blin and the girls? He felt now that he loved them more than ever, turned for home, one deeply troubled man.

Blin was a little late. He heard the front door open and close. She walked into the kitchen as he was busying himself preparing their meal. He looked up. 'Hi. Good day?'

'Hello to you, too. Good day? I'll pass on that one. Where are the girls?' She ran her fingers through her hair, shook it out.

'Upstairs. Supposed to be studying.'

'You've heard the news?'

A great lump seemed to have formed in his stomach. 'No. What news?'

'Our lovely little Swedish friend, Johansson. It's all over town. He's, well, David they say he's, he's dead.'

'What?'

'Dead, as in dead and gone. Silly man was found in his hotel room in the Midlands somewhere.' She picked up an ivory handled vegetable knife. 'Seems he was discovered in what they politely call compromising circumstances. Stuff about ropes and an orange, all very lip-licking salacious. There was a girl involved, apparently. Long gone of course by the time they discovered the body.'

'Oh, my God, Blin. I don't know what to say.'

'Well, I shouldn't think *sorry*'s quite the word, would you, Dave? In all the circs? Pass me those carrots, will you?'

He'd hardly slept and then had overslept, grabbed the mail on the way out to school with the girls. Miracles happened. Maybe one of his job applications had come back positive. At the school gates he kissed each of them a more than usually fond fatherly goodbye, hurried off. Once he stopped to look back. Molly was still standing there looking after him, frowning.

He waited in the Seagull for half an hour, checking his watch, chatting to Sandy. Lew still hadn't arrived. Finally he paid for his coffee, got up to go. 'I'm sorry Sandy,' he said, can you tell Lew when he comes in I've had to go, please?' She reached down to her belt to adjust the hearing aid. Must have been too soft for her. Or too loud? He lowered his voice. 'Be an angel, tell my friend I'll call him this evening?'

She smiled up at him, strangely in control. 'I don't think he'll be coming in here, Dave. I thought you knew. Didn't like to talk about it. The police...' She flicked a spot of something off his coat lapel. 'I've got to say I don't like him at all. He comes on to me when you're not with him. It's always the ones you don't want ...' She looked at him directly, still smiling, but that word kept on banging around inside his head … police… police… police.

Coach to Gatwick, just in time for the 13.20 to Malaga. He walked from check-in across the vast concourse, stopping only to take as much cash as he dared out of the ATM, then down the boarding ramp, stomach churning, expecting at any moment the hand on his shoulder. But once in the air with half his bottle of champagne drunk and the other half waiting, he relaxed a little, thought once again about things at home. Remembering the mail, he took down his bag from the overhead locker. Mail! Just junk and a few bills that he'd need to send back to Blin. She'd prefer it this way. She'd understand. No police to bother her or the girls, no trial with all its awful publicity, no prison visiting. There was enough collateral in the house to tide her and the girls over until he could reconstruct his life, bring them out to join him in Spain. And if he couldn't do that? Well, to hell with it. 'It's the river,' my friend, as Lew would have said. For the thousandth time he wondered; how long would it take for Lew to accept a deal with the Law, inform on his collaborator?

There was one other envelope. A plain one postmarked the day before yesterday. Private and confidential, for the attention of Mr David Lockeridge. He turned it over, ran his thumbnail under the flap. The letter was from X-Fabriqué plc, very short and to the point, very Sven Johansson. Oh, God! Soon there was no sound of engines, no feelings of fear, no movement in any part of his world. Only the alcohol and the words, read and re-read… *'Dear David.'* The 'David' was hand-written. *I am sorry it has taken so long but finally, following a change in Group policy, my efforts on your behalf have resulted in a settlement, without prejudice, according to the attached summary. This money has now been transferred to your account.* Paragraph. *I am now able to offer you the thanks that are your due. The thanks of myself, my colleagues here and the owners of the business that you were instrumental in creating.* Paragraph. *My best wishes for your future.* Paragraph. *Yours Truly* ... The man's film star face seemed to be there in his signature, the look on it as without emotion as always. But ... accusing. He turned once again to the attached summary.

At Malaga airport he bought a mobile with a pre-paid time card, found a hotel right on the beach. Time, that's what he needed. Time to sober up, work things out. He sat on the balcony of his room with another miniature of Scotch and a Budweiser, looking out over a sea turned all the reds in the world by the setting of the sun. Blin answered the call straight away. He could hear the strain in her voice, tried hard to think straight. He'd need to concentrate. He said, 'It's me.'

'You? David? Just where the hell are you? I've had the police here. What on earth's going on?'

'I'm in Spain. In a hotel. Don't ask me - Listen, there's money in our account, Blin, almost a quarter of a million. Christ - it's ours, Blin. Johansson came up ...' It was all such a jumble, all coming out so stupidly. The sea and the sky waved and heaved like a bad TV picture. 'But, police? What do the police want, Blin? Did they tell you?' He'd already thrown up once but needed now to do it over again.

'Spain? You're in Spain? David, what's going on? You're asking me what do they want, the police? I should think it's whatever you're in Spain for, wouldn't you? But a quarter of a million pounds? Is that what you said?'

'Pension rights, bonus and so on. If only...'

'You're drunk, Dave.' Her voice seemed softer, yet somehow more remote. 'Listen to me. I don't know and I don't want to know what you have or haven't done. Hold on for a moment. Let me think.' There was a long pause. Dave gulped back the rest of his Scotch, shook his head. 'All I know is, they've arrested Lew Davies and that they say you've been seeing the guy, and that it's got to do with

97

what happened to Sven Johansson yesterday. One thing I *can* tell you; the woman in that hotel with him - it was Joanna, would you believe: Joanna Davies, Lew's lovely wife? That's how she's been earning all their money. *Earning*'s probably the wrong word. Been at that sort of thing for years apparently. Rumour going round is that some waitress overheard Lew, well, incriminating himself, I suppose. They say the waitress has a hearing aid, turns it right up to eavesdrop on the clientele, the nasty little so and so. Anyway she calls the police who make the connections with Joanna and Johansson.' She paused to let it sink in then, turning the knife, 'Yes, I think it must have been her on the phone to me a minute ago. She was asking for you. Sandy.'

'Me?' he whispered.

'Yes, you, husband. I suggest you stay right where you are unless the police somehow manage to force you out, get you back here. I'll send you a bit of cash from time to time so long as you're in Spain. And I'll be changing the joint account to my name only. You'll need to sign up for that. Oh, and I'll give your lady friend your contact details. No doubt she'll be on the next plane out. Enjoy her, and good luck to you. Send us a postcard. Sometime very soon, like tomorrow. Don't forget your address.'

The end

I myself was a company director who was fired (made redundant, same thing,) in circumstances similar to David Lockeridge's in this story. The meetings with ex-colleagues in seafront cafes were real enough but that's where reality ends and fiction begins. Bitter and twisted doesn't last long enough to think about this story's kind of retribution. And as one dream fades and dies another one, more glorious than the last, begins. And I can assure my wife that there was never any Sandy!

Mrs Diane Boden has always fancied the once-famous rock star, Harry O'Shea even though, years back, he had dropped out of the business and turned hairdresser. Even what Harry had done to her friend all those years ago hadn't changed anything. Now Diane Boden has a plan. Yes she would get some satisfaction. At last. And the hairdresser would get a long overdue surprise...

A Wave Hello

The face close to hers was well lined, a bit saggy under the eyes and around the mouth but still unmistakably his. 'We used to go to the festivals specially to see you, Harry,' she continued, 'Me and my friend Mary? You know, Ringwood, Beaulieu, over on the Island later on, even up to Earlswood? You were great. We all had a thing for Harry O'Shea.'

He grinned at her in the mirror. Snip, snip, snip. Quick and sure, shaping her fringe, the sound of the hairdresser's salon. 'Hey,' he said. 'I seem to remember something about all that. But thank you, you're good for a man's morale Mrs ...er...?' Again the grin. The teeth were still good and the look in the eyes still bad, if you liked that sort of thing. And she did.

'Diane. I'm Diane.'

'Thank you, Mrs Diane.' He glanced over his shoulder at a departing client. ''Bye now, Mrs Poulter. Take good care. But if you can't, well, you know what...' Harry the hairdresser; king in his sweet-scented palace, happy with his rotating harem and they with him. The face might have gone home a bit but the hair was the same. The same blonde, the same length, exact to the shoulders, the same desolated waves; the lot. He turned his kingly interest back to her; 'Yeah. None of the drugs now, not much rock and roll any more but the sex, that's still OK. You know, I'd figured you must be new to these parts, Diane. Funny that, I'd have surely remembered your face if I'd seen you before.'

'Cambridge,' she said. 'I came across by train.' She took a deep breath. 'But, oh, you've seen me before, Harry,' she said. 'All there is of me.'

A hush worked its way across the salon. Amazing. Even those who hadn't really heard somehow knew she'd said something worth listening to, were trying hard to hear more. Harry had stopped snipping, started groping for some words. Smiling, she went on, 'Yes, you saw all of me and all of my friend Mary and God knows how many more of us. Great, wasn't it? You and Rod the Mod when he was still a jazzer. And Monty and Acker and Kenny Ball. Don't look so worried. I've no problems with any of that. They were very good times. Pity about my friend Mary, though.'

'Mary?' he whispered. Some of them had switched off the dryers now. 'Listen, Mrs - , why don't we meet up at the Lion, lunchtime? This isn't exactly private.' He glared around, very much the king under siege at this point. They all set about their business again - Harry O'Shea's business.

She smiled at him in the mirror, quite relaxed. He had not, of course. He hadn't seen her naked but with any luck he would. She giggled. But Mary he'd seen all right, all over. He really should not have done it to a girl of sweet sixteen.

Viewed in the soft mirror lights behind the lounge bar of the Red Lion, she could see that Harry had done her hair very well, she had to admit that. She didn't look at all bad, not for fifty five. He was coming through the swing door behind her. 'Hello, Harry,' she said, 'Now, what can I get for you?' And that's another first, she thought. First time she'd ever offered to buy the first drink for a man.

'This is down to me,' he said. 'It sounds like I might owe you one anyway.' His customary smile seemed just a little bit strained.

They took their glasses over to a window table, chatted about places and people and some of the better things that had happened to them since the sixties. She didn't at all mind that the talk was mostly about him, the famous Harry O'Shea, Lothario supremo, guitarist very good but not quite extraordinaire, fast rising and slow falling star of the sixties pop charts, today the somewhat less brightly shining star of the Wave Hello Ladies Hairdressing Salon, High Street, Upminster Somerton.

'So listen,' he said, 'I do apologise for not remembering you, Mrs Boden.' He must have picked up her surname from her cheque. 'Or your friend. Her name was - is - Mary, you said? So whatever *did* happen to her?'

How wonderfully casual. She put down her glass, took her wallet from her handbag and extracted a photograph, laid it face up towards him on the table. 'She did,' she said. 'She happened to Mary, Harry. This is Theresa and according to my friend she is your daughter. Lovely, isn't she? She's thirty eight now and actually she's really been my daughter because my friend Mary died giving birth to her.'

'Oh my - what can I say to you? Except this child was not mine, Mrs Boden.'

Her knee touched his beneath the table, stayed in contact. 'I couldn't have any children of my own, not with my husband anyway.' She shifted in her chair, saw how his eyes flick down to the working of her fingers on the stem of the glass.

He was frowning; darting about like a fish on the hook, she thought, probably trying to decide whether to come on to her or continue his retreat in the face of the Theresa revelation. Finally he said, quietly, firmly; 'Diane, I'm sorry but you have the wrong guy.'

'I do, do I??' Of course he was going to deny it. They always did. Didn't matter anyway. Theresa wasn't the point at all. 'Cheers.' She raised her glass. 'That stuff I said in there about me, it was wrong, Harry. You never looked at me. But Mary told me all about it, you know. About you and her making love in that cornfield? And then after that in the hotel rooms.'

'I don't know why this Mary said that stuff to you, Mrs – I mean, Diane, but it all sounds pretty X rated; you could make a few bob having it published.' His knee had moved away. He must be wondering what was coming next.

She giggled. 'Really? Me, I'd never even been inside a hotel room at that time. Mary had me green with envy - when I wasn't worrying myself sick about her, that is.' She sipped some of her wine, looking at him across the rim of her glass. 'I could buy a whole hotel now if that was what I wanted,' she went on. 'My husband may not have been much good for me in the bed but he's been brilliant in the banking department. All these years I've fantasised about it; about you, Harry! You know, me and my rock star. Better late than never? What do you think?' Harry shook his immaculate head, for some reason his sense of endanger-ment clearly receding.

The pub door swung open again, to admit a group of regulation suited businessmen. Damn! Jeremy was with them. Not that she had to worry too much about that. She sighed. The moment might have gone but she'd get it back. Her husband had seen her at once. He excused himself, came across, smiling. She started to introduce Harry but he cut her off.

'Darling, I know Mister O'Shea,' he said. 'I damn well should do. The guy's picture was pinned to my bedroom wall alongside the classic Marilyn Monroe avec skirt high in the air and a *terribly* sulky Jimmy Dean. So, what are you doing with my lady, Harry? Not leading you astray, is she?'

Harry said, 'No, of course not. What do you think of your wife's hair-do? I have to get back to the salon now. Si I'll see you next time, Mrs Boden.' He stood, finished off his drink. 'By the way, your friend, this Mary, she must have been on some wavelength all of her own. Look, your husband will explain. I'm sorry. Really.' He waved goodbye.

Jeremy said, 'Nice guy. Must have broken a few hearts. You knew he was gay, of course?'

'Harry O'Shea? Gay?' She laughed shakily. 'That rhymes, doesn't it? But that's ridiculous.'

'I don't think so, darling. Harry and I, we've been seeing each other for years, off and on. Can I give you a lift home?'

The End

A lady near and dear to me, when in her teens, met some soon to be famous rock stars at one of those sixties festivals. The rest is my fiction but it is a fact that I had my hair cut for years by a guy, by no means gay, who could boast of having had a number one hit record called 'Kites'.

A Wave Hello

Zara is a Hungarian vizsla, one of the oldest of the gundog breeds. She is also a successful young showdog. She lives with her sister called Pegan and the golden retriever, Barnaby. In this narrative 'He' and 'She' are of course their human owners … In championship dog shows a dog or bitch has to win his or her class and, if successful there, be rated best of sex in all classes. Then he or she must compete with the best dog or bitch for the title 'Best of Breed'. If winning that, he or she has to compete for Best of Group (gundogs group in this case). And finally, Best in Show. So, the best of the best of the best of the best!

Zara's Day

(One day in the life of a Hungarian Vizsla)

Again I hear Them move. I lift my head,
slow-blinking in the early morning dark.
as Pegan shifts and sighs within her sleep
I rise, I leave her warmth and stretch and yawn;
then slant of yellow light from opening door
- this is the way my golden day is born.

Soon Peg and me and big blonde Barnaby
agree that something special's going on.
outside I sniff the stars and smell the old
brush-tail: I whimper low, my body shivers
I yearn to hunt him down across dark fields;
and deep inside, the slit-eyed she-wolf quivers.

Oh yes! He has those keys, my brush, show leads
and wears the things that mean we'll soon be at
another place where comes from far and wide
dog's of many races in one giant pack
where Zara's part of Him and He of she -
where I shall stand then run triangle track.

Content within warm noisy-moving thing
we curl together, Peg and me, at rest,
hear both their voices soft above the drone,
the swish along deserted crow-black roads.
and in Her low-pitched voice we hear the thrill;
in His the contest: what the day forebodes.

In Them we trust to take us where They will.
soon misty dawn through misted windows shows;
new light now turns the black fields grey then green,
past windowed cliffs and caves from concrete made
we turn into the crowded gathering place
to which have come the brave and those afraid.

What sounds and sights and oh what wondrous scents
around the boxy rows, the roped off squares
where stand already many hunting breeds!
it's good to smell where some friends take their walk,
their scent on clothes of they who stand like trees
in groups as He and She with others talk.

There's solemn Blaze On Chest, my sister's beau.
here, Angel Face, she's not so very smart.
this big new boy's so sweet, so very shy;
'Though not for long,' laughs knowing sister Peg
'*Shy Boy* is what from now you're called,' I cry
he runs his lead around his person's leg.

This strongest of all scents! We quiet down
look round and there he is, The Distant Lord,
his glance disdainful takes in me and Peg
I hate myself for how he makes us feel.
'I'm Zara,' soft I speak; 'I shall not beg
of *you* : this bitch won't dog your lordly heel.'

Zara's Day

She stoops and has Her arms around my neck
my She who smells of foreign fields and oils,
I cock my ears, in vain to understand
her sounds although their meaning's always clear.
I peer into Her bright and shining eyes
once more see all the love for us that's there.

He walks into the ring, me by His side
I know this place of judgement's our's today.
I trot a circle, head held level, high,
tight feet loose -reaching forward for the ground:
we stop in line, He touches me to stand,
I am a rock whilst only one moves round,
this person starts and stops and stares and stares
and I can feel her staring now at me
though Angel Face' bum is all I see.
'neath tail and jaw I feel His fingers tense;

The staring Person comes, I'm waiting for
the hands to lift my ears, my lips and hence
run down my back and legs and touch my feet
that's when I like it least - and like it best
when trotting the triangle on our own.
I long to run, to leap, I feel so good
but if I did although my friends would laugh
I'd anger Him, I'd not be understood.

It points to me, the finger of power!
I know that Person's chosen me the best
mine is the glory, His red rose the Flower.
and I'm allowed to jump just for the joy:
I watch His happy face and feel his hands
and here's the smile that nothing will destroy.

Outside the ring She touches face with me
and laughingly with Him; and Pegan sighs.

107

'Why all the fuss?' she asks but proud, she is,
and says; 'You're back soon for another show.'
side by each side into our box we jump...
now I'm so tired...my weary head sinks low.

It fades, this place of many sounds and scents,
of yells triumphant , other noises loud
and so I sleep … *and in my sleep I dream*
and in my dream I'm running and walking
in sunshine 'cross a meadow-land with he,
the boy that Peg calls Long Tail Talking.

This strong and lazy boy likes me and Peg
and that Fast Girl, the wild one who's his mate
and golden coated handsome Barnaby
but Long Tail Talking doesn't think it right
for boys to get too close to them or me
so grumbles his false challenge to a fight.

!! From right in front of me a Long-ears leaps
out of his hiding place, the bounding form
a blur of brown and I am off, head down,
the grass stems whipping past my foam-flecked jaws,
others close behind: I hear His shout -
how simply flying paws ignore the Laws!

It's me and fair Fast Girl, oh what a race,
the speeding swerving tail so close ahead,
from ears laid back and gathered haunches comes
that strong, sweet smell with which our heads are filled
and we can hear the oldest song of all;
to chase: to kill or by hunger be killed.

We breast the rise full tilt: Oh no, too late
I see the Long-ears tumbling into space
and cannot stop or turn so follow him

and, falling, bounce from ledge to rocky ledge
and Fast Girl too, white water far below,
the others' faces peering o'er the edge.

I whirl through space as smaller, lesser grows
my fear; for what will be, will be. I close
my eyes against onrushing fate, recall
gold-shafted sunlight slanting through the wood
where scent of Cackle-wings to us is strong,
where White-tails tease and Dapples silent stood:
there's many-coloured Dancers in the air,
I hear a Cuckoo's urgent note, so clear
from hill-top crowned with mighty fan of trees
and through my pads I feel the moisty earth
the moving growing company of things,
the fading and the living and the birth...
now back in our unmoving cave, the bed
wherein I curl up safe to dream and where
the scents are those of He and She as we
await with patience Their homecoming sound;
the upsprung joy as one of Them appears,
our tries at holding back the forward bound.

....Then o'er the rush of air comes Fast Girl's cry;
'Zara, just stretch out and soar - for we can fly,'
and suddenly I know that this is right:
we're sea and earth, the keening wind; and fire
as, effortless, we wheel around a cloud,
as one, to point the stars, reach ever higher....

I wake, heart pounding and my throat is dry
and drink so deep, my sister still asleep
but They wake her and walk us to a crowded
place where just The Distant Lord's alone
'Right, Peg,' I shout, 'Let's find what he's about!'
I slip my lead and, head down, hurtle on.

I know he sees me, hears Their anxious shouts
but stands unmoved, unmoving till I swerve
to miss, brush past his heavy head so close -
but how disdainfully he leans, so neat
and how I tumble, just as in my dream,
how slow he strolls as I get to my feet.

'All right,?' He asks in that deep rumble voice.
I dance a bit to show him I don't hurt
although I do and do feel stupid too;
'Yes but through no thanks to you,' I say:
my He and She rush up, Their tones are harsh.
Lord says; 'Next time don't be a fool, OK?'

They place the thong around my aching neck.
although my shoulder hurts I shall not limp
and soon I'm in the ring again with Him
and with four older girls, a lovely lot,
each of their Persons wears that certain flower,
that's red like His, as round and round we trot.

The pain burns deep within my tender frame
but no-one knows for I stay on my toes,
stand still and tall, I know He wants it so.
the Person in the middle of the ring
is looking most and thinking most of me -
I know that she to us the prize will bring.

Around, the Persons' faces smile and cheer
as to my He the bigger flower is given,
with all the clapping of the Persons' hands,
but Zara's pain's too great to celebrate
our further victory, so in His eyes
there is surprise: I see his worried state.

Zara's Day

We are alone in that now-silent ring
I stand with Him and with the worsening hurt
I almost whimper out aloud. He comes!
The Distant Lord comes here to challenge me!
that noble rested head, that smooth-fast trot
so now's my time to face reality.

My aching stride's too short, my head too low
I feel I've let Them down, I am not fit.
The Distant Lord, contemptuous, turns around
to smirk - but then I hear The Fast Girl's tone
and yes, I fly! My feet carry no weight
and all the pain is gone: and we have won.

That night in our unmoving cave, in bed,
old Barnie asks about when, later on
I met the Blondie in the biggest ring
and Blackies too, and all the gundog breeds?
'Although we did not win that time,' I say,
'I did my best and that is all He needs.'

The lights go out, our place is cosy-warm
out of the dark speaks Pegan, sleepily;
'The Distant Lord came up and spoke to me,'
she said; 'He knew you hurt yourself in play:
he said although he liked your style, next time
he'd win.' He may - but this was Zara's day.

Zara, Pegan and Barnaby belonged in the nineties to some friends of ours and this narrative verse was written for them. We have ourselves owned Hungarian vizslas for more than thirty years - and have shown one of them at the highest level. Not as high, though, as Yogi *the world famous vizsla dog, biggest dog show winner of any breed, of all time, and who won the coveted Best of Breed at Crufts in 2010.*

111

Zara's Day

This one is about a hunted man, a killer deep underground. He is in the pay of his service, at the same time is hiding from them and from his own past. This is pre-EEC Dublin's fair city. But for how long can you stay out of sight …? Can the answers for the soldier / hitman / poet really be found in the gun or the knife? Or at the bottom of an emptied glass?

A Walk Downtown

Yellow lights like insubstantial islands in the dark.
A feeble, cast-off string of loose connected thoughts.
Paving cracked and worn and, rain-pricked, shining.
Still ... no wind to snatch away, to hide the sound
Of the stagger in your step, the catch of your breath,
Nor sweep you on your way to unmade bed, cold-lined,
Nor gust aside the trace of those that you just left
Who nightly seek the answers they can seldom find,
Pretend to know more than they understand and,
Grinning, clutch at immortality from glass in hand.

In Brian's Bar they watched you, saw you as you wished;
Young and strong and sensitive to most that's going on,
Dress casual poor and stubbled by design, not miss;
A man of quiet note, intriguing watcher of the scene.
'Not doing over much,' they say, though not to you,
'Writing or something. You know, poems and such.'
Heads shake and shoulders shrug; 'Bit of a loner though.'
Avert your eyes: now twist your father's crested ring
And wonder will they gain from what you will relate
Or ever learn to cease their chanting hymns of hate?

Thrown from that warm redoubt we're all outsiders now.

A Walk Downtown

Even the damn singer: tensed, you hunch and shiver,
Remembering Mairie's smile on him and touch on you
Whilst you drink and stretch your mind and think
Of his account of Dublin In The Rare Old Times.
He traps you at the bar and asks; 'How are yeh, boy?'
Traps you in the crush so you give him back the lie;
'It's good I am and sure it's great you're looking, Roy.'
But lie the singer's lies so shallow in his face,
In eyes you cannot hold, with bad that thickly laced.

Your foot-steps stop; impatient fumble with the hose.
So good to watch piss merge with rain-ringed puddle;
This glory town's in dirty-mirrored tones of night,
Long-gone its heroes, shining swords, their words.
Where are they now, lost keepers of your gallantry?
'Ireland, the liveliest and the loveliest member,' so he said,
Kraut speaking of his bureaux-ugly ee ee cee
That spreads itself within your body and your head,
Ejaculating poison loaded overpace
So who in thee, ee cee, can know how rare your Grace?

You, Dieter, bragged too much about Mercedes Benz.
No steel fantasia can hope to wipe that slate
Whose marks indelible were burned from racial hate.
Our marks; for you and we they say are bound by time.
Never will they be enough! Not your drive machine,
Your reclamation scheme to justify more crap
Converted soon to nightmare from our User dream.
You never felt it, never saw through tears the trap?
You hear no music rhyme behind the noisy beat?
Right, Dieter, here and now in this so silent street?

Zipped again and on your way and singin' in the rain.
But soft, no window-lights, there comes no angry shout.
Did woken lovers just re-turn to making love?
'I'm ha-ppy a-gainnn just,' Just think of them in bed,

A Walk Downtown

Hot gasping working up so wasteful in the dark.
'Oh yes,' she cries coming maybe to that place where
You have not: Not since that with Mairie in the park,
Long grass, sky shining through the curtain of her hair.
'Lie still,' she laughs although you have her breast.
'If he finds us, your man is sure to want the rest.'

No no, oh yes, Beth floats into your troubled mind,
Her wide awakened face, confettied titian hair
Her soft and gentle form that night so light so sweet
A thing amidst the gathering darkness of your youth
To have and hold in perfect love from this day forth
Together walk the golden foothills of our lives
And then the baby John who would become life's worth
The only son from whom so soon all hope derives:
Oh Beth! they took you 'ere our babe was weaned
On crying stones that bear your blood, uncleaned.

You breathe in deep and pause and hold on tightly to
Cold iron street light, fingers stiff and tense and wet
Feel rough paint flake and the warm soft skin of her.
Smell sweet/sour weedy Liffey; the female of her.
Let go, good man y'are; let her go, that story's told.
Take care on slick wet road, cross to the riverside
But slip, lights whirling like a broken band of gold
And so from shrieking tyres you cannot hope to hide,
See three-arm star rest smug inside its silver ring;
Say, 'Sorry Mister Benz if any problem I may bring.'

You've no real hurt on you but on the driver's face
Revolves shock then fear, understanding then fury
As you hold to his car, climb to your feet, un-hit,
His curses fluent; 'Move your bloody arse, eejit!'
Now safe to the bench although shaking and wet
And in dreams it's not real to feel unbroken bones
...Mairie's real, so she is, as this your last cigarette,

As The Pogues and the Rats and those English Stones
As the heat in her and the ground and mid-summer air,
And the joy and the shame and the pain; now your fear.

.... Bloody wheels ... that routinely can inspire such fear
Boast freedom as they lock you up in motor debt
So you may go from where you didn't want to be
On roads that are a threat to all that walks or flies,
To places new from which so soon you'll need to haste,
Despoil with engine gas the world in hateful din
That goes unnoticed, or as worthy of the waste
Of lives and space and peace and grace to live within.
Forbadest He thou to engage in false idolatry?
He could not have meant thy bloody motor, could He?

This seat's all wet... remember that pale-faced fellow
In Brian's? Too much of the Jameson's drunk too fast
And shined-shoe well-suited men of business
Drinking with men of trade, even with men of work!
Spending so casually, each other over-talking
Eyeing hot-eyed Sinead, Brian's' cold hearted bar-maid
Telling false stories of whatever they're hawking...
Yes, tales of derring-do, fine men y'are getting laid.
Then into your firms' cars, fast forward to your wives,
Excused by strong drink for such poverty of lives.

Look up: Your eyes can feel the crying of this night
The stars and light all lost behind that wet black face
Whose tears descend to spate the darkly moving flood.
Hey, that Mercedes man? you wonder could he know?
If so where do you go when death is just begun?
Mother 'tis true you have to reap but what you sow?
He is bad seed who is your husband's only son?
Though yet his clay's un-ploughed, nor has it felt the hoe,
But he fears now that his bursting crop of untold things
Will stay untold if Mairie to the singer sings.

A Walk Downtown

What purpose has that urge that blots all other things,
And drains the mind of all except a certain she?
That has you risk your life to find that old glory,
Grows, some fresh pink rose in thorny secrecy
To prick you, have you bleed no matter what you give?
This agony, it moves from just a thing of glands?
'Forsaking all others:' But a rose that's not your own,
Is a fire at which those lost may warm their hands?
Questions like black shadows leap ahead across the way.
Lost answers swirling in chaotic shades of grey.

Before the film began and lights and music faded
Carefully she'd asked; 'What was it like, the fighting?'
You stared at her in silence as she held your hand.
She could not know but just suspect and find it thrilling.
Eyes fixed to filling silver screen she'd said no more
But as the skirt had pulled across soft-rounded thigh
You thought; Joe said 'it is a war like any war,
Long-waiting years, then final seconds rocket by'.
And he, this bed-sit soldier, pondering on cowardice
Had felt no glory in himself, none in the Judas kiss.

There is Joe's face, rain-mirrored in between your feet.
The eyes, black pits observing all but asking nought,
Not even yet to know the hand behind the hand
Behind the gun that killed another mother's son
Rather than take a prisoner once the bomb was stayed
From stripping bloody tissue from the hard white bones
Of any other close to he whose life they craved.
In his glass house Joe'd seen no danger throwing stones,
Knew not the cancer in his soul nor realised its death
Caught not that whiff of sulphur on the fighters' breath.

Hear that distant tread? Your head comes up to listen.
Your jeans are cold and soaking wet, your legs like lead.

Nothing; the bastard's stopped and may be listening too?
Flick your fag-end out into the stream and stand and
Stumble on; look not you back nor think to run
But stop half way across the bridge, now do not turn
It matters not to me my friend so come on, gun,
One puny splash then no-one's left to care or learn.
Make it easy. Yes, look down into that blackest boil,
That flood that eats your blood-beloved island's soil.

Fresh early morning dew on creaking, bending oars
Dead storms yet surge and writhe uneasy in the brine.
From on wet floorboards with the rods and tangled line.
Atop his straining hands you watch your father's face.
He winks and grunts his exultation at the waves.
You smell the sea-weed as you're passing by hard rock,
And hear the mewly calling of the sea-king's slaves
And kneel to try to see your home down Belfast Loch.
'Look well, son,' Daddy says; 'This place is surely yours
For always, son; however else the lion roars.'

Blink rain spray from your eyes and wonder how your boy
Looks now at eight years old - does he remember you?
And have they told him yet of why his daddy's gone
And why this father and his son shall never share
A wink, a secret smile, an extra special day,
Nor track the dewy meadow in the early morn;
Tell why the bombers' chance explosion stole away
The gladness from his father's heart at being born?
Your nan and grandpa will look after you, my John,
Please hold no pistol, John; please detonate no bomb.

'Tis nobler, son, to close your eyes or turn to fight?
The steps are drawing nearer in the night; who cares?
'O.K?' The voice has sharp anxiety; Garda,
If some fool jumps he might feel bound to follow.
'Sure, officer, I'm listening for the lion's roars;

A Walk Downtown

I own this place or did he say I'm owned by it?
Say, Ireland's now more yours than was the dinosaur's?'
'Right, fellow, move,' the garda says; 'Don't need that shit.'
'I'm gone,' you say, not wanting trouble with the law,
'The trouble is the drink is at my bollix of a jaw.'

Remember how when you had fish upon your hook
You'd always shunned self-questions on the lives you took.
For when the killing grips who needs to know the answers
Like there tonight those tattoo'd kids in Brian's Bar -
Just brawlers but had sensed the germ in you, for real
(That you knew fine should really not infect a poet.)
They'd seen the out-burst spores advance your killing zeal,
Knew how the will to hurt gains ground by being hurt,
Thus how small pain can turn into a thousand kills
With none to end such exponensis 'till He wills.

But fear you dying more or any less than living?
'It is as un-natur-al to live without war
As it is right to die waging war,' old Joe had said,
But after you'd typed his words you tore up the page
And dropped the pieces in the bowl and pissed on them
And tears had washed into this would-be poet's eyes
Who knew could not from stone form any shining gem,
No more than manufactured words make truth from lies.
Now turn into your street; again you hear the tread,
Behind you something moves that's neither quick nor dead.

Inside, lean back against the door, your beer eyes closed
Against harsh-bright, un-shaded light and un-made bed.
New dampness holds the cold smoke smell of the place
Now gather your pages and read once more with dread;
> *'In hot beginning rock hissed in a sterile sea*
> *That pulled its tides from other worlds, explosion turned,*
> *And in the space foreverness of chemistry;*
> *Mothered by salts and sired by sun at last life burned...'*

Jesus, some battling tom-cat's agonising scream
Has yanked your startled senses from that deep dream.

With care re-place your work beside its silicone womb
These words could just live on beyond your early tomb.
In re-made silence look around just one more time,
Oh yes this barren place yet held or holds out hope.
Now leave the door ajar, switch off the naked light,
Full dressed, lie calmly down and do not touch the knife,
In darkness ponder on the past and what was right,
Will your shadow dance again to greet next morning's life?

Upon your face, how soft night's drafty fingers play,
Oh son oh father, whither goes this John MacRae?

The End

I used to travel widely on business around Europe. Pre-EEC Ireland
was one of my favourite destinations. I had good friends both north
and south of the border but nowhere in those days could you escape
what used to be called The Troubles. One evening a British Army
officer threatened those at our Belfast dinner table with a .38 revolver.
He was very drunk and was duly taken awa y… But pre-EEC
Dublin was my favourite of favourites. Ah, the Guinness there!

When life turned around and bit star footballer James Earling - bit off both of his legs, actually, there didn't seem to be much point in anything any more.

On The Bench

The seat by the footbridge over the river was unoccupied. He made his way there. Slowly. Quickly wasn't an option. The almost new bench had been bolted up from good, solid oak with a brass plaque set into its back rail. *Donated by Robert C Walters*, the plaque read. Beneath that; in quotation marks, *2,780 miles to Long Berrow*. He settled down on the bench, let go of the crutch. The pain loosen up a bit. Thank you to Robert C Walters. But that inscription. How come? Long Berrow was only twenty two miles away.

There wasn't much in today's paper if you weren't bothering with the back pages. Close in by the reeds a pair of swans took turns dipping heads under water. In the middle where the river flowed out from under the bridge it was five metres deep. He should know. In between football sessions as a kid he'd often fished there. Oh yes, in those uncomplicated days when St Kilda's had been home to him how often he'd leaned over the parapet to peer into the depths. Now he wondered how it would feel when the river closed over him; when all his stars at last went out.

Sitting on this bench, mothers walking past with their pushchairs would often smile at him, wish him a good morning, reassured by his relative youth and by his being a tin-legged cripple with quite a nice face underneath all that scarring. Sometimes one would stop, try to chat. And how often that had seemed a sure-fire signal for their dogs to

121

piss on his bench or his leg. Then the mums would apologise and when they did he told them that it was all right: He didn't mind and Robert C Walters wouldn't, either. He'd point to the plaque and they would smile their puzzled smiles and nod and say goodbye and walk on.

Most of the men passers-by knew who he was all right. The aged and the unemployed would often sit down alongside him, try to talk football. Of course they would even if he really didn't want to talk with anyone, especially about football. And besides that they all called him 'Jimmy,' which he hated. Maybe *James Earling* had had too much gravitas for a footballer, even a one legged ex-footballer trying hard to forget what he'd once been and what he was now.

He put down the newspaper, thinking about the upcoming insurance appeal. *'They may be more generous than they need be,'* the lawyer had told him, *'in the circumstances.'* Bollocks. The guy hadn't needed to mention the level of alcohol in the bloodstream of a story-book young striker straight out of St Kilda's orphanage, rising star of Marlebury Town Football Club. Nor had the lawyer said anything more about the red hot Mondeo going much too fast into that rainy night, nor about the little blonde with the eye-popping chest who'd been a lot luckier than him, 'though still unlucky. All of the above a write off and soon, any time now, so would he be. So? When? He shivered, thinking of the drop from the parapet, going deep, trying to suck in cold and muddy water to end it as quickly as possible.

'I see United done it again, son.' An old guy he hadn't seen before. 'That Giggsie, he's just a bloody marvel. Mind if I join you?'

'Be my guest, mate.' James moved his crutch to a more amenable position. Please, please, do not go on about Ryan Giggs or Beckham or bloody Pele or any of them.

The old man sat down, parked his stick, went on; 'Yes, like walking it through a door it were, that third one. You seen it, Jimmy? He's got one of them going one way and the other the other; walks straight through the bloody middle. The goalie's dived too soon and he's lifted the ball over and it's in the back of the net. Wonderful.'

'Yes?' Anything to change the subject. 'That's a great stick you have there.' The stick was made of very dark wood, almost black; ebony or something. It had a man's head carved into the end of its handle.

'You'll recognise who he is, then?'

He shook his head. 'Can't say I do.'

'You don't know the greatest outside left England ever produced, son? The Ryan Giggs of the forties and fifties? That's Sir Tom Finney. *The Preston plumber* they called him. Seventy six caps and thirty goals for England. And plenty more goals for Preston North End. That were the only Club the man ever played for, barring war-time of course.'

'Tom Finney? Yes, I think I've heard of him.' but would he ever get away from football speak?

'You're sitting on his mate's bench,' said the old man, quietly.

'What?'

'Bobby Walters. It says it on here. Robert C Walters.' He turned and pointed to the plaque. 'He was Tom Finney's mate in the war. Tom and Bobby, they played a lot of games together. A team of soldier lads. Army called them *The Wanderers*. Mostly ex-pro's. He grinned. 'Powers that be reckoned football was good for our boys' morale. Didn't do much harm to the Wanderers', neither.' He sighed, pushed his cap back, rested his chin on Tom Finney's head. 'Anyway, when Bobby Walters finally turns up here again after the war he were in a worse state than bloody Russia.' He checked himself visibly. 'Oh, bloody 'ell. Sorry, son.'

'What for? I've been asking people about it, I mean about him whose name's on here.'

'Bobby Walters? He were born same year as Tom Finney, nineteen twenty two. Turned pro and played for Marlebury a few times before he joined up, like most of the pro's did. That would have been nineteen forty. Never come back 'til a couple o' years after the war were all over. Everyone who remembered about him thought he must have copped it in the fighting.'

'That right? You said he was in a bad state?'

The old man nodded, grinned. 'Not that it stopped him too much, you know? Not with the ladies or nothing. Matter of fact he'd tell anyone he'd done some of his best work here on this bloody seat. Well, in actual fact he meant the seat that were here before this one.'

'What was this Bobby Walters' problem then?' For some reason it seemed important to James that he should know.

'Bobby?' He hesitated. 'When he come back he hadn't got no legs, not down from the knees.'

'Poor guy. Bet he had them all queuing up to watch.' He laughed, the harsh cynicism in the sound of it appalling even himself. He realised he'd half shouted it.

One of the mums who'd normally have stopped to say hello now hurried by, leaving her little boy and their fox terrier standing there staring at him. The woman called out; 'Jonathan, do come along' but the dog, predictably, strolled over to cock his leg up on the bench. James took a swipe at it with his crutch and the boy burst into tears, ran after his mother, the terrier in unharmed pursuit.

'I'll be on my way then.' The old man levered himself up with the aid of his ebony Tom Finney stick.

'No, please, I need to know more about this guy, Walters. I'm sorry.'

'Sorry? Listen to me. You should be ashamed of yourself, son. Get yourself up off your bloody backside and see what you can find out for yourself. The state you've got yourself into? You're not fit to tie Bobby Walters' bootlaces if you don't mind me saying so.' He turned away; 'As a footballer nor as a bloody man, neither.'

James tried to get up but fumbled the movement and fell back on to the bench. The old man didn't even look back. Through the new pain he shouted, 'Well, you fuck off, then, why don't you.'

The woman behind the Town Hall reception desk looked up, frowning, inspecting him. 'The bench in the park?' she repeated.

He said; 'Yes, the one near the bridge. It was donated to the town by a guy called Robert C Walters. It says so on the brass plaque. I'd like to find out more about it, about him.'

She picked up the phone, dialled an extension, murmured something he couldn't catch then handed him the instrument; 'I think Mister Brown can possibly help you.'

The voice was that of a busy man talking to a time-waster. 'Good morning, Mister, er, Earling?'

'Yes. Good morning.'

'I can tell you that the bench in question was donated to the town under the terms of the Will of Mister Robert Cedric Walters. The terms were quite unusual,' the man went on, his voice betraying its owner's distrust of anything at all unusual; 'The interest on the donation was to be used to maintain the bench that was there at the time of his death. When, in the view of Civil Works the old bench needed to be replaced, the capital sum itself was to be used to purchase a new and improved one and the residue passed to a children's home.'

'Is there any record of where Mister Walters was buried, or anything?'

'Just one moment.' The impatience was becoming more evident. 'No. Our records show he was cremated. His bank manager was sole Trustee. No known next of kin.'

'Thank you. But why the '2,780 miles to Long Berrow?' Any idea?'

'What? Oh, I'm sorry but I can't help you with that. Perhaps it was his birth place?'

He said again, 'Thank you', replaced the hand-set, tried a smile on the non-receptive receptionist and turned to leave, the rubber foot on his crutch slipping a little on polished marble.

Long Berrow was only an hour away by bus. Refusing the usual offers of help he got himself down and out of it, looked around. Just a few cottages straggling along the bottom of this shallow valley and that nicely kept village green, saucer shaped with a cricket pitch in the middle and edged around with mature chestnuts. And there was a little church with a well tended war memorial in front, and a pub, *The Cart and Horses*. So why in hell was he here then? He crossed the road, clumped up to the bar, ordered a tomato juice.

It took the barman all of fifteen seconds to chance his arm; 'You're Jimmy Earling, aren't you?' James nodded. The barman said, 'I knew it. It's really good to see you, Jimmy. I'm John O'Donovan. That's my name over the door and this one's on me.' He snapped the cap off a bottle; 'Worcester sauce, ice?' James nodded. 'Did you catch the Giggs goal last night?'

'Thanks for the drink but no, I don't keep up with the football these days. I was wondering if you could help me?'

O'Donovan took no time at all to recover from no beer and no football; 'Sure. If I can I will. We all will.' The two other early drinkers nodded, murmured their provisional concurrence. 'You know, Jimmy, Marlebury Town's not been the same since, well, since your accident and everything.'

'No?' He levered himself up on to a bar stool. 'I was wondering, have you ever heard of Robert C Walters?'

'Of course. It's on the War Memorial over there. He came from here some time before the war; world war two that is. Someone told me he played for Town like yourself.'

One of the drinkers said, 'My Dad used to talk about Bobby Walters. He was born and brought up over the road. Dairy Cottage, right? Brilliant right back. Lovely man by all accounts. My Dad said he'd often wheel himself in here for a pint or three and have a good laugh with everyone, specially about the memorial. It was put up while he was missing but it turned out he'd only been injured. Right at the end, on the run in to Berlin? It was bad enough, mind, From what my Dad used to tell me you'd better believe it. Seems, after getting wounded he'd got taken and held by the Russians. My Dad said he'd never talk about that bit, nor about his V.C..' He pointed at James' empty glass. 'You'll have one with me, Jimmy?'

'That's kind of you but no thanks. One juice is enough Don't drink anything else much these days. Contrary to - but did you say Bobby Walters had the Victoria Cross?'

'Right. Posthumous, except it weren't posthumous by about bloody fifty years' The man laughed. 'Like I said, they all thought he was dead and gone 'til he turns up wheeling along on this home-made trolley thing of his, laughing his socks off. Not that he needed any, mind; socks?' The speaker took a deep draught from his pint, wiped his moustache; 'Sorry, mate, that wasn't intended.'

The war memorial was of grey granite in the shape of a cross set on a plinth with a dozen or so names in alphabetical order, some of them same family. Right at the bottom, *Walters, Corporal Robert C, V.C. : Royal Fusiliers and The Wanderers.'* The cross was facing the bench by the bus stop. By now the sun was partly behind the cross and the trees. He screwed up his eyes. Underneath the names there was an inscription: *'At the going down of the sun and in the morning / We will remember them.'* Crows argued with each other in the tall beeches. He could smell mown grass, food cooking in the pub. Lights were coming on in a few of the windows, warm yellow in the gathering dusk. He felt the tears. Couldn't help it, couldn't understand why. There was just this weird sense of - well, something ... the Marlebury bus came trundling down the hill, drew to a stop with its doors opening. He didn't move.

'You getting on, Jimmy?' the driver called. 'Can I give you a hand?'

'No thanks. You can give me a foot if you like,' he joked. So odd, this strange laughing at things, at himself. 'Seriously, thanks but no. I'm going back over the road for a pint and something to eat. When's the last bus?'

His insurance appeal had been thrown out. But more importantly he really was getting to grips with the prosthetic leg. More like a friend these days, less of a hated enemy. And this morning he'd screwed himself right up, left his crutch behind the front door, made his unsteady progress to the paper shop then all the way to Bobby Walters' bench. He'd fallen only the one time, laughing about it both times now he'd learned how best to roll with it, taking care to reassure passers-by that he could get up by himself, thanks, however unsteadily. He sat down, opened the paper at the football pages. Marlebury Town FC hadn't started off their season at all badly. The new kid in midfield wouldn't last long though, not with half the Premiership watching him. He'd seen the spotters down at the ground on Saturday. They were supposed to be secret but everyone knew who they were. And now himself. Now he was to be one of them, a spotter for the club. He grinned, stood up, turning his back on the river to watch a horde of muddy schoolboys rushing around on the pitch, many of them shouting for the ball at the same time. The little wing back had all the push and shove and something else, some movement, some kind of balance as he sent the opposition first one way then the other, belted the ball down the touchline, took it infield through a crowd of legs, tried to chip the goalie. The lad must have been watching Ryan. He took out his notepad.

He hadn't heard the old man coming up. 'Puts me in mind of The Little Bird - you remember, Garrincha? What's happened to your crutch then?' Tom Finney's head took all the weight as its owner sat himself down.

Jimmy said; 'Crutch? I'm hoping it's history. Listen, I've been waiting for you to turn up. I wanted to apologise.' He held out his hand. 'But you never did tell me your name?'

The old man shrugged, gripped James' hand with surprising strength, looking up at him from under the peak of his cap. 'Name's Bellamy. Folk generally calls me Ben. This guy you was asking about?' He cocked his thumb at the brass plaque; 'He were my father.'

'What, Robert Walters, your Dad?'

'That's right. He and my Mum could agree on that, at least. She were the Bellamy name, God rest her. She died when I was still only in my early teens. After that I were brought up where you were, son, at St Kilda's. I was going to tell you.'

'You were? I'm - I'm sorry. I don't mean about St Kilda's, I mean about your mother. You *should* have told me.'

'Didn't give me too much of a bloody chance, did you?' The old eyes wrinkled and twinkled.

'Yes', Jimmy said, 'I wanted to tell you. I spent time in the library checking out on a few things. Like the mileage from here to the camp where the Russians held him. It was in the Caucases. I worked out the route he might have taken across Europe and back to Long Berrow on his skate board or whatever it was. I've got the map in my place. Two thousand seven hundred miles, just like it says.'

'Is that right? I've not been much of a travelling man, myself.' He frowned; 'In case you might be thinking it, he didn't what they call abandon me. He weren't a bad man or anything. It's just, he didn't want to burden me with his problems. Not mother either when she were still around.'

'I can understand all that now I've spoken to people. And I've read all about his Victoria Cross. What he did was just incredible.'

'He wouldn't never want to talk about that V.C.. Said they just drew lots for 'em.'

'Like hell they did.'

Ben Bellamy chuckled; 'Bobby Walters and Douglas Bader, eh? Talk about wide eyed and bloody legless.' There was a good deal of high pitched cheering from the pitch. Little Garrincha had finally scored. They watched him take his theatrical dive, get himself covered over with mud and a struggling crowd of team-mates. 'You recognise that lad?'

'Can't say so.'

'Think back to when you had your little tantrum. You hit his dog with your crutch.'

'Please don't remind me.'

'Anyway he's got *it*, whatever *it* is. You know and I know. Some of like what you had, and Sir Tom - my Dad, too.'

'They've got Bobby Walters' picture in the Club,' James said; 'The Chairman told me he was supposed to have been as good as anybody, maybe better than anybody.' He hesitated, shifted more of his weight on to the tin leg. It didn't hurt much any more. 'I wouldn't say this to everyone, they'd probably have me inside, but when I was sitting in front of the Long Berrow War Memorial something happened. I don't know what, but something definitely happened to me.' He grinned; 'Don't worry, I wasn't hearing voices or anything. I went for a couple of pints then waited in the church on my own while the last bus came. There was definitely something…'

'What they call 'born again,' eh? I wouldn't be surprised. You know, my Dad mightn't have had no legs but there wasn't much else wrong with him. He helped a whole lot of people in his time. Maybe still does. Who the hell knows?' He flicked something off Tom Finney's head, polished it with his sleeve; 'He went on damn great sponsored walks, or 'rolls' as he called them. 'Sponsored rolls.' Did John O'Groats to Lands End once over. All the proceeds to St Kilda's and most of his pensions, too. Not that the pensions were all that much, not after he'd paid support to one or two ladies more than just my Mum.'

Jimmy laughed; 'What? Hey, he could have been my grandfather.'

'Dad could be anybody's, any footballer's anyway. That whole bloody team's over there for all I knows.' The old man's hands curled, one on top of the other, taking a firm new grip on his ebony Sir Tom. 'I loved him, you know, my old man. Everyone did. Legs or no bloody legs. He used to tell me, All you need is love, son. Those Liverpool lads weren't first with that one.'

The end

We used to walk our dogs in a Winchester Park much like the one in On The Bench. *In this park were a number of football pitches and wooden benches, each of them bearing an inscribed donor plate. One inscription included a seemingly irrelevant place name. I sat on that bench and wrote this story outline there and then - on the proverbial back of an envelope.*

On The Bench

A very old man returns to Wester Ross, the scene of his youth in World War Two. This is Loch Ewe where the convoys assembled to begin their perilous missions for the relief of Russia. Eddie Colman is coming back to where, as a serviceman in the war, he met his late wife, Dolly. And where he last saw Charlie, the friend (or ex-friend) who died on the convoys. Charlie: the man of whom he and Dolly could never, never speak…

Not talking about Charlie

He'd not thought he could get this excited any more but here he was, nearly ninety and back in Dolly's country. Fifty long, long years ago; six years after the war and up here on the Norton five hundred with Dolly holding on like grim death and all their holiday stuff in the panniers and the kids left at home with mother, bless her. As the bus ground its way around the margins of the lochs he gazed out at the passing land and sea scape. Very little had changed. No houses or anything, not for miles and miles. Autumn in Wester Ross. Eddie blinked back the sudden sadness.

'You have come from far?' The big old boy in the window seat across the aisle had leaned across as speaking in the clear, soft accents of the native Highlander.

'Rail from Norwich to Inverness, now the bus. Far enough, I reckon.'

'The last I heard, it was Adelaide you were at, Eddie, but you'll be remembering this road well enough. You are Eddie Colman, I'm thinking?'

He hesitated, recognition dawning. 'You know me? Jesus; just wait a minute … I don't believe it. You're Murdo, Dolly's brother?'

'Oh yes; but do not take the Lord's name in vain, brother-in-law.' The man's grin had in it all of Dolly's. They shifted towards each other, shook hands across the aisle. 'Ouch! The old right hand is still good, so it seems,' Murdo murmured. He chuckled. 'I was bigger and stronger than you, but you had the quickest right hand. I never did see it coming, Eddie Colman.'

Eddie laughed. 'You've saved me some searching, Murdo, old mate. I've been meaning to come up to see you all for bloody years, ever since I came home from Aussie after ... well, after she died, you know?'

'Yes.'

'I'm sorry I didn't get up here 'til now. Tell you the truth, after I got back to England I wasn't looking for much in the way of socialising.'

He nodded. 'Well, never you mind. You'll be staying at Aultbea?'

'At the hotel.'

'You've come up in the world.' Murdo laughed again. 'Only the officers at the Aultbea in those days, so I am remembering. I hope we shall be seeing the bottom of a glass or two whilst you are here?'

'O yes. But the rest of the family? How are they all?'

Murdo shook his head. 'Just myself and Donal now, but he not able to get out and about any more.' The bus had slowed, the driver sounding his horn to move a few sheep off the road.

Eddie chuckled. 'Dolly, she used to call the sheep woolly maggots.' He looked up at the hill. 'In between the Murmansk runs, me and Dolly, we used to go walking up there. It was good to get away from everything going on with the military down by the loch.'

'I would think it must have been for you. Good days and bad days they were for all of us. And you are still in touch with your friend Charlie, I hope? In spite of you know what...?'

He shook his head; 'No, I'm sorry. Charlie was killed on the convoys.' He didn't know for what he was sorry but it didn't matter, he never talked about Charlie. They lapsed into a not uncomfortable silence then said, 'I'm a bit tired. Trouble about getting so old, Murdo. You're asleep more in the day and less in the night when you should be.' Murdo nodded. Soon enough he felt the closing of his eyes. *Already he'd slipped back into Aultbea Village Hall, the place he so often was when he slept, the dreams brighter and more real than ever when you somehow know most of the time it's a dream you're dreaming. He was the raw young fisherman who'd run off with his pal, Charlie, from the Great Yarmouth herring fleet just a couple of years after war broke out, the two of them finally arriving at the naval land-base HMS Helicon on Loch Ewe. Some of the locals at the village hall dance didn't even speak much English. Gaelic, yes, not much use for him and Charlie with the girls. But the beautiful black haired one with the cheeky eyes who told them her name was Dolly, she could speak English all right. Her voice came sweet and low, seeming to sing the words and even now, when he knew he was asleep and dreaming, the sound of her voice affected him. He stirred uncomfortably. But that bloody young Scotsman. Cheeky sod, trying to warn him off. He hadn't realised the lad was the girl's brother, this Murdo, and looking after her like they all looked after each other up here.*

'Oh, isn't this just exquisite?' The Englishwoman in the seat in front had woken him, speaking to the boy alongside her. The bus was climbing steeply, low gear grinding away. He blinked, shielded his eyes with his hands against the setting of the sun, looked through the window down to a chain of rock-bound beaches.. The sea stretched out flat calm, a sheet of fiery glass the same as the low part of the sky so you couldn't tell where sea ended and sky began. A short way offshore Gruinard Island humped up, dark and menacing. Murdo interrupted his thoughts; 'I'm thinking you'll be remembering this all right, Eddie?'

He blinked again, cleared his throat. 'Where the hills end right out over there on the left? That's Greenstone Point, right, Murdo? And Loch Ewe's only just round the corner from that, so we'll be at Aultbea in two shakes of a lamb's tail.'

The woman in front had overheard them. She turned around, smiling, 'Isn't it absolutely wonderful?'

'Well, it is that,' he said, 'Except that island, there. That's not. That's where the brainy boys from Porton Down came to do their germ warfare experiments. Yes, anthrax, top secret those days.'

Now the boy turned around, suddenly interested: 'Anthrax? Please sir, tell us about it.' Eddie didn't dislike the 'sir.'

The boy's mother frowned. 'Mark!'

'Oh the boy's all right, lady. Most of 'em don't want to hear us old codgers going on about the war and all that. Murdo chuckled. Eddie went on; 'Just before I got up this way for the Russian convoys, and that was sixty years back, lad, these hush-hush men from the War Office took over that there island. They put a load of sheep and goats and some cattle on it then they killed every last one of them with some kind of new gizmo. Yes, and top secret 'til after the war was done and dusted. But they only said what everyone'd already got to know, like, about how this anthrax stuff was lethal. Its spores or whatever would stay alive in the soil. Almost forever. No-one could set foot on Gruinard, they said, not for donkey's years.'

The boy said, 'Wow!'

Murdo broke in. 'It was cleared by the government about ten years ago but you wouldn't catch me on that island still, no, you would not.'

The boy squinted out of the bus window, looking into the sun. 'There isn't anyone there now. I can't see any houses or sheep or anything.'

The woman sighed. 'Talk about *where only Man is vile*.' It's horrible.'

The boy had knelt up on his seat to face Eddie. 'What's a convoy, sir?'

'Mark!' His mother looked at Eddie apologetically, shaking her curls: 'I'm sorry.'

'No problem. A convoy is a group of ships, laddie, all of them going in the same direction at the same speed. We were taking all kinds of war stuff from here right the way up through the Baltic to Murmansk. For the Russians, see. They were supposed to be on our side so we needed them equipped to fight the Germans.' They'd topped the hill, were now descending into the tiny village. He spotted the first bit of Loch Ewe, felt the adrenalin kick in, the upsurge of old memories.

Murdo said, softly; 'They were brave men on those ships, son, very brave. Many did not come back.'

When the bus pulled up near to the pier Eddie got to his feet, as irritated as ever by the small, slow pains of his age. He nodded to the woman, shook hands with the boy. The boy said, 'Goodbye, sir,' came smartly to attention, saluted the two old men.

Murdo joined him in the bar most evenings. The two of them talked about Dolly and her family and what had happened to them all. And he told Murdo something of how it had been in Australia and something about the time when, not that long after he'd retired from his post-war trade as a printer, Dolly had just looked across at him and smiled and had told him in that gentle way of hers that she was going to have to leave him, but that it was all right. Everybody dies, that they would both be all right. They had been lying there side by side in bed at the time. It had been another blue sky Sunday morning, the Adelaide church bells calling out. It had not been a total surprise and he'd put down the newspaper when she told him, saying nothing at the time; couldn't. Just reached out for her. She'd been sixty three and as beautiful then as ever she had been and they had made love with none of the clumsiness or the guilt with which they had made love that first time, up here on the hill. And afterwards he had cried the first of his own thick salt tears and that was when she'd tried again to tell him about Charlie but he'd put his finger to her lips, smiled, shaken his head. He knew. Every time he looked at James, their first born, he knew but didn't want to know.

Most days of his holiday Eddie walked miles to visit the old camp sites, gun emplacements and suchlike. And of course the village hall. Sometimes Murdo came with him, their walking sticks tap-tapping in unison along the single track roads. Both of them were still pretty fit, considering. He looked for the start of the hill trails up which he had climbed with Dolly and sometimes with Charlie. Once he tried going up there but after a few hundred yards it proved too rough for him. And once he walked to that secret place under the bridge where he and Dolly had first made their frantic love, stood there looking at it for a long time, thinking about that lovely girl who had been his first, the one who would be his last.

Murdo had a small open dinghy with an outboard engine. Hadn't been used in years but the two of them went over everything together, pronounced it seaworthy, got a couple of the village lads to help get her afloat. She started first time. They puttered off around Isle Ewe then motored all the way across the quiet waters of the loch. He'd always loved being in any kind of a boat on the sea but had never taken the sea for granted. Too many of the mates he and Charlie had grown up with on the East Coast fishing boats had gone the way of Davey Jones. You couldn't be a fisherman without respect for the sea, could you?

They visited the tiny settlement called Cove, close by the headland on the other side of the loch, there to visit the memorial for the men of the North Atlantic convoys who hadn't come back; Charlie included. He sighed, shook his grey head.

Back in the boat they followed the rocky coast, re-landed at the half derelict crofting settlement where Dolly and

Murdo and the others had been born and brought up. No electricity or phones or even any tap water in those days. The cottage was now just another ruin. Murdo left him to his thoughts, walked back down to the beach in search of bait. They had decided to try the fishing tomorrow if the weather held.

Eddie picked his way in, sat down on a pile of fallen stones, lit a cigarette, watched smoke drifting up through where the roof had been. He enjoyed the smoking. It hadn't seemed to make much sense, giving them up. Not after Dolly.

He thought about that evening between convoys when he'd rowed across to look for his girl, expecting to meet her people for the first time. He thought about the big fight after he had surprised his mate Charlie, for Charlie had got here before him. He hadn't known about what his friend had been up to. Himself and Charlie wrestling, punching, rolling, locked together down into that stream, or burn as they called it up here, with Murdo and the other brothers and her father all looking on in silence. Dolly had run off, crying. He could have killed Charlie that day and damn near did.

Well, what he'd started the Germans had soon enough finished, hadn't they? His ex-friend's convoy had sailed the next day without him. He had been left behind in hospital at Gairloch. 'Fell from a rock-face,' that's what Charlie'd told them, loyal as ever, except - Eddie took one final drag on the cigarette, blinked, dropped the butt on to his mother-in-law's once so carefully swept kitchen floor. He thought about Charlie going out on the first available convoy after he'd come out of hospital, the SS bloody *St Agnes*. The one that'd disappeared with all hands, 'position unknown'. Enforced radio silence in those days.

A mile away, over across the loch, was the pale strip of Slaggan beach; Slaggan the long since abandoned settlement to which he and Dolly had walked the day after he'd put

Charlie in hospital. They'd sat side by side on a rock by the shore, saying nothing until she'd burst into tears and told him she was pregnant. He remembered standing up without a word, striding away up the sandy beach, his mind in an unruly turmoil, then going back to where he'd left her. She'd been sobbing, her face in her hands. He smiled, now, remembering how he'd actually got down on one knee to ask her if it would be all right if he asked her father if they could marry. Sitting here in her ruined cottage he could almost feel the wet sand through his uniform trousers. He'd just received a posting down to Portsmouth so it would need to be soon, he'd told her. When she'd taken away her hands and looked down at him the tear stained beauty of her and the look she had for him had told him all he'd needed to know.

Not much ceremonial in Portsmouth about those war-time marriages. Afterwards he'd sent her to live with his mother in Norfolk whilst she carried baby James. Himself, he'd gone off sailing the seven seas for the duration of the war. He didn't ever want to know about what she'd been up to with Charlie. Charlie had been his friend, would always be, never mind the bloody fight. And really, there'd been no point in talking about Charlie, not even with his wife. Not then. Not ever.

At breakfast time the nice young receptionist came in to see him. 'Your friend, Murdo,' she said, 'He's just been on the phone. Not feeling so well this morning. He says he's sorry but he won't be able to come out fishing with you.' She shook her curls. 'Fishing, just! For goodness sake, what were the two of you thinking about?'

Eddie said; 'Now listen here, young lady, I've had more days out at sea at the fishing than you've had hot dinners.' He thought about all the fresh bait Murdo had got together, the old rods and tackle he'd got out and cleaned up, the engine all fuelled and ready. He looked out through the window.   The weather had held good. 'I shall go anyway, so it's fish for supper; all right?'

'Popeye the sailor man, so you are, but I don't think we'll be holding the menu. Myself, it's my day off. It's me to Inverness to have my hair done. You keep an eye on the weather, now, Admiral Colman. It's called your weather eye, is it not? Mum says it's coming in. She knows more about weather round here than the telly does.'

Murdo's dinghy cut nicely across the long, low, glass-like rollers. Slow rise, slow fall. Seagulls and fulmars wheeled above the V of his wake. A wilderness of dull green and bracken hills ringed the loch, here and there patches of dying purple. Passing the last scattered buildings of Mellon Charles he wondered if anyone there could hear him singing. He hoped not. His voice was still not bad but the songs were mostly snatches of half-remembered ballads best confined to the below decks. He looked around. Yes, this would do it. He cut the engine, tackled up, baited the hooks. Once he'd got going on that first, almost wind-less drift he stopped singing, concentrating, tuned well into the silence, to the tremors and bumps of the lead weight dragging far below on the sea-bed in concert with the surface rise and fall. 'Must be a storm out there,' he told himself, talking out aloud; 'Wouldn't get these rollers, else.' His rod tip bounced twice then curved hard down, jerking spasmodically. He struck to set the hook, feeling the life and the power of the fish far below. 'Yes,' he shouted out and struck again and, 'Whe-hey, get the bloody chips on,'

Reeling in as quickly as the fighting fish would allow he grabbed the leader, swung his fish inboard; a nice three pound haddock.

That was the first of a half dozen good fish but as soon as the tide slackened the fish stopped biting and a south easterly breeze got up to spoil the drift, converting the swell into a relatively uncomfortable chop. Time to go home. He was about an hour and a half away from the slipway at five knots. He looked down at his catch, leaned forward to lay his palm on one of them. Beautiful. Perhaps the last living fish he would ever touch? It would be dark in an hour or so, seemed to have become a few degrees colder. He looked up at the thickening cloud.

The engine started all right. It started first time. Trouble was, he couldn't get it into gear. Each time he tried it choked and died. Peering down over the stern in the failing light, now with the aid of the torch, he could see the length of weeded up old rope that had become caught up around the prop, preventing him from tilting the engine to get it off. He couldn't reach down deep enough with his knife so he tried tying the knife to a section of fishing rod. His bindings didn't prove up to much. The knife disappearing, glinting, into the dark, dark depths. By then they were drifting in the gloom along Greenstone cliffs, threatening to be blown out into the Minch. Thirty miles to the Outer Hebrides and too bloody deep to anchor! And to make matters worse the outboard was now refusing to fire at all.

He threw back his head, laughed out aloud, yelled, 'Balls to it, then.' A single remaining seagull rocked his wings on the stiffening breeze as if in understanding, just a pale grey spirit in the last of the light, calling out to him once, as if in goodbye.

Forget about the bloody engine, Ed. Time to break out the oars, shipmate, right?' Who the hell was that. He looked all around. Nothing. Just the steepening seas, black and white. 'What?' he shouted, but no reply. Christ, he must be going nuts. That had sounded like Charlie's voice. He picked up the oars, fitted them into the rowlocks, began with all his diminished strength to pull for home.

With the still increasing wind came the darkness and then the rain, spatterings of it at first and then a solid, slanting down-pour that hit you in the back of the head and made you gasp for breath. If it wasn't for the sometimes

salt in it you wouldn't have known if the water lashing your
back was from the sky or from seas breaking over the
bows. He'd almost forgotten it; this once so well known
taste of the savage sea. On the convoys and before, in the
North Sea after the herring, there'd been times when he'd
tasted salt for days on end. He'd known what it was to be
scared. Scared shitless they used to say. But he was not
scared now, not for himself anyway although he knew well
enough that this was an old man fighting a losing battle.
Out of breath and almost out of hope he stopped rowing
and used the torch, flashing out the old dot dot dot, dash
dash dash, dot dot dot. Not that there was likely to be
anyone on shore to see his SOS on this deserted coastline.
The wind was still pushing him out into the Minch. If he
missed the Hebrides it would be hello, North America. He
grinned into the darkness and the weather. At the rate the
boat was trying to fill up he'd be swimming long before any
landfall. The weird and wonderful thing was, he was almost
enjoying it all. He laughed out aloud. He finished the latest
SOS, held tight on to the gunwhales as the boat fell
sickeningly into the next trough then rose, steep-to. *'Take it
easy, Ed,'* Charlie called out; *'You'll not pull back to Aultbea.
Best save your strength to keep bows on into the weather. They'll be
out looking for you any time now.'*

Eddie laughed again, shouted; 'Piss off, Charlie, you
bloody know they won't be out looking. Only the hotel girl
knows I'm out and she's in Inverness.'

'Yeah? You all right, mate?'

'Oh, lovely,' he shouted; 'What the bloody hell d'you
think? Don't worry about me, Charlie boy; just a bit cold,
that's all.' The rain and spray had penetrated right through
to his skin. He wondered if Charlie had felt any of this after
the *St Agnes* went down or whether it had all ended nice
and quick for him.

'No, it wasn't that quick for me, Ed,' Charlie said, as if mind
reading. *'Not 'til those white coated bastards came, it wasn't.'*

'What?' he shouted. What was that?' No response. But he'd been keeping an eye on the compass and now there couldn't be any doubt about it, the wind was definitely veering, pushing him more to the north east. Depending on how far he'd drifted, he'd either hit the rocks at Greenstone or go flying past them into Gruinard Bay. Nothing to say or do bar keeping the old baling arm going between strokes on the oars, trying to keep her headed into it. He'd not done much in the way of praying in a long time but now, with the bilge-water slopping around his lower legs he took time out to thank God for his life, for all the wonders of it. He didn't ask Him for any salvation or for forgiveness or for anything else. He'd already asked enough of God, hadn't he? Had received from Him enough for any one man, for any one life. Dolly had been much more of a blessing than her death had been a punishment when all was said and done.

Above the wind he thought he could hear a growing thunder of waves on solid rock. Yes. He leaned forward, appalled by what he was beginning to see. Not far away, directly on the line of his drift, huge, semi-luminous seas were rolling and rearing high up against great walls of rock. By the wavering, fast dying light of the torch he thought he could just catch glimpses of this one tiny interspace in the cliff. Possibly a steep-to, stony beach? The dinghy rose one last time, hovered on a breaking crest then rocked and tipped and dropped and then there was just the crashing , rolling and tumbling about in salt-stinging seawater and darkness. But all he could think was, Sorry, Murdo. I've wrecked your boat.

Charlie was with him, though. Yes, grinning that lop-sided grin, telling him he was going to be all right. All was calm, all was still as Charlie told him; *'She wouldn't let me, you know that? I would have, but … your boy, he really was yours, Ed. Not mine worse luck. So listen, I'll be seeing you. Not yet, but I'll be seeing you, all right? Her as well; Dolly. She still loves you, Ed. Only you. Lucky bugger.'*

Once more the cacophony. He found himself crawling up a smoothly pebbled rise, called out, 'You still there, Charlie?' But came no response. 'Thanks, mate.' he bellowed over the uproar, crawling further up the beach out of the grip of the sea. His hand seemed to have been cut, coming into contact with what felt like a rust-pitted metal structure, some kind of a broken hulk? And his right leg hurt like hell. Broken for sure. Jesus, did it hurt! He felt his slow, slow way into the metal shelter then dragged together a rough wall of stones and bits of grassy turf to protect himself from the worst of the wind. It had stopped raining. Didn't matter when you were as wet as he was.. His watch was still working. Its luminous hands told him it wasn't even eleven o' clock yet. There was this smell of wet salt on rusty steel, the immense rise and fall sounds of the sea and the gale, small comfort lying in here on his stony mattress.

Precisely at midnight Charlie said, *'Happy birthday, boy, and welcome to Anthrax Island.'*

'Gruinard?' He'd known it. 'Oh shit. Well, why the hell not ...' Jesus, he'd forgotten about his bloody birthday. But both of them thought it funny; the brand new ninety year old with the painfully broken leg and his permanently twenty year old friend, the two of them chatting their way through the night as if a little thing like anthrax mattered a good goddam.

He dreamed that, soon after daylight, there was this great beating of wings and someone was shaking him awake and he opened his eyes to see close up the face of a young man, full of concern. He looked past the face. A helicopter hovering sharp and dark and incredibly noisy against a clean blue sky.

Before they got him out and stretchered him up into the chopper he insisted the young man scrape away the accumulation of stones and turf around what, he now realised, had been the bows of an old, upturned steel lifeboat, his makeshift shelter. Some of the letters of her name were still readable. Yes, definitely. This lifeboat had once belonged to the *SS St Agnes*.

Murdo in his best suit sat on the edge of his chair alongside the bed. 'They're going to let you out soon, so they say,' he said.

Eddie nodded. 'Bloody good job, too. Us Highlanders don't much care for hospitals nor for any big cities like Inverness, do we?' He winked at his friend. 'My grandson's due up tomorrow with his wife. They're planning on driving me home. You know, home down south? Listen, Murdo, I'm sorry about the boat. Should never have taken her out single-handed. Course I'll pay you, mate.'

Murdo raised his hand in denial: 'Boats should not fade away. They all should go like that. But yourself, you are not forced to go, are you now?' He glanced around before slipping a bottle of beer and a flat half pint of whisky under Eddie's bed covers.

Eddie said, 'Hey, you're a real pal. Thanks for this. No, I'm not forced … but listen, I was going to ask you, was there ever a boat wrecked on Gruinard Island? Sometime in the war?'

Murdo shifted on his chair; 'Oh yes. I have many times myself seen it where they found you, the one that I believe you used for shelter? But you remember what it was like in the war. Top secret, yes, and with all the wickedness they were up to over there…?' He gazed carefully out of the hospital window. 'I am not a man for rumours but they used to say that one of the convoy ships was attacked and sunk by a U-boat not too far off Greenstone, that she had gone down at once with no time to signal. They say some of the men might have survived and come ashore.'

'Yes? What happened to them?'

Murdo hesitated. 'Dead and buried: with all the sheep, so it was said,' he murmured.

Eddie's felt himself holding his breath: 'You mean there were men off that ship who died? Died there on Gruinard?'

'Died or got killed, who is there to know? I told you, Eddie, no-one talked about it or about the things they were up to. There was a very great fear about this contamination thing.' He shook his head. 'And also those in charge would be concerned about panic. As I said, just, there was a war on, was there not?'

'Perhaps, but... now ...' Eddie felt his anger now. Real anger. 'So, *vengeance is mine, sayeth the Lord.* I'll be turning over a whole lot of old stones my friend. Or my son James will. He's in a good position to do that for his father.'

'Yes, 'mine,' He sayeth; right enough, Eddie. He does not say, 'thine.' Your friend Charlie - it is him of whom you are thinking?'

Eddie nodded. 'I'll be out of here tomorrow. I'll come back to the hotel. Maybe I'll try to find a place to live up here. My folks won't mind. They're good people but they don't need an old codger like me around too much. Listen, mate, when I get back to the hotel I'll buy you a wee dram and a pint and I'll tell you all about Charlie. And after that, don't you worry, Murdo, I fancy I'll be doing something about him, too. Just to help the Lord along, see.'

The end

We walked our dogs for one or two hours every day up here in Wester-Ross, finding many out of the way, mostly off-track routes,. We gave them names. The walk along the bouldery undercliff at Second Coast we called The Caves *for obvious reasons. One day we sat there with our flasks and sandwiches looking out at Gruinard Island, thinking and talking of its grim World War Two history. This had been the site of our government's not so wonderful experiments with the dreaded anthrax. Dee said, 'You should write something about that place, Bryan.' So I did.*

Not Talking About Charlie

Rose Feather is determined to succeed in the game of snooker - in what had always been, especially at the highest level, very much a man's world. She is looking for help from her father, the ex snooker star and hell-raiser, American Henry. And from her friend, up and coming Italian star Roberto D'Amato.

Rose Feather

His car smells of real leather. It's so quiet she can hear the tick -ticking of the wipers above the faint grumble of the engine. Snowing again, swarms of tiny white parachutes floating out of the blackness, criss-crossing each other in the lights of the hotel. The windscreen was almost covered already. 'Thanks for dinner, Roberto,' she said; 'Very nice.'

'Is OK, Rosie.'

'I can get a taxi out to my father's house from here.'

'Why not you stay? Good hotel,' he said.

'Thanks but no thanks; naughty boy you are! Look, this match tomorrow. Please - oh, hell, I don't suppose you can call it off? If I ask you nicely Roberto? I don't think my father can afford it if he loses.'

'*If* he loses? You think maybe he can win?' He laughed. 'I am pro, yes? Henry Feather is pro. Maybe not so good no more.' He shrugged, returned to his main preoccupation. 'But forget taxi. Stay with D'Amato tonight.'

She shook her head again. 'I told you, forget that. But listen,' she urged, 'You *could* pull out. It's a real mis-match.'

Roberto had turned towards her, his left hand had moved carefully around the stubby gear stick, settled light as a small bird on her thigh. His voice came soft and throaty; 'We don't need no talk about it. Why not you stay with me, huh?' The small bird moved a short and vital distance on her leg.

Always they had to try to put their hands there; 'I've told you before, lovely man; I don't do that stuff. Not even for you.' She took his hand in both of hers and lifted it from that area it had almost reached up into the street light, cupped it under her right breast. 'I think I know a good way to pass some time, though. Drive on a bit? Somewhere less public?'

He gunned the Ferrari into a wheel-spinning star, soon enough swerved into a deserted car park beside a blacked out supermarket, switched off the lights. Leaving the engine running he turned to kiss her. It did not take long to do for him, for his maleness, the things with her hands that other men had taught her to do. Italian stallion or not, he quickly accepted where he could go and what he was allowed to do and soon enough came his climactic, agonised groan into the valley between her breasts, bare now for she had rolled her new red sweater high up to her neck. All that strength and power and maleness had come and gone as every time it came and went. She looked with simple fondness upon his temp-orary helplessness. 'Better now, you lovely champion, you?'

Slowly he sat up. 'Jesus Christ, Rosie,' he muttered, 'You - beautiful. You sure are something.'

'Oh, don't be silly,' she said. 'It's just hand sex. That's all. Everyone does it. I mean, all the time. Not like it's something special just for you or me.' Smiling, she kissed his cheek

He looked across at her now, his eyes black pits in that pale outline of a handsome face. 'OK,' he said, 'But I don't know about you, Rosie. Beautiful, beautiful girl. Never … '

'Don't say it, Roberto. And call me *Rose* please, not *Rosie*.' She rolled the sweater back down and smoothed it over her breasts, feeling with pleasure the nipples still swollen. 'If you don't call me Rosie I won't call you Robert.

And if you tell me about how it is to be rich and famous I'll be prepared for it when I get to be rich and famous, won't I?' She opened the window to throw out his handkerchief. Freezing air and thistledown snowflakes drove into her face. She laughed out aloud. Twenty years of age and a virgin, how weird was that?

She was nearing the end of a best of five when her famous - more aptly infamous father walked into his club. American Henry Feather looked as good and as stylish as ever. It was very important now that he should see her beating his Brown Ball club's star amateur. She knew she was playing close to her best. Why was it you never seemed to have to think about the shots when you cued the balls this well? Such a great feeling when the cue seemed to be without weight, just an extension to your arm and hand as it impacted the white ball, shot after shot, with perfect force and direction. She finished the third and final frame with a clearance of the colours, shook hands with the much older man who seemed a lot less than happy about being trounced by a young woman. Perhaps especially if that woman happened to be half black? she wondered.

She joined her father at a table with a cup of coffee. He was drinking something stronger. 'Well, what do you think, Pops?' she asked.

'You're looking great, Rosie.'

'Yes? I mean about my game?'

Henry Feather shrugged his shoulders. 'Great. I think your game's come on a lot. Hell, sweetheart, you're damn near as good as you might be thinking you are.' He laughed to lessen any hurt. 'But those guys were looking more at your butt than your cue action.'

Rose felt the smile fading from her face. 'I always play better when someone's watching, don't you, Pops?'

'No. Just between me and my cue. Nothing else.' He spoke carefully; changing tack. 'Yeah, I've heard all about

151

how you've been playing.' The eyes that had seduced a million female hearts on the television screen bored into hers. She blinked. 'But it's a damn hard path to follow for anyone, never mind a pretty lady. Hell, but you're serious, aren't you?'

'Very serious. As serious as I can be,' she said. An unusually violent gust threw hard snow or half rain against the window-glass with a sound that underlay the crying of the wind like soft brushes wiped across a drum skin. She shivered. 'I think I could be very good indeed.' She leaned towards him, speaking with real conviction. 'That's just it. If I could work here with you for a while I'd learn such a lot.' She had a sense that the couple at the neighbouring table were eavesdropping, looked at them and at once they resumed their own conversation. 'You wouldn't mind me staying with you for a little while, would you?' she continued. A winner's shout and the fast repeating thump of a fruit machine disgorging its jackpot shattered the club's click-clicking tranquillity.

'How long is 'a while'?'

She said; 'This is it. I've left home. I left after Christmas and now I've packed up my digs. I have everything I need here with me.' She hesitated. 'Roberto D'Amato gave me a lift up from London.'

'D'Amato? Christ. I'm playing him in a big bucks challenge tonight. Hey, wait just a minute - you knew about that?'

'Yes of course I did. And I hope you beat him. And before you ask me, I've chucked in my job.'

'Oh my God.' He shook his head, took another swallow of whatever was in his glass. 'Your mother? Lucille knows you're here? And she knows about your job - like, not having one?'

'Well, not just yet,' she admitted. 'I wanted to hear what you said first.'

'So what the hell you plan to do, Rosie?'

'Snooker. I'm going to play snooker. I'm going to make a living from it, same way you used to.' If he'd noticed the past tense he said nothing. 'Sorry,' she added, 'Like you still do, now and then. See, I'm beating scratch players now.'

'That right, Rosie: I didn't know there were any women scratch players.'

'No, not women.' She looked at him. 'Women's snooker isn't a necessary part of my game plan. That's what I need to talk to you about. Woman, man or Martian, I don't much care. Why is that such a problem for people to understand? There wouldn't be a problem if I were a twenty year old man, would there?'

He thought for a moment, gazing down at the palm of his big right hand, then, 'We can talk about it. I've no problem with you staying on at my place for a day or two more. But you should know - there's this friend, she sometimes stays with me.' He emptied his glass, peered into it as if in search of problems and answers. 'Mind, you have to let your mother know what the hell you're up to. She's still with that guy?'

'Of course she is. Mother doesn't pick people up and put them down so easily.' She hadn't meant it but it came out as a rebuke nonetheless. 'Sorry, Pops. Your friend won't worry me, but remember I'm not anybody's little girl.' Angry, she turned round and the eavesdroppers, fearful of her intensity, once more hurried back to their makeshift conversations. 'And by the way I have to tell you - you're mad, challenging Roberto for all that money. He's number eleven in the world, for God's sake!' She stood up. 'And you ...'

'Sit down please, Rosie,' he said.

'No I shall not, and my name is Rose, remember.'

'Please? Rose?' She was on the point of turning away when he added, 'I need your support. This D'Amato match? Look,' he ticked off the reasons on his fingers. 'One, I need the dough. This place isn't doing so good. If I lose, maybe I could lose the club.' He shrugged, forced the customary grin. 'Second, you know I can play a better game than the kid ever heard of. And last, he could really use a good whupping. I need to talk to you some more. Maybe we should take a walk. Let's get the hell out of here, shall we?'

Walk? He wasn't going to tell her about his lost driving licence or about having to sell his beloved E-Type, was he. 'Car's in dock,' her father added, by way of a lie.

Road-sweeping machinery had piled dirty snow into miniature mountain ranges alongside the kerb. A bus drove by, too close in so that its heavy tyres splattered the trouser legs of a man walking up ahead. They had seen it coming, moved away but now stopped at the kerbside, looking for a gap in the traffic. A white van slowed for them. Her father nodded his thanks. The driver grinned and winked at her.

The pub smelled of wet coats and old beer. This guy stood up, said; 'Good to see you, Henry. I recognised you from when your matches was on telly. Bloody great you was.'

'Gee, thanks,' Henry said. 'Good memory you've got.' He smiled, eased himself and her through the crush and up to the bar. The noise had ratcheted up a couple of levels. Raised voices and shouts of laughter over-rode each other from every direction. Heavy rap pounded out from the juke box. In un-successful competition a bearded, rheumy-eyed drunk sitting slumped up to a corner of the bar was croaking on about *Bonny Mary of Argyle*. He sounded as he really meant it, as if he had known the lady personally.

'That,' pronounced the heavy Birmingham accent close up to Rose' ear, 'Is a wanker of the first water.' A group of young men mostly with more stubble on their faces than there was still on their heads pressed in on them. Henry turned around, 'You think so?' he said. 'Get to be an expert in the third grade these days?' And she could see it was trouble; yet more trouble for this trouble-prone father of hers.

One of them said, 'We wasn't talking to you, grand-dad but we might have been talking about you, see. We was saying as what's an old puddin' puller doin' with a nice bit o' the blackstuff like her. And he wants to watch who he's bargin' into.' He appealed to his friends; 'That right, Smudger?'

'Oh yes,' said Smudger, grinning. Yellowed teeth, snake-tattoo'd neck. 'That is right.'

The barman said; 'That'll be all from you lot. Five pounds seventy six please, Henry.' He didn't need to shout it. Much of the talking in that part of the pub had died down. 'O.K. boys, you've had your fun. Good thing Mister Feather didn't hear you. Now let's all relax, O.K?' A very large and expressionless man had appeared at his side behind the bar.

'Let's get the fuck out of here,' Smudger said. 'We know you, Mister kiss my arse with a fuckin' Feather.' He addressed his mates. 'Brown Ball, right? We'll play a frame or two there, right lads?'

'Wrong,' Henry said. 'You best keep the hell out of my club.'

Rose grabbed hold of his arm, feeling the tension in it, the hardness of his biceps. The old drunk had started with a new song: *My-aye-aye heart is like a red red rose …* 'Let them be, father,' she said, 'Just let them be.'

With whoops and yells and a slamming of the pub door the gang departed, one of them singing *See you later, alligator.*

She hadn't wanted to come to the match, had delayed it and delayed it but here she was. Better late than never - or maybe the other way around? The Brown Ball Snooker Club's damp stair carpet smelled of the dirt carried in from the street on the soles of a great many shoes over a great many years. She unbuttoned her wet raincoat. At the top of the stairs she opened the door, slipped into the dimly lit room, overcrowded and silent. She made her way as quietly as she could through the spectators to the bar. Behind the bar was a big-busted blonde woman she'd never seen before. 'What's happening?' she whispered, not really wanting to know.

The woman sighed. 'You want a drink, dear? It's a money match on. The Italian boy, Roberto D'Amato.'

'Yes,' she interrupted, not meaning any rudeness, 'I just wondered who was winning.'

A man sitting on a stool, his back to the bar grunted; 'Well it ain't our old H, that's for bloody sure. Two nil now, good as.'

The bar-lady tried again, addressing a point just over her shoulder; 'You want a drink or not?'

'Thank you,' she said to the man, smiling. Then to the woman, unsmiling; 'No. I don't need anything to drink.' She turned and made her way towards the match table, back-tapping the men, seeing their annoyance changing into some-thing else as the faces turned. 'Sorry,' she whispered, 'Sorry', and they were glad to make room for her until she could see the table, watch the players at their one-sided game. The man at the bar was right, it couldn't last much longer. She shivered. Even with the street cold still in the fabric of her clothes she wanted to go. Her father's defeat was going to embarrass her. Even from here she could see the drink in him, in his face and his demeanour. She shifted, knowing at once that the man standing next to her would probably have misinterpreted the momentary contact.

Dinner jacketed Henry Feather was sitting just within the edge of the cone of light spreading out from above the brilliant green table, legs crossed in pretended nonchalance. He had his cue resting against the arm of his chair and his right hand was wrapped protectively around a glass half full of what might have been water but was definitely vodka. He still looked great, though, her father.

Roberto potted another black. The white cue-ball went spinning off into the cluster of reds, spreading them out nicely. Henry Feather nodded appreciatively, tapped his glass on the arm of his chair. Nobody else applauded. Why does it have to be you doing this to him, Roberto? she thought. Thanks for the lift but no thanks for this. I don't need much more of this and besides, any minute now I'm going to have to be rude to the idiot who will keep closing in on me and whose body smells are beginning to sicken me.

Roberto D'Amato finished off his break with a neatly contrived safety shot, taking no risks, giving no chances even though he had the match all but won. Someone in the audience coughed loudly and somebody else tried a tentative hand-clap. A few joined in the coughing but no-one reinforced the applause. The Italian sauntered over to his chair, making his couldn't care less arrogance all too obvious. He sat down, leaned back, examining one of his finger nails with undue care. Henry Feather swayed slightly as he got up, wiped down his cue, advanced slowly to the table. From the gloom of the audience a deep, Midlands-accented voice called out; 'Come on, let's go, America!' It was said lightly but it was truly meant. A murmur of unconvinced support ran around the room.

The man next to her grunted 'No bloody chance,' lifted his pint glass, drunk noisily. Almost as if in agreement, American Henry Feather failed in his attempt to make a touch contact with his targeted red. It hadn't been that difficult. 'What did I bloody tell you?' the man muttered, almost in triumph. It was time to go. She had no wish to be here at the bitter end. She re-fastened her raincoat belt, made her way out as quietly as she could, tip-toeing through the silence.

She was woken by the telephone, jumped out of bed, went to bang on her father's bedroom door, opened it. He wasn't there. She looked at her watch. Three a.m. The telephone was still repeating and repeating its strident carillon. She picked up, cleared her sleep-tinged throat, said, 'This is Rose Feather. My father's not here. Can I help?'

Briefest pause, female voice, 'Sorry to disturb you, Miss Feather. I'm Detective Inspector Sanjit. We were told you were staying with your father. Look, I'm very sorry to tell you this, but there's been a disturbance at your father's snooker club. Your father has been taken to the General hospital. I'm afraid his injuries seem to be serious.'

'What?' She was having trouble separating dream from reality.

'Yes. Your father is in hospital, Miss Feather. Look, we're parked just outside. Didn't want to disturb all the neighbours by knocking you up or anything. Can we take you to see him?'

On the way there, slip-sliding along icy roadways covered in snow, Inspector Ellie Sanjit told her about how a gang of youths had come into the Brown Ball club after everyone but Henry and his manageress had left, about how a serious fight had developed, about how her father had been hit by a bottle and kicked into unconsciousness, about how the manageress had given the police very fair descriptions of the assailants. 'One of them,' she said, 'had a very obvious snake tattoo'd around his neck. Don't worry, we will get them. All of them.' But American Henry Feather, ex snooker star extraordinaire, had died of his head injuries by the time of their arrival at the hospital.

****

The YWCA hostel was OK. Rose Feather took a deep breath, stood up, went to the telephone. Roberto answered on his mobile. She could hear the well-bred muttering of the Ferrari engine; snooker star on the road again. 'Hey, Rosie' he said.

'Thought you might have forgotten about me, Roberto. I saw you there - you know, at the funeral.'

'I try speak with you but - shit, you know like, how it is.'

'Yes, Roberto, I do know. Too many people. Look, I don't care what he did or didn't do or what the papers said he did. My father was a good man. You saw how many there were at the service. I never knew all that stuff he'd been doing for the kids. I didn't know any of that ... '

'Yeah, I saw. Many many people. So I can help you now, Rosie?' There was an unaccustomed gentleness there.

'Well yes, maybe you can. You own the Brown Ball now, Roberto. The last thing father managed to do was lose it to you. The one thing he had left.' Except me, she thought. She took a deep, slow breath. 'I'd like to challenge you; to play you for The Brown Ball club.'

'You challenge - play Roberto? You crazy? Sorry but hey, how come - you have money?'

'No I don't. Listen. This is the deal. You give me a one black ball per frame start and we play best of five frames. If I beat you, then you sign my father's club back to me - '

'Oh yeah, right - but when I win, Rosie?' There was a puzzlement, a looking for the catch. She couldn't hear the car's engine any more. He must have pulled over.

'If you beat me, Roberto D'Amato, I'll go to bed with you. You can be the first. You can have the only thing of any value that I still have.' *Apart from my talent.*

For a few seconds there was this silence. When at last he spoke his voice had thickened and somehow she knew he would accept. 'You are something, Rosie.' he murmured. 'You sure? You serious?'

'Yes'

'Let me think. You call me Saturday, yes?'

'Yes. Thanks. 'Bye now. Roberto?'

Yeah?'
'Sweet dreams.' She replaced the telephone in its cradle, wandered into the TV room. Three or four girls were watching an old Pinewood Studios war film. She sat down as far away as possible from the cloud of their cigarette smoke. Afterwards she found an Automat annexe where she bought herself a chicken sandwich with pickle and a boxed apple pie and a can of Coke. She locked herself into her tiny room and undressed. Using the hand-basin she washed out three pairs of panties and two bra's and the socks she'd worn today and draped them over a painfully hot radiator.

She turned out the lights then drew back the curtains and stood naked for a moment, bright white moonlight slanting in on her through dirty glass. It wasn't ten thirty yet and the big city was hardly into top gear. She sensed the challenge that was out there for her and she felt happy, really strong. She climbed into the bed. Sitting up in the half light she ate the sandwich and the pie and drank the Coke, thinking about her match and about Roberto whilst a number of radios or television sets infiltrated junk sound faintly through the walls.

When she'd finished her dinner she licked her fingers and lay down on her side and pulled the coarse, well-disinfected bedclothes tight to her ears and drew up her knees and close-wrapped her arms and hands around the warmth of her body. Like that she clung to her dream, riding it like a wild horse into the night.

The End

The game of snooker fascinates me. Many years ago one of our daughters decided that if I could take our son to my club's Saturday morning teaching classes then why not her? There should be no reason why a female should not equal the men at this game. So why doesn't it happen?

Mrs Lucy Brothers and her two children have been on their own since her husband went - actually, since she had kicked him out of house and home. She should be OK, though, for she's well secured. But what next? Something tragic happens three thousand miles away to suggest an answer, reawaken all those memories, good and bad.

The Mending of Marion

'*This is the eight a.m. BBC News for the ninth of December nineteen eighty… John Lennon has been shot and killed. Last night as he entered his New York apartment building …*'

She didn't hear, didn't want to hear any more, not now; just reached up to switch off the radio then held on to the towel rail on the front of the Aga, eyes tight closed, back towards the kids so they wouldn't see her face.

'You all right mummy?' Alice: as ever first to know when something seemed to be going wrong.

Through a mouthful of cornflakes James said, 'Why are they always shooting people in America.'

'I'm OK, Alice,' she said, although she was not. 'And James, please don't speak with your mouth full. No they don't … always shoot …'

'Don't cry, mummy, it's my birthday,' James said, changing tack in that small boy way. 'And daddy's coming home for my party.'

'That's what he told us.' She took a deep breath. Three weeks to the day and it wasn't getting any better and now - now this … oh, John, John, what have they done to you! She forced herself to turn around, tried a smile. 'Ten year olds are supposed to be pretty grown up, aren't they, James? Grown ups don't talk with their mouths full. Now hurry it up, both of you. I've to get things in for the party.'

Alice stood up, came around the table to give her mother a tip-toed hug, her fast burgeoning young breasts pressing in. 'I'm sorry, mummy. About daddy and about John Lennon. You told me you knew him once, didn't you? You used to like him.'

Lucy Brothers kissed her daughter's uptilted forehead. Warm, soap-scented, lovely. 'Yes that's right. I do - I did. Come on now, we don't want to be late.'

The talk on their school run was all about the party although she had seldom felt in less of a party mood. All she wanted to do was to be alone, to listen to the Beatles tape. Listen. Remember ...

She'd never had a problem with driving because it forced her to think of other things, normal things like road safety and the upkeeping of her beautiful, empty house. Thank you, ex-husband Bill. Thank you for the big Ford and the bricks and mortar and these two little people, only not so little any more. Thank you for my broken life, I mean broken heart, empty heart, whatever. She heard again her husband's words, not meant unkindly, she knew that now. *'Yes, Lucy, she may not have your looks or your mind but she turns on all the lights for me and - I have to have light. Warmth. It's tough enough out there, you know?'* He'd seemed on the verge of tears but she'd still wanted to hurt him then, badly hurt him, so she'd turned her back. *'Go on then,'* she'd said. *'Why don't you. We'll be OK. I should have married your friend John. He understood - about me and lights and everything. I could light him up and he could light me up. So why couldn't you?'* Not the truth of course. Not in that way, the way the magazines said, the way her husband meant. For her that kind of thing had always been just a duty of love and marriage.

She pulled up the car. 'Here we are then. Have a nice day, darlings.' The kids got out of the car, hurried inside the school gates, became instantly absorbed into the general, navy blue melee, 'See you at three. Be good,' she called after them to nobody.

It was only thirty miles or so to Strawberry Field children's home. *Her* home. Well, ex-home. She shuddered, thinking about it, frightening herself all over again. *The nights were frightening, when the lights went out. And sometimes the days, too, especially when it rained and especially when Major called you into his office. You were always frightened then but you weren't allowed to cry. If you cried He sighed and shook His grey straggled, shiny bald head and sent for She, Mrs Major, who would take you downstairs because that's what He told her to do because He'd given up on you when you wouldn't do everything He said and do your best to look happy or excited about it. Downstairs was underground without windows and without proper furniture, only a few bits and pieces of broken tables and chairs and rolls of old carpet so when She switched off the light and went out and you heard the key turn in the lock,* Please, madam, *you would whisper,* Please. *But it would never be any good. She wouldn't say anything at all to you and you were there in the blackness, feeling for somewhere to sit down, somewhere that wouldn't mess up your clothes too much which would make everything worse.*

Along the busy East Lancs road it began to rain, spitting at first and then more heavily. The Liverpool bound traffic quickly and noisily degenerated into stop-start mode. Thus far she'd resisted the temptation to play the 8-track but now she touched it on and listened, windscreen wipers beating rough time with that strangely beautiful east-west intro, then John with his lovely, nasally scouser's voice: *Let me take you down, 'cause I'm going to Strawberry Fields ... Nothing is real and nothing to get hungabout. Strawberry Fields forever.* She felt the rise of whatever it was that was trying to make the tears, trying its best to turn her breathing into sobs. John, John, John. 'Strawberry Fields Forever,' he'd written. Except it wasn't Strawberry Fields, it was Strawberry Field. Singular. And it wasn't for ever, was it, John Lennon, aka Robin

Hood, because now it's you that's gone. Forever. Thank you, God.

She'd had this vague plan to park up by the big old gates, padlocked closed between their massive stone pillars. She and Bill had been by there a few times over the years but only the once since they'd pulled down the old Strawberry Field and built the trio of family units in its place. But they'd left the gates alone, and she knew most of the trees inside the grounds were still there. She thought about how she'd sometimes sneaked out through the kitchen door against all the rules and walked through the copse of until she could see the road outside the iron railings from a safe concealment, could watch the passing cars and cyclists, wondering about where they were going and how it would be in those homes where the drivers and passengers and the cyclists lived. Like where she had herself once lived in her small house with her brother and her sisters? With a garden and with fields at the back to run and play in and where was daddy and why had mother left her here?

She braked to another stop, windscreen wipers slashing away; dissolving, resolving, dissolving the brake lights of the car in front. She turned off the 8-track and turned on the radio, listened to the reports from New York and some of the interviews thinking about her own first meeting with John Lennon *'Stand and deliver'*, had shouted the fat boy with the big stick. He and another one holding a bow with some arrows in a kind of sling around his neck had sprung out of the undergrowth in front of her. She'd quickly recovered her composure. *'What are you doing?'* she'd retaliated. *'You're not allowed in here.'*

'Neither are you bloody Strawberries.' A scorn-filled voice had come from above. *'You naughty, girl, you. If you go down to the woods today,'* he sang, *'You're in for a damn big surprise.'* Then his laugh. She'd looked up and there he was, John Lennon, up in this big old chestnut tree, grinning down on her. *'Who do you think you are?'* she'd said. *'Robin 'ood,'* he'd said, missing

out the H, Scouser style, *Who d'you bloody think?* He'd dropped suddenly, swung by his fingertips, spindly legs in short trousers pedalling almost directly overhead, then he'd let go and fallen, crouch landing with a natural grace in front of her. He'd been chewing gum; she could smell spearmint on his breath. *'So come on. Tell us your name and what you got for us, OK? We rob the rich and give it all up to us poor, right boys?'*

'Lucy', she'd told him. *'I'm Lucy and I haven't got anything but if I had you wouldn't get it, see.'* She tried a laugh. *'I suppose this fat one here is supposed to be Friar Tuck then.'*

'Right, Lucy,' John had said. *'How did you guess? And this is Will Scarlett. Bill to you. Bill Brothers. So come on, what you really got for us then?'*

There was such a crowd of people there, some under umbrellas. One of them held a lighted candle in a kind of lantern, others just stood around in the cold getting wet. She drove a little past them before stopping. She switched off the engine, looked up, adjusted the rear view mirror, dabbed on a little lipstick. Mrs Lucy Brothers, forty, housewife, mother; sometime Mrs Marion Hood, because Robin had said she had to be Maid Marion and, after she'd met up in the wood with the Merry Men a few times had suddenly and unilaterally announced their engagement and the next day he and she had been married under the greenwood tree, Friar Tuck officiating. Robin had told them all to sing *here comes the bride all over wide* and some other rude words of his own, and then had told the others to bugger off because he and Maid Marion needed to go to bed now they were married. She recalled the sick misery of that moment in the den underneath the rhododendron after they'd left and he'd grabbed her hand and tried to put it on his thingie, just like Him in there, and even now she could smell the flowers and feel the danger and see that bad look of strength and masculinity on the suddenly less kind face of her friend and pretendy husband, John Lennon.

She shivered, reached over into the back of the Zodiac for her sheepskin coat, shrugged herself into it, pulled the hood over her head and got out of the car. The pavement was slippery wet with the last of the fallen leaves. A few more people were coming to swell the crowd, some on foot, others getting out of cars. The man with the lantern was singing *Imagine*, quite well, too, so was attracting attention, but most just stood around, not a few of them in tears. She could feel all their anger, all their impotence, all their grief at the loss of something good, something important. There were all sorts here, all types and ages. The prosperous and the not so prosperous, some of them grown up flower children, some with their own children. All the lonely people, just like her. She turned away, towards the wet and wintry trees and undergrowth, took hold of the railings, tasting with her tongue the iron and the paint of them all mingled with fresh rain and with the salt of her tears.

The voice from behind. 'I knew you'd be here.'

Without turning around, 'Bill, go away. You don't have to see me 'til this afternoon; James' party, remember?'

'Yeah, of course. Come on love, let's take a walk? Please? You know where.'

How awful she must look, for once not caring. She shook her head, setting free many droplets as she turned. He didn't look too smart, seemed older, more lined, not his usual well-shaven self. Still a good looking man, though; still very much the businessman beneath the rain-slicked hair and the belted Gannex. She shook her head. 'Take a walk? With you? What about your lady, then, the one with all the lights?' But she sensed that her voice had betrayed her and she put up little resistance to the encircling arms.

'Don't cry, Mrs Brothers,' he said, 'John wouldn't want you to ... you know, cry? He wouldn't have hisself, mind.

Not John. At least I never saw him. Come on, you remember the place we can get in. Where we used to. Me and Friar Tuck and Robin Hood, OK?'

All but overcome by a maelstrom of conflicting emotion she walked with him along and around the corner of the woodland grounds of Strawberry Field. Behind the bus shelter he stopped, looked around, saw the coast was clear then took hold of a railing, lifted it up and out to create a gap. 'John and me and Alex broke the welds,' he explained. 'But somehow I don't reckon we can get through here, not any more. Not me anyway.' He grinned, patting his stomach. 'Didn't reckon on that.'

She smiled in spite of herself. 'Put that railing back, Bill,' she said. 'If you want to get inside there's an easier way.' She led him around the grounds and into the yard behind the new buildings, to all appearances intent on some official mission. Through one of the windows she could see a woman at her housework, her head bent, and two little faces looking out at them. She led him on to the place behind the gardener's shed, located the rough footpath into the wood. It was much as it had been those years ago, almost thirty years ago. So was the chestnut tree but the banks of rhododendrons had considerably enlarged. By now her face must look terrible. She didn't care.

'A great tree climber, our Robin Hood', Bill said. 'He'd been right to the top of this conker tree before you come along. There was a missel thrush nest up there, see.' She looked up through a network of twisting branches and a tracery of lifeless twigs to a pregnant cloud base, weeping steadily. 'Hey, listen,' Bill went on. He seemed excited. 'I remember now. He carved his initials somewhere here.' He walked around the trunk of the chestnut, examining it closely, good shoes muddied, rainwater from long wet grass spraying his trouser legs. 'Yeah, it's here, Lucy, right here; come and see.'

The letters carved into living bark had all but grown over: *RH* then a heart shape then *MM*. 'Robin Hood loves Maid Marion,' he interpreted. He looked at her. 'And he did that, didn't he? Oh Christ, Lucy,' he whispered. 'What's happened to us all? Come here girl. Please?'

The rhodedendrons had grown up and outwards, long ago filling in the old entry to the den, but they'd managed to force a passage anyway and in this hollow centre of the great bush, in amongst the root-like branches it was gloomy dark and the ground was relatively dry. Saying nothing, he took off and spread out his Gannex. She sat down on it, not much caring about being wet and cold, and when she felt him shivering she took off her own coat to cover them both. "What's that hymn?' she said, '*When to the days of our childhood returning*'? This is crazy. What am I doing here? Forty year old separated mothers of two shouldn't ...

'Lucy,' he said, 'Just shut up and don't try so hard to rationalise things. For me, for John: for once, please?' He touched her face. She tensed, resisting the automatic recoil. 'Love me do,' whispered her husband. 'Like here, like, with him?'

'I didn't,' she whispered. 'With John. Not like that. I couldn't.'

'What?' He sat up. 'He told us about it. He said you did it here. Consummated, he said.'

'Well I don't care. It wasn't true.'

'But you told me.'

'I know but people make stuff up, Bill. John must have. And so did I. You were my first, well ... ' She turned her dirty, rained on face away from him.

'Well, yeah, I forgot. The dirty old bastard in the Home. You told me about that, just the once over. The one that went and hung hisself.'

'Yes, him.'

'I reckoned our John had something to do with that. You know he kept in touch with me now and then, years back?'

'Yes. What do you mean? Something to do with Major … ?'

'He told me he'd written the guy a letter. About you, what you'd told him. He was always great with words, were John'

'You think so?' She rolled back towards him. 'Oh God. I did tell John … not everything, you know … but he and you were the only ones who knew anything about it - about Him and his … about Her. I don't ever want to talk about that or think about it. Not now. Not ever.'

'But you have to, to someone if not to me. It's the only way.'

'A bit late for you and me to be telling each other our secrets, Bill, don't you think? But I wouldn't be surprised, what you say about John and his letter.' She shook her head, cold wet hair sweeping across her face. 'Who can ever know now? Our Robin Hood wasn't exactly short on words or imagination.'

'No, he were not. One great guy. Another thing you didn't know, girl, because I didn't tell you. it was him give me the cash to start up the business.'

She sat up then and put her arms around his neck. 'No, I had no idea. Now let's be quiet for a moment, shall we? Will you let me shine a little light for my husband? Please? And I'm not a girl. I'm a woman. You can feel me if you want to.' And so for the first time Lucy Brothers made love to her husband instead of him making love to her, in there amongst the gnarled and twisted branches and the scent of wet rhodedendrons and with the sounds of passing traffic from a short distance and the sound of the man with the lantern who'd started over again with his version of John Lennon's *Imagination*. Very good. She wanted to cry out, to tell him how good it really was. They lay together for a long time afterwards, saying little, content to be with each other and in thought with their lost friend John Lennon. Late in the morning they scrambled their way out of the bushes, brushed each other down as best they might, grinning their guilty, child-like grins.

They walked out past the buildings, studiously ignoring the puzzled looks from a couple of adults and a group of children. Back by her car he kissed her, said, 'So, Maid Marion, will it be all right if I bring my things with me this afternoon?'

'Why, Will Scarlett,' she said, feigning surprise, 'Are you thinking of stopping over with us then?' She didn't want to ask any more about that other she. Perhaps there wasn't one, wouldn't be one any more.

'Yes', he said, 'But can we do Strawberry Fields forever? Please?' There was dirt on his face along with the grin and he was all over as soaking wet and muddy, as she was herself.   'But, Mrs Lucy Brothers,' he added, with unaccustomed gentleness, 'I do love you, you know that. I know what they say about his son Julian's school friend Lucy being the *Lucy In The Sky*, but it were you. You were his diamond. You are *my* diamond. 'I'll see you and the kids later.'

The end

I wrote the first version of The Mending of Marion *in response to calls for entries from that great short story website www.Shortbread.com. The entries had to be themed on one of the Beatles' songs. I have a second hand but highly personal knowledge of at least one poor little child's life within that long gone Strawberry Field. Not 'forever', thank God. Not Strawberry Fields Forever.*

The old and the lonely tend to take comfort in two things: their own past and their own special routines. Especially at Christmas time.

On The Feast Of Stephen

It took her so long to get ready these days, even longer when she had to be at her very best. Well, you would have to be at your best, wouldn't you, even if you *are* now eighty years old. Church this morning and the Queen on the radio this afternoon. She smoothed down her good red dress, looking at herself in the mirror, turning this way and that.

Ruff was waiting at the bottom of the stairs. She stopped to strike a pose halfway down, 'Well, what d'you reckon then, Ruff?' she said, and the big old dog slowly wagged his tail, looking from her to the front door. 'Now then do come on,' she scolded, 'You know well we don't go out walking 'til after church, not on Christmas Day.' She opened her front door to breathe in of the damp grey air of Millsbridge High Street, vaguely disappointed by the absence of snow in spite of the cold. Not like in forty five, was it? Today there was only the pictorial stuff on the red and white plastic Father Christmases with their sleighs and reindeers hanging listlessly between each pair of lamp posts, doing their best to relieve the general dilapidation of the town.

She looked up. Bonnybreck Hill loomed over all, as it had for the first twenty years of her life and now for these last twenty as well. She sighed. In the forty years between, just America and Steve, God bless him.

Across the road the new young Reverend emerged from his church, stooped to pick up an empty beer can. He

171

straightened, smiled and waved to her. 'Good morning, Mrs Solarno. A merry Christmas to you.'

'And a merry Christmas to you, too, vicar,' she reciprocated. He wouldn't be able to see the sadness in her, not from there.

'Your family's not been able to come over this year?'

She shook her head, forcing the smile. 'No, there's just me and Ruff this time.'

'Oh, well. But I expect we'll be seeing you later then?'

'You will that.' She shivered, waved goodbye, went back inside and closed the door behind her. Only a light tidying around would do for today, taking care not to spoil the dress. Afterwards she set and lit the coal fire, made herself a cup of tea, sat down in front of the blaze then took out her hankie and had a good cry. It was the years with Steve; they were the lost years making her cry; those years and the memories of their girls growing up in the small town over there in Jefferson County, Washington State. She thought about other Christmases just after the war. She and Steve, newly weds. They were happy times. Ruff sat there looking at her, his head on one side, something of understanding in his liquid brown eyes. 'Oh, I'm just a silly old woman,' she told him. 'Take no notice of me. Anyway it's *The Great Escape* tonight. We always like that, don't we? Apart from the ending. They shouldn't have had him back in prison. Have I ever told you my Steve looked just like Steve McQueen, Ruff?' She smiled and dried her eyes. 'Of course I've told you. I've told everyone, haven't I?'

Through the window she could see Bonnybreck Top. Perhaps there were traces of snow up there, after all. 'It's going to be a cold walk and a long one,' she said. 'You still all right for that, old guy?'

The dog cocked his head, eyebrows raised, then followed her back into the kitchen, wagging his tail and watching as she busied herself getting the two frozen turkey legs out for thawing. As she prepared the veggies, the telephone began to ring. She wiped her hands on her apron, went out to the hall, looked at herself in the mirror, plumped up her hair then picked up. 'Hello, this is Tryphena Solarno. Who's this please?'

'Happy Christmas, mother.'

'Angie? Is that you?'

'Yes, mother, and I've got Jemmy right here beside me. How are you?'

'I'm very well, Angie. But ... you're in Seattle?'

'Sure we are. It's still Christmas Eve for us, remember? Listen, mother, Stephen's in London. I think he's planning to come up to see you. We just wanted to make sure you're at home.'

'Your Stephen? In London? I thought he was working down in California or somewhere? Those film people?'

'That's right, he is. He's gone to England on assignment. They're making a movie there. Anyway, we're all just fine and missing you. Jemmy wants a word, then all the others. Here she is, but mother?'

'Yes, dear?'

'You'll be going to church then watching the Queen?'

'Of course I shall, Angela. Of course.'

'That's good. And are they running *The Great Escape* this Christmas?'

'Oh yes. Wouldn't miss that. Why do you ask?'

'Oh, nothing. It's just, we were looking at some old photos. Us and you and Daddy, you know?'

'Were you, Angie?'

'Yes.' She hesitated, then, 'You always said it, Daddy sure did look like Steve McQueen. My Stephen has the look of him, too, now he's older. You'll see it.' The old Angie smile had come back into her voice. 'All the Steves on this St Stephen's Day, right?' Without waiting, 'Here, I'll pass you to Jemmy.'

She spoke to them all, in the end worrying about the cost of the call and hurrying to finish. Finally putting down the phone, she went back into the kitchen and turned to Ruff. 'See how lucky we are, all of them doing so well? But they all have their own lives, Ruff.' She bent down to stroke the silky smooth grey head, cup the old grey muzzle in her two hands. 'And we have ours, right?' She remembered the last time they'd all been over here, young Stephen sixteen years old. Yes, he'd had the look of his grandfather, no doubt about it. It was mostly in the deep-set, cold blue eyes, the quickness of that lop-sided grin. She shook her head, dropped the last of the carrots into the saucepan. That time when they'd all got back from the traditional climb up Bonnybreck the lad had done his best not to let her see the bored, *when are we going?* glances at his parents.

The first clap of the church bells startled her. Then came the outpouring of the first ragged carillon. 'Right then, Ruff, that's me,' she announced, taking off her apron, 'I'm off now but I'll not be long.' She always said that, even if she was going to be gone all day. Dogs were lucky. They had no real concept of time. Only of routines.

She put on her grey hat and her best coat, the black one with the thick fur collar that Steve had long ago bought for her, trying not to notice the well-worn look of it. 'Mother,' Angela had said on her last visit, 'Whenever are you going to let us buy you a replacement for that old thing?'

She had not wanted to seem unkind or ungrateful but, 'Never, Angie,' she'd replied. 'Never. You know I'll not take charity from you nor no-one else. And besides, your father saved up a lot of hard earned dollars for this coat.'

As usual she was one of the first into church, perhaps because she was the one living nearest. She slipped into her place on the pew she thought of as being her own, the one immediately below that certain brass plaque. She knelt down and closed her eyes and said her prayer to God and to herself then sat back on the biscuit thin cushion.

Looking up, she read the inscription, the one she knew by heart…

In memoriam
To the twelve officers and men of the United States AirForce
who died here on Bonnybreck Hill
25th of December, 1945
'In the service of their country and their fellow Man:
And now in Christ's good care.'

She closed her eyes again, the better to remember it: Christmas Day in the morning, sixty one years ago, herself just nineteen. She remembered helping mother with the dinner things after church and the dull *crump* that must have come from somewhere high up on the top, invisible in the falling snow. She remembered people coming out on the street, running around shouting about there being a plane down, up on Bonnybreck. She remembered how she and Mum and Dad had hurried to get up there with thermoses of tea and blankets and things. Half the village had battled up the pathway through those drifts. She'd been so young and so fit and was one of the first to arrive at the crash site. It was awful. As others got up there on the Top they all gathered into small groups, horrified and helpless in the face of the heaps of hot, tangled metal, the already dying fires; and the bodies. All the horror of it.

Triphena had wandered off by herself, crying, seeking nothing more than solitude in the lee of that huge boulder. But that was where she'd found him. He was the only one still alive: Steve, *her* Steve, Lieutenant Steve Solarno, pilot, U.S.A.A.F., unconscious, torn and bleeding, thrown clear by what fluke of physics no one would ever know. She'd covered him with her blanket, shouting for assistance. All at once his eyes had opened and cleared, light blue, and there was the trace of that cockeyed grin and the slow wink. 'Hi, Honey,' he'd whispered, 'Steve Solarno: You some kinda angel?' She'd said she was called Tryphena, adding, irrelevantly, not knowing what else to say, 'It's from the bible'. He'd muttered something about how the good Lord knew it was sure a pretty name before falling back into unconciousness.

But when he'd been discharged from hospital he'd come back to Millsbridge looking for her as, somehow, she had known he would. She had been waiting.

The thunder of the church organ died away. Tryphena used her hankie to dab away the signs of tears as the new vicar ascended the pulpit steps.

Ruff always started off dashing about like some great big puppy but that didn't last long, not these days. As they climbed higher and the pathway got rougher the old boy was reduced to an amble, his breath pluming out into the still, cold air. Before they were half way up he was moving in front of her legs, which had always been his standard way of suggesting it was time to turn back. But she had to get there. She needed to reach the top, to see what was still left there and to think about Steve. Because that was what she always did on Christmas Day. Always, even if the going did get harder and harder with each passing year.

The much corroded bits of aluminium engine cowling were still there, sticking up out of a sparse snow-cover. So were the two, now almost unrecognisable engine blocks with their twisted remnants of propellers. She went over to the edge of the tarn, with the toe of her Wellington boot scraped away the snow. Yes, she could still see it, still down there under the ice and a foot of ice clear water; the oxygen mask with the rubber hose. She wondered how many thousands of times others had seen it, perhaps picked it out, meaning to take it for a souvenir but unaccountably , carefully putting it back. Perhaps not so unaccountably though. Perhaps there was some sense of respect left in this world after all.

Realising that Ruff was not with her she looked around, called out his name, tried a whistle. He didn't come. So unlike him. In dread she stumbled over frozen tussocks and rocks half hidden beneath the snow following his paw-prints. In some peculiar way she knew. She knew where he'd gone and, yes, he was there by the big boulder, the one behind which she'd found Steve, the one where, each year since she'd come back to Millsbridge, she had placed her single Christmas rose. The old fellow was lying down, all curled up as if to sleep. She choked off the scream, the cry for help, knowing at once that nobody would hear, knowing that something inside the dog was giving up. She didn't want to frighten him. So she sat down on the snow with her back to the rock, unfastened the buttons of her coat, gathered up his head and pulled as much of him as she could close in to her. He would normally have objected to such an impertinence, even from his beloved mistress, but not now. Now the only response was this, very faintest, wag of his tail.

'There now, you damn great daftie,' she said. 'I can't carry you back down and no way shall I go without you. I'll not leave you here on your own, you know that. So it looks like we're a bit stuck, doesn't it, old lad?' She took the Christmas rose from the lapel of her coat and laid it down on the snow: for Steve and now for Ruff and maybe for herself as well. It didn't matter. She wasn't cold, not up here with Steve and Ruff, even when she suddenly remembered she'd be missing the Queen's speech. And it wouldn't be long after that, until dark, until *The Great Escape* came on the telly. She closed her eyes. Amazing! She could hear the motor bike, snarling and hiccupping as Steve raced it up and down the German-Swiss border wire. With her usual sense of growing panic she saw the soldiers coming for him, all fanned out across the sunlit fields, whispered, 'Oh, my poor Steve. But you'll get out when it's all over. Like, when the war's finished. They're not going to kill you, not like the others. Put up your hands now. Oh, please, please put them up.'

Steve was looking down at her, his eyes betraying the depth of his concern. Suddenly she realised it was her Steve, not Steve McQueen, and so very, very young again. 'Oh, Steve, love' she whispered, 'I just knew you'd come back.'

Steve said, 'No, it's not him, Grandma, it's not Grandad. It's me, Stephen, your grandson.' The eyes, so very blue, so filled with concern. 'Hey listen to me, you'll be OK now. The reverend saw you starting out. That was just as well. I remembered the way. Let me have old Ruff, Grandma, will you, please? I'll take good care of him.'

'Stephen? You're Angie's Stephen?'

He leaned over to kiss her cheek. 'Right, Grandma. So this is hello. Hell, I'm so sorry about this old boy. Can I take him now, please?'

Ruff's eyes were closed. There was a coldness and there was no life in him. Somewhere else. He'd gone somewhere else. An awful sense of desolation filled her with pain of a strength and a depth she'd not known since this boy's grandfather had himself gone somewhere, over there that day in that other land, in those other hills, and with such equal finality those twenty one long years ago.

She could hear her grandson downstairs in the hallway, talking on the telephone, telling them all about it; 'Yeah, I sat her on the pillion and managed to wheel her back down. … Yeah, she's fine now. The doc checked her over. Don't worry… Right, and I'm going back up first thing in the morning, like I promised. I have to bury the old dog … Yeah, up top where I found her, you know, the place where she first found Grandad?… OK… Yeah, I'll be here for a week or so; I'll make sure she's still OK. 'Bye, now, mother.' Tryphena heard the phone being replaced, his feet on the stairs, the knock on the bedroom door before he came in. 'Hey, Grandma, you're awake. How you feeling?'

'I'll be just fine, Stephen. But I don't know what on earth I think I'm doing here, lying in bed like this.'

'Listen, I'll be working over here for a while. You better get used to seeing me around, if that's all right? Hey, I almost forgot. I have some gifts for you.' He went off downstairs, came back up and sat on the edge of her bed with the packages. She unwrapped the books and the bottle of perfume and the minute pair of binoculars, *'for your walks on Bonnybreck'*, Jemmy had written.

Finally the gift from Stephen himself. She tried hard not to think of the other present downstairs, the big bone she'd wrapped up for Ruff. She'd have to get the boy to take it up to Bonnybreck Top for him. Inside Stephen's parcel was a video of *'The Great Escape'*. She smiled, put her arms around her grandson, gave him a big kiss. 'Thank you all, especially you for this, Stephen. I watch it every Christmas, you know, and I missed it yesterday. Now I'll be able to get dressed and come down and we can watch it together if you don't mind being with an old lady for the evening instead of out chasing the girls? Please?'

He'd bought some cans of beer for himself and with the fire going nicely, a pot of tea at her elbow, she turned down the lights, put the film into the video player and the two of them settled down to watch it. For a while she was even able to forget Ruff. It was better, being on a video, because she could stop it and go back over parts she'd not properly understood before, or the really good bits. She had her hankie out and ready as the end of the film approached. McQueen stopped his motor bike, looked back at the Germans, made up his mind. He twisted the throttle, accelerating away, the engine stuttering and roaring. She watched in resigned anticipation, awaiting his fate.

What? No! She leaned forward, puzzled then astonished. Up and up on his bike he'd soared, flying the wire just like some mighty, god-like bird, standing up on the pedals with one arm raised, fist clenched in triumph, coming down into Switzerland, making his Great Escape. In silent disbelief she replayed that part and again and then again. It was real. She let it play on as Steve disappeared from sight over the green and sunlit fields to freedom, the theme music swelling as *The End* appeared and the credits rolled.

She said nothing but her eyes had filled with tears. Stephen came over to squat down by her chair, take her hand. 'They told you I'm working with Paramount now, Grandma, didn't they? I got to meet the big boss there. Mother told me about what you'd always said and I mentioned it to him and, hey, they let me do it, filmed me jumping the wire on that old bike then cut in the new ending. My gift and their's. Just for you.' He grinned that old Stephen grin; 'And by the way, the big boss said to tell you, Grandma; he said he likes your ending best.'

The End

Many who visit Wester-Ross come to know of the crashed USAAF bomber whose wreckage lies to this day scattered over the hill and in the clear waters of the Fairy Lochs, high above Gairloch. The rubber oxygen mask and tubing referred to in my story is still there, too, last seen. The accident happened in 1945 as eleven men set out to fly home to the USA, their war in Europe over.

An old fisherman - an unusually rich old fisherman - thinks about his own life and about the legacy paseed on to him by his grandfather …

L.U.C.K.

People aren't often disrespectful enough to ask an old man like me, even though most of them would like to know where my money came from. But if they do ask I tell 'em the truth; that it was originally a legacy from granddaddy Mitch. 'Lucky bugger', you see them thinking. Anyway I've never elaborated beyond that. Keeping a secret runs in our family! Until now, that is.

See, it was one night in '72 in *The Royal Albert*, the dockside pub at Eyeby up on the north east coast. I was at the fishing then, o' course, just as my grandaddy'd always been when he was still working. But it was blowing up a right hoolie that night and my boat was tied up. I found grandaddy Mitch in his usual seat by the window in the Albert so I bought the old boy a pint and one for myself, sat myself down and got ready to listen as he rattled on about how the weather outside was nothing compared with the great storm fifty years back when he'd first started out on the *Annie Harvester*. Anyway I liked to hear his stories about the old days fishing mainly under sail. 'Them days, being a fisherman was being a real fisherman,' he says.

'You'll have heard tell about my skipper, Jack McVeigh, lad,' he told me, 'And most of it would be no more than the truth. Best man at sea I ever heard about, him. You know, aside from during the war when I were in the Navy I fished with that man twenty six years straight. Oh yes, Jack

McVeigh and my first skipper, Ross Buchanan, both of them were good, but McVeigh? Well, he were just a natural born fisherman.'

'You got lucky when you got to crewing for him, then, Grandaddy?' I said. We all knew Grandaddy Mitch had made plenty more than a bob or two.

The old man looked at me, suddenly serious, pulled a few banknotes out of his trouser pocket. 'You should know better than use that bloody L word, son,' he says, and he was right enough.No fisherman up there would say the word that's spelled *L ... U ... C ... K.* 'Well, never mind,' he says, 'Here, let's have another.'

When I was sat down again with the pints he leans forward, 'Listen to me; I'm going to tell you what I've told not another soul, not even your daddy, God rest him.' You maybe know his only son, my father, was lost at sea when I were just a nipper? No, well never mind. Fishing's the most dangerous job there is according to the insurance. Anyway granddaddy Mitch, he's speaking real quiet with the gale outside rattling the pub's leaded windows and howling like a banshee when someone comes in, before they could get the door pushed to behind them. 'Since I were just turned fourteen I'd been a deckie learner on Ross Buchanan's old boat, the *Miss Candida,*' he tells me. 'Dave Seymour and Denny Hardaker were Ross's permanent crew. All three of 'em big and strong. Big, big drinkers, too, and well known for their fighting as well. Not welcome in most of the pubs round about here. Ross hated Jack McVeigh, probably because Jack weren't any way afeared of him. Jack won medals in the trenches. Afeared of no-one and nothing were Jack, and no man worked harder at the fishing. That, and his natural way with the sea. He were near always top boat in these parts. When he offered me a full deckie's job on *Annie Harvester* I didn't wait around deciding, but that caused one hell of a bust up between the two skippers. Like world war two with world war one only just over!' He chuckled; 'And all ending up on the night of the big storm of '22 right here in the Albert.' The old fellow took a deep drink from his pint glass, went on; 'See, Jack were the only one used to go out through the rough to fish the slack weather centres in the weather systems. Course, we didn't call them 'weather systems' then; just damn great storms. Skipper, he was able to read them like an open book. *Annie Harvester* would make more money fishing a couple of days like that than in any normal week. Less fish, higher prices, you know that story, lad. But dangerous. You had to know exactly what you were doing and you need that L word even them.' He chuckled, shook his baldy grey old head. 'Anyway, the great storm were just building when Jack comes in here looking for me. I were just sixteen by then and having a drink for old times with my ex shipmates, Ross and Denny and Dave. 'Come on, son,' Jack says, all quiet like. 'We've work to do.' Well, right off I could see where things were headed so I left them to it. Don't get me wrong, I were pretty handy myself, them days, young as I were, but I wouldn't want to take sides against my old crewmates, would I? Later on I was told about the set to. Denny Hardaker made the mistake of pulling a knife. By the time Jack walked off from here all three from the *Candida* were laid out and well out of it.'

'That were one time skip *did* get it wrong,' he says. 'I never seen seas like them and very few has, not in a forty foot stern sail trawler, not and lived to tell about it. The *Annie Harvester* lost her engine one day out. We had to take a real hard pounding. No radios, mind. Not in them days. We spent three days and nights trying to keep her head into the winds under just a scrap of sail. Jack never left the wheel. In the end we had to hold him up in his chair, all of us at it in turns and slapping cold water into his face to keep him awake.'

Grandaddy took a deep drink, put down his pint pot, sat back again, sighing. After a bit he went on, 'Well then, with the worst of it gone we found ourselves blowed right down south, put into nearest port. Lowestoft, right down south. And bloody pleased to get there, I can tell you. The harbour-master used his telephone to tell our people we were safe. But … well, the man had to report to skipper Jack that his father'd died. Heart attack, he said. It were one hell of a blow, was that, coming right on top of what we'd been through. Couple of days later, after we'd had our engine repaired we set off back north. But you know we'd no sooner made fast and Jack getting set to rush off to his mother's than comes even more bad news. They told us Ross and them had taken *Miss Candida* out when the storm was dying down, and she'd just been spotted at first light, up fast on Skean Dhu rocks. They'd seen her all broke up and slipping away. Gone now, they said, and all the crew gone too. Without another thought Jack puts straight back out to sea.'

'The others had been damn quick to jump ashore but I stayed on board with him, so there were just the two of us. When we reached the Skean Dhu's, right enough there were nothing left there of Ross' boat, but it's not too far to Tern Island from there. See, Jack had worked out that were where the tides would have carried anybody still afloat? When we got there to the island, sure enough we spotted somebody - or maybe just a body because it weren't moving, high up on the beach. Skipper helped me get our dinghy afloat. Of course he had to lay off with the *Harvester*, leaving me on my own to pull like hell for the shore.

Denny Hardaker were still alive. Only just, mind, and in one hell of a state. I'm not just talking physical. Those eyes … *Hang on*, I told him. *Just you hang on, shipmate, while I get you into the dinghy.*' Denny mutters, *Oh, Christ, Mitch, you're real We thought you'd all gone down with the Harvester.* Then, quiet now so I could hardly hear him over the surf and the gulls, *Reckon I'm a goner. Hurting bad. Real bad. I've got to tell someone.*

'Well,' Grandaddy says, 'Denny told me then what I've never told nobody, not 'til now; never even told Jack. Nobody.' He finishes off his pint, smacks his lips, looks to the bar but went on, 'Seems like after the big fight Ross and him and Dave had got themselves well drunk and made for Jack's father's house. Ross were certain sure that Jack had found himself a new, unfished trawl line out there somewhere. Everyone were looking for one of those them days. All of us. That's how Jack McVeigh always come out top of the landings, Ross reckoned. He thought Jack's father might know the lines - the chart positions.' He chuckled. 'Of course only paper charts? Weren't no chart numbers and bottom fishing lines clicking up on no television screen in those days, son.'

My granddaddy accepts another pint, takes another mouthful of beer, leans forward. 'Me, I still think because that drunken lot couldn't get back at Jack for what he'd done to them they thought to try it on with his dad. Anyway, things must have got out of hand because Jack's father collapsed. Stone dead. But listen here, before he died Denny said he'd told them what they wanted to know about the unfished trawl line. Still there on that Tern Island beach he told me the three of them quick tidied things up and sneaked off out of it. They laid low on the boat 'til the storm started to ease up then put out to sea, but it weren't long 'til they'd taken to arguing amongst themselves. You know, about which one were to blame for Jack's father? To make it worse, when they got to Jack's father's mark and shot their trawl, inside five minutes they knew he'd had the last laugh on them. Their trawl net come up real tight on a fastener. The old man must have just invented any old position just to get rid. Anyway, up comes the net, all ripped to bits with nothing but a load of rock and weed and bits of old wood in the cod end.' Grandaddy Mitch leaned still closer to me across the table. 'That's when they knew they'd come fast on an old wreck, lad,' he whispers,

'Because one of the bits of what they thought were just rock were a bunch of coins all crusted over. Gold, son, gold.' He sighed. 'According to Denny that's when the real trouble started, specially as they had the drink aboard. Ross said it'd be the usual fishing shares for him as skipper and them as crew, which meant Denny and Dave would get a lot less than Ross. In the end Denny and Dave were teamed up and Ross had himself locked up with the gold in his wheelhouse. Well, the two of them managed to break in and - see, this is how Denny told me it: *Ross got hisself killed*, he tells me.

He tells me the two of them threw the body overboard, tied to an old anchor. Burial at sea, he said. Then they steered by the compass for home meaning to report the skipper lost at sea. Not so unusual in them days. Trouble was, neither of them had much navigation, not much sense neither, going in to land by compass alone and at night. Reckon it were the gold and all the booze done for their bloody brains.

Now, according to Denny, lad, Ross'd rigged the boat's compass on purpose to about ten degrees off. So next thing was, they'd run into Skean Dhu and that were the end of *Miss Candida* and the end of those two as well. Denny died right there on the beach, lad, his hand held in mine.'

'And you never reported what he'd said?' I asked; 'Or about the gold?'

'Nay, lad, never did. Now listen, why d'you think I applied for Navy diver in the last war?'

'Don't tell me: you came back and dived down off the Skean Dhu's?'

He grinned. 'Too bloody right; after the war finished, I did that. Sackfuls of gold coins. Sold them off here and there a few at a time so no-one would take too much notice. And let me tell you something else: the bits of wood they'd trawled up? They were still down there on the wreck of the *Miss Candida,* still fast in the cod end. One of them were engraved with some letters. 'NTA', then a space, then 'LU.' Look it up. The *Santa Lucia* were the Spanish Armada's treasury ship. They reckon she carried upwards of thirty boxes like the one the *Miss Candida* brought up.'

I waited while the old boy drained his fifth pint glass. 'After I finish telling you, it's your round again, son, I reckon.' He winks at me. 'Don't you? Anyway, he says, there must be a whole load more coins out there but just the one off the *Miss Candida* were enough for me. Never went after any more. Fishing with Jack Buchanan were my life, see? I didn't need much more.' The tough old guy sat back, told me, 'The other boxes must still be down there, where Jack McVeigh's father told them that time. By pure accident of course.' He shook his head, took a piece of paper out of his wallet, handed it to me. 'So anyway, lad, this is for you. Do with it well.'

I looked down at the map reference that was Jack's father's L.U.C.K.; now my inheritence. Her Majesty's Treasure Trove? What the hell does that mean here in Barbados?

The End

Commercial fishermen surround themselves with superstitions. They won't wear white socks; don't ever allow a female on board, don't ever use that four letter word for 'have good fortune' for instance. All four of our sons left school early to go to sea. A tough, tough life and at least partly down to me because they all grew up with me in small boats, rod in hand, off-shore in the waters of the Solent. Eventually one of them got himself a small oyster dredger. Sometimes his dredges came up with things of greater value than oysters: barnacle encrusted bottles dated all the way back to 1710, thrown overboard by sailors.

L.U.C.K.

This is an xxx rated story. Lady Margaret McCorquedale is a shareholder in her family's major industrial company. She is also a psychopath and her own psychopathic sister, Catriona. Catriona is the very worst kind of a man killer, one without mercy and without motive other than the sheer pleasure of taking random revenge on the male of the species - one of them in particular. A serial killer clever enough to keep a good few steps ahead of the law - in whichever country she chooses to operate, this time.

Cat's Kind of Loving

Now it's the best bit. She has him as she wants him. Naked, wrists and ankles safely tight-corded to the corner-posts of the bed. He's willing, helpless, spreadeagled; grinning like a silly boy, ashamed of his situation but near to bursting with excitement. Catriona smiles down at him, turns around, bends over to wriggle out of her panties. The man groans. How very predictable. Be happy man, be happy. She places the panties carefully on top of her neatly folded pile of outer clthing.

What's his name? Walter? Yes, down in the hotel bar he'd introduced himself as Walter someone, President and Chief Executive Officer, Fabrikenplast something, rain-water fittings? Yes. 'Sshuuush, Walter, shush,' she whispers. Still smiling, she presses the piece of carpet tape neatly, quickly across his mouth. Now his eyes have opened wide. He's saying something - something unintelligible, naturally. He's shaking his head from side to side. She climbs on to the bed, making as if to straddle him. He stops the head shaking. A curtain of auburn hair from her crinkle-waved wig falls to frame the wide-eyed face below. She can see the good looking young man behind the skin-folds, behind the tired greying of the years, behind all the business meals and the alcohol, behind the lack of physical exercise; behind the selfishness, the greed and the competitive abuse of others. The man's face is flushing now, pink into dull red into crimson.

She's still smiling but her thoughts have turned to uncle George, damned George. Smoothly and very quickly she applies the nose clip, the comical one as used by all the synchronised swimmers; maximum strength spring. How very ridiculous! How Walter really would hate it, looking quite this panicky, this ridiculous. 'I'm sorry about this, Walter,' she whispers, 'But you can blame my unlovely old uncle.' With some difficulty she unstraddles the bulky form now thrashing and heaving away with the usual weird grunts and whimperings - keening, yes, that seems the right word for it; keening. She watches him carefully. The erection is of course no more. Walter's last stand! At this stage most of them just panic but some, like this Walter Someone do their absolute best to think it out, try to snort off the nose peg or use their shoulders to brush it off. Not possible the way she has him tied. Do they think her stupid? None of them ever accept their hopelessness, helplessness. To a man they all bring forward and use up their last reserves of bully boy strength but in the end, just this, this nothing. Flabby and old or taut and young or somewhere in between, all the power and any glory, all the driving sex in them, all of it finished, exhausted, dead. Like you, like now Walter Someone, king of pipes and guttering.

She picks up her glass. The champagne's still bubbling merrily, smells and tastes so sweet and sour and salty. Wonderful. 'Slainte,' she murmurs; 'Or maybe it should be the Austrian: *Petri Haag*'. I don't suppose you would have had too much of the Gaelic.' Herr Walter Someone's right thigh twitches as if in positive response. 'Anyway here's to number seven: unlucky Number Seven.' As she raises the glass, as always there's another quick response, the air now suffused revoltingly with the dead man's evacuated bowel gas.

Catriona hurries with her empty glass into the hotel bathroom to wash it free of fingerprints, DNA , any escaped body fluids, whatever, then to repair her makeup in front of the wall to ceiling mirror. Yes, she definitely likes this particular wig. She'll use it again. The long, random wavelets soften the planes of a face not that young any more but still heart-shaped, small and pale and still pretty even though she says so herself, even with the faint, two inch line of scar tissue zigging and zagging down from the outside corner of her right eye. She supposes Walter must have thought her attractive, even if he'd not actually said it during that one hour conversation between strangers, the atmosphere growing thicker, filling up minute by minute with sexual excitement. His excitement of course, not hers - well, not for real anyway.

George had said she was beautiful, hadn't he? Breathlessly, croakily telling the little girl who owned the original of this face about how beautiful she was and about how beautifully she did the things she was doing. Those secret, exciting, frightening, disgusting things that he wanted her to do. But of course he had also told her how he loved her and even now she feels the beginnings of the tears and of all those other feelings, remembering.

She passes her hands down each side of her body, slim where it should be, not at all slim where it should not; not according to men anyway. Oh yes. In the mirror she sees her body smooth and flawless if you discount the near invisible under-breast scars left by the boob job. Well, you have to have the right bait when you go fishing, right? So where do you look different, Cat? Where do you look worse than when you were thirty?' Or when you were twenty? Or even when you were twelve with George first telling you how beautiful you were? Perhaps around your eyes? Yes, undeniably there is a difference in you eyes, and of course in your expression right now because in it lies the fevered look you can't stand to see for more than a second or two and actually will not have to, for very soon all excitement, all ferocity will have vanished from this face. As always. That much you do know. 'Like you, Sir George, gone like you; because you're next.' She smiles to herself, speaks again. Out aloud; 'Walter here - he really was the last of the random practice. And you, George, you're going to be the first and the only non-random one.' She giggles. Already the face is blanking out.

She takes her time removing all trace of her presence, concentrating even whilst thinking some of the old thoughts about her life and about the life of Margaret McCorquedale, about what happens when things like tonight are finally over and done with and there's no more of this - this ... whatever. She looks up to the mirror again. Catriona's face looks back at her, frowning. Lady Margaret McCorquedale blinks, shudders, does not really much like her sister Catriona any more.

She goes back to the bedside to get herself dressed: nonsense little thong then dark stockings, plain wool skirt, calf length chamois boots; white linen, high collared shirt over bare breasts; country tweed jacket. Yes, Catriona McCorquedale, quintessential high class hooker or well-heeled sex adventuress; take your pick. She's been very careful in here but still she uses the impregnated yellow duster bought especially to wipe over every square centimetre of any surface she might have touched. She hates this next bit, washing any trace of herself from the dead thing that hangs its head between his thighs. Finally, when she's ready to go she removes the nose clip and the carpet tape and the cord bindings in that order, the usual order, then stows them safely in her shoulder bag along with the man's wallet. Another red herring for you, officers. She shudders, remembering the one who'd proven at this stage to be not quite dead, the nose-clip having been inexactly applied. It had taken all of her strength … She shudders again, remembering how he had actually shat the bed even with herself desperately trying to re-apply the death-clip. Quietly she closes Walter's hotel room door behind her, turns away down the vacant, silent tomb of a corridor.

As the elevator opens on to the hotel lobby she's repairing her makeup in a hand mirror. Well you would, wouldn't you, after all the bed exercise? She glances at her watch. Two thirty. The night porter looks tired, possibly even unwell, in any event shows only a simple commercial interest. The sexual predations of his charges have, she assumes, long since sponged up the last of the man's potential for shock. She remembers to speak to him in that heavily Germanic French, tells him where she wants to go. He picks up his phone, calls one in; 'Oui, á l'hotel Beaufort,' he mutters. He replaces the phone, accepts her guilt sized tip with good enough grace.

How long would they have the porter and the taxi man under questioning? How long before the Beaufort and this hotel would be allowed to resume their proper function as night-time retreats for the powerful, the wealthy, the worried, the lonely, the excitement-hungry? Not long. And Interpol would not take too long after that to have Herr Walter safely installed inside their computer program: 'Serial Murders - International - Current'. File; 'Sex Bond', or something more appropriate, some title cleverer than that. Of course they would be discreet about it. As discreet as possible. Neither the families of the dead men nor the hotels in which they'd died, nor businesses like Walter's would want to allow more than the most cursory, most necessary public mention of the fact and never mind the circumstance of these deaths. So very much easier for them with each 'incident' being in a different country, spread over three continents.

She pays off the taxi outside the Beaufort, stands there checking inside her handbag until it has driven off then walks without hurry around to the rear of the hotel. The Renault is just as she'd left it. She unlocks the passenger door, gets in, angles back the seat. She takes off the wig and all the make-up, holds her breath to rip off the fake facial scar. Quickly she removes her clothing, re-dresses herself in Lady Margaret's plain cotton panties; de-emphasising brassiere; nice, conservative silk top; dark grey trouser suit; finally the low heeled business shoes. As she re-applies a minimum of make up, so very different from Catriona's comprehensive works of art, she's checking and re-checking the street. Nothing. She stows the discarded stuff in the brief case. Using the car's vanity mirror she pats and pushes her short cut, greying hairstyle into better shape, turns the ignition key and drives off. Five hours from start to finish and now the two hours back to Dusseldorf in time to drop off the motor, spruce up and breakfast in the hotel, good and ready for the meeting of the Board at nine.

The prim, the proper Lady Margaret McCorquedale is ready for her step-father, Sir George Farlow. With a certain kind of savage sadness she's ready for that man's last hurrah.

Home again. The Board Meeting had followed its inevitable course. She'd known and so had George that there would be no point in fighting it, herself with only the fifteen percent left her by grandfather Mac. After the meeting, by the time she'd been lunched, checked out of the hotel, headed for the airport, arrived home and switched on the PC, today's Board Minute was on-line and waiting:

McCorquedale Publishing Group plc
Minute of an Extraordinary General Meeting of the Board
09.00 11th October 2005: Corporate offices, Dusseldorf
Present: Sir George Farlow (Chair)

Lady Margaret McCorquedale
Mr William Munro (Managing)
Herr Dr Otto Schneider
Mr Leonard H Zachariah

1.   The Chair noted the Apologies from Lord Brentcliffe and from Sheikh Fawad Al-Kharqui.

2.   The Chair expressed his regret in respect of the short notice for this meeting.

3.   The Chair confirmed that the sole item on this agenda was the formal Offer for the Company submitted 4th October 2005 by Messrs Blackstone Wardley on behalf of the bidder, Zendlemann Corporation of New York, USA. Their offered price per share was confirmed at UK pounds sterling 560 (five hundred and sixty) pence, valuing the Company at £235,655,000 (two hundred and thirty five million and six hundred and fifty five thousand pounds sterling) as per the papers distributed to Board Members.

4.   The provenance of the Offer having been ascertained and attested by the Company's legal advisers, discussion focussed on the acceptability and/or otherwise of its terms and conditions.

5.   Mr Zachariah proposed a motion in support of the offer, Herr Scheider seconding. Having taken into account votes by proxy received from the absentee directors the motion was then carried by five votes to one, Lady Margaret McCorquedale the dissenter.

6.   The Chair declared the resolution carried. He would be writing to all shareholders stating the Board's recommendation of the Offer.

7.   The Chair will confirm this action and cover off the matters arising by visit to Zendlemann in New York.

The meeting closed at 11.30.

Margaret switched off the PC, stood up, removed her coat. She was close to tears. 'Sorry, grandfather, everybody. I really am so sorry,' she whispered. 'He's finally done it, the bastard. Nothing I could do.' She poured herself a good measure of the malt whisky, added the usual slurp of water. 'Not yet, anyway.' The whisky smelled and tasted of the clean-running burns and seaweedy shores of the Hebridean island estate in which both it, and she, and of course her sister had been born. Savouring it, glass in hand, she stood by the window looking down on a Princes Street almost deserted this late on a rainy mid-week evening. She turned, lifted the house telephone.

Moira the housemaid had obviously been waiting for she picked up and answered at once. 'Good evening, madam. Welcome home. I hope your trip went well.'

'Thank you. Everything here's fine, thank you, Moira. You can stand down now. I'll see you at breakfast, yes?'

'Yes.' The hesitation, wanting to enquire, not doing so. 'Thank you, madam. Goodnight.'

'Goodnight.' Lady Margaret McCorquedale put down the receiver, pulled the coffee table to a place in front of the fire, arranged a chair to each side. She placed her glass and the decanter of whisky on the coffee table and a second tumbler into which she poured a measure, topped it up with a tiny splash of the good water.

She took her seat. Catriona was of course mow sitting opposite her, as bright and as high class tarty as always behind the blue tinted glasses, the blonde wig, this time the ragged cut one. 'Well, hello, you,' murmured Margaret.

Catriona raised her glass. 'And hello to you. So, 'slainte', my Lady.'

'Yes, slainte.' Margaret sipped at her drink, hesitated., 'I thought you did nicely last night.'

'Practice, M. Makes perfect you know?'

The two of them sat back in silence, each watching the play of firelight amongst the tawny facets of her crystal tumbler, each with her own thoughts. Finally Margaret said, 'Well, so finally it's George, our own wonderful Sir George; and you the dragon, Cat.'

Catriona giggled, nodded. 'Yes, right. But look, I was wondering if I shouldn't do one or two more, after him? You know, literally bury our lovely step-father in the middle instead of at the end of the list? All the better to obscure the trail?'

'Cat, you really are something! We agreed you should do two or three at most and then George and now you're already up to seven and want to kill - to do some more of them!'

'Yes. But I do wish you wouldn't, you know, use that word?' Cat sighed. 'Oh well, maybe we can think about it later?' She smiled her sweetest little girl smile. 'Anyway, next it definitely is our George's turn and, M, I'd like to cut off his dick. You know, afterwards? So there won't be too much bleeding?'

'Oh, do come on! We agreed they all had to be the same, didn't we?'

'Yes, but it's for mother, Margaret. I want to cut it off for bringing our mother to our bed, for making her - you know.' She still couldn't bring herself to use any of the actual sex words. 'Yes, for all that and for having stolen grandfather's Company. He jolly well deserves it.'

'I know he does. Of course but, Catriona, he wins, you see. If you get yourself caught he wins and nothing's better.' Lady Margaret found her eyes awash with tears. 'You promised me!'

Catriona shook her head. Spears of fair hair fell across her face. 'Cry baby, Margaret.' She sighed. 'Oh, but all right; when and where, then, for our dearest uncle George?' Deep within the orange white bed of the fire an out of place piece of stone cracked and spat.

Margaret searched inside her handbag for a tissue. Here was that Walter's expensive, brown leather wallet. She dabbed at her eyes with the tissue then took the wallet, dropped it into the fire, watched as it curled and split, blackened and burned and became nothing, just like its erstwhile owner. The smell was of burning flesh. 'George will be in New York tomorrow for the best part of a week, tieing up his Zendlemann thing,' she went on. 'He always stays at the Manhatten Maritime. I thought we'd go down to Heathrow then fly Amsterdam New York. Using your own passport, of course.'

'Tomorrow?'

'Yes, tomorrow.'

'Jolly good.'

'I'll book us into the Kennedy Hilton.' Margaret thought about it for a moment, uneasy with her sister's light heartedness. 'Anyway, so I'll do the usual. I'll call the Maritime and explain about my back to find out exactly what kind of beds they have. If it's one of those with no suitable tie points we'll just have to wait on another chance.' She took out from her bag the coils of thin nylon cord. 'But if it's one of the ones we know about I'll adjust these accordingly.' She laid the roll of silver coloured tape and the nose-clip alongside the cording. So innocent. So final. She finished off her whisky, stood up, arched her back, stretched out her arms. 'Talking of beds, I'm going to find mine now. Oh, I'm *so* tired... How about you?' Catriona really was attractive with that wide open smile. No wonder they all wanted to follow her - upstairs, if possible. She went around the table to stroke her sister's hair; 'Cat?'

'You're going to ask me again, aren't you?' Catriona said, 'About me and our mother?'

Margaret nodded, her eyes downcast.

'Look, I don't know, M. I really don't. But she'd had enough of it by then, more than enough of her bastard of an ex-gardener; our wonderful sex-father.' Catriona didn't often use language like that. 'But it was all too late. Daddy not two years dead and she's already married to the bugger and he has his strangle hold on our business. God knows, on each of us, too. And - and I think she really might have wanted to end it for all three of us that night,' She looked up. Pin-pricks of reflected firelight danced within her eyes, dark behind the tinted contact lenses. 'It was just your luck - and George's bad luck that he managed to keep a hold of you, M, when mother and I ran off. It was raining. I was so cold. We only had on our coats. I've told you all this. Mother was drunk. She was driving much too fast. I might have been only thirteen but I knew it. She was sobbing, not making any sense. I couldn't stop her...' She lowered her head. Reds and golds haloed around the pale blonde urchin cut wig. A whirring out in the hall preceded the first musical boom of the grandfather clock's striking of the hour.

Margaret said, 'I'm sorry, Cat. I shouldn't have asked you again. Come here, I want to cuddle you.'

Catriona stood up. Lady Margaret McCorquedale put her arms around her twin sister, kissing her face, tasting her own salt tears. 'He had only me after that night, Cat,' she whispered, 'With you and mother - dead and gone. How I hate, hate, hate him.'

Ms Catriona McCorquedale checked into her room at the Kennedy Hilton at nine in the evening, immediately phoned the Maritime hotel. Yes, Sir George Farlow had checked in, they said, and no, he was not in the hotel right now. She washed and changed into the light grey mohair trouser suit, retaining the dark, full, bob cut wig, the one with deep red highlights in which she'd travelled. Finally she put on the expensive, plain glass designer specs.

She took a taxi downtown, walked into the Maritime Hotel, smiled and nodded to Reception, took the moving stairs up to the lounge. No Sir George in there but if he followed his usual habit he'd be here, right enough, sooner rather than later for his night-cap with whichever business friend he'd dined. She settled back with a drink and a paperback, her eyes roving the page, not seeing the words. It took all of several minutes for one of a group of well dined conventioneers to summon the courage to detach himself, walk across to her watched with ill-concealed merriment by his friends. Ricky Shapiro, manager of Whitemark Dental Services (Eastern) really was world class in good, old fashioned, boring arrogance. But he'd do fine for her to practice the New England accent. Margaret had told her; 'You have the gift of tongues, Cat,' and she'd dropped her eyes, laughing. 'Oh Ricky', she thought, considering him carefully over the rim of her glass, hardly hearing his words, you really are the lucky one. On any other night than this…'

Shortly after eleven Sir George Farlow walked in with two older men and a youngish woman. Catriona felt the quick acceleration of her pulse, the sudden drying of her mouth of the hungry lioness spotting the well fed wildebeest. But what about the girl? What if he wasn't intending to spend the night alone up there in his penthouse suite? For a moment George stood there looking for a suitable place, very much the dominant male. The flash of an eye contact. She couldn't help the shiver. Which one the lion, she wondered, and which the wildebeest? She returned her attention to the dental man, realised he was staring at her, awaiting her response to a question she hadn't heard. She apologised, leaning forward to give her new friend a fair view of the promised land, reaching over to touch his hand by way of further compensation before offering him a sweetly smiling 'Good night'.

As she walked out she had to pass close by George whilst hesitating, feeling inside her handbag, ostensibly looking for her room key. He looked up, smiled, nodded. She thought he was going to say something but then both she and the moment had passed. There'd be no problem with the girl, of that, now, she was sure.

Margaret was there of course, waiting in their room at the Hilton with the bottle of malt whisky. They drank a fair amount of it and talked a lot, too, and afterwards clung together, like always; in bed, in sleep, and in their dreams.

In the evening Cat got dressed. 'Dressed to kill', she joked, but Margaret wasn't laughing. She wriggled herself into a thong then the dark stockings, brick red cashmere skirt, calf skin boots; high collared shirt unbuttoned down between bare breasts; country tweed jacket. All the good hunting kit. 'How do I look, sister?' she asked.

'Wonderful,' said Lady M, 'But you forgot these.' She held out the pair of plain glass designer glasses. 'Come here. I want to kiss my sister good luck. And I want to tell her it has to be no different from all the others. No different. Does my sister hear me?'

The dental man, Ricky, he isn't here in the Maritime lounge to bother her. Probably with the rest of them, off to some club or singles bar, looking for excitement. Whatever, Sir George Farlow and company *are* here, night-capping, talking animatedly around a glass topped coffee table.

This time she chooses to sit up at the bar. She orders a gin and tonic, something slow to drink because she doesn't care for the taste of it and hates its perfumed smell. She takes out a notebook, scribbles in it, falling easily into her part as the hyped up socialite remembering something really important like her nails of the hairdresser. She glances now and then into the bar-back mirror; watching and waiting.

It doesn't take long for Sir George to get to his feet, signalling his group's end of evening. They finish with their handshakes and their goodnights and as soon as the others have all gone he comes across to the bar, calls for a brandy and soda. As it's being poured he sighs, murmurs as if to no-one in particular, 'End of a perfect day.'

She looks up, unsurprised. Catriona is never surprised by any approach tactic. She says nothing but puts away her notebook.

'I was wondering whether you'd care to join me? A nightcap?'

She considers her glass, looks up at him with just the trace of a smile; 'Well, thank you,' she says. 'Just a quick one, tomorrow being another day and all that.' The accent feels right; pure Kennibunkport. The barman's a real pro. He's already at the mixing of it.

The greater the self-importance the shorter the time lag between introduction and invitation. Tonight, Sir George Farlow breaks the record. Ten minutes and already she's been made to understand all about his humanity and his modesty in the face of the success, his urbanity and his lovely sense of humour. Most of all she's been made to understand about the man's exceptional virility. In return she's made little secret of her interest in sex, hard sex, and of this brief window of opportunity pending her movie director husband's making it back from the Coast to his wife, Shelley. She has decided to call herself Shelley tonight. She feels the quickening of her pulse as the big fish circles the bait. Sharks? Sharks and lionesses, no wildebeestes. She smiles. He's scribbled something on a tab, passes it across to the barman. By the time they finish their drinks and reach his room the champagne's there, on ice of course, ready and waiting.

Closing the door he says, '*Shelley;* oh, you really are something.' He laughs, expertly attending to the bottle. 'But listen, I think, now that our little disagreement is all in the past we're going to have to stop meeting like this, Lady Margaret.'

'Why? You know you like it,' Catriona says. She hears the unsteadiness in her voice, the trace of a reversion to the Scottish. She takes off the spectacles, sits and bounces on the side of the bed. The bed is the Swanpillow Tornado, just as advised. She takes out of her handbag the four leashes, walks around, clipping them to the posts.

'Seriously, Margaret, why can't we cut out the charades? We don't need it. Not away from Edinburgh anyway.'

She says nothing but badly wants to tell him the truth now. She wants him to know that she isn't cry baby Margaret pretending to be someone called Shelley, that Shelley really is the lioness called Catriona, Cat, the one he thinks died with her mother, his new wife, all those years ago. But not yet. She won't tell him just yet. She unzips and shakes off her boots then performs the usual strip-tease for him, taking care with the folding of her things, with the careful positioning, the slow movements of her body.

Exploding champagne fires out its cork. White foam ejaculates from the neck of the bottle, falls to the carpet, sinks back to a dribble. George laughs, fills up the flutes, picks one up, raises it to his face. 'Anyway, nice one, Mrs Shelley: slainte!'

'Later,' she whispers, 'Come here.'

And now it's the good bit when she has him as she wants him, naked, with his wrists and ankles safely tight-corded to the corners of the bed. She's across and fucking him, riding the wild ride close up to its tumultuous conclusion. He's willing and helpless, spreadeagled, eyes closed and grinning like a silly boy proud of himself, bursting with the excitement of his upcoming orgasm.

She presses the piece of carpet tape neatly, quickly across his mouth then hesitates, fixed by the sudden power of his widened eyes, of the knowledge and then the savagery there, then the fear and all the pleading.

'Now,' whispers Margaret; 'The nose clip. Now!'

'Yes?' Catriona asks, 'Now?' Her tears themselves are the profession of a kind of love, falling, glistening, rolling through the hairs down there on the heaving chest. She cannot believe how very, very hard it is to stay on top of him, how very difficult to do the next thing. She raises her hips, releasing him, and with some athleticism moves up her knees, one to each side of his head, her thighs stronger by far than his neck, giving him a last view of his paradise, of that mother place from which he'd come, into which he would never come again.

'Now!'

The End

Anyone who has sat in enough first class hotel residents' lounges would have sometimes noticed the late night ladies at work. And most company executives would have witnessed in recent years the company takeover frenzy; most often of benefit mainly to the bankers who inspire and feed so richly upon it. Of similar relevance to Cat's Kind of Loving, *one of my colleagues who shall remain forever nameless, (other than to a few of us), sacrificed his family and his marriage to his business. As a result he would go home to an empty house. According to instructions the housekeeper would have left the coal fire ready to light, in front of it a coffee table bearing two large glasses of whisky with two opposing chairs. The man would then be able to converse with himself, moving from one chair to the one opposite as he asked himself questions and gave himself answers about the day gone by and the one to come. Yes, truth can be stranger than fiction!*

Living a lie is never easy. Gordon Wylie leaves home at eight twenty every morning, briefcase in hand as usual, ostensibly on his customary way to the office. But in reality he's wondering how to fill in the hours of the day and worrying when the evil day would come - when Melissa would find him out; would discover that her husband was one of the great army of jobless.

A Ticket To St Nazaire

Fear. Fear of failure, of disgrace, of Melissa. Not here though. Warm, welcoming, respectful. Nine o clock on the dot. Automatic doors clicked, swung open. He went in, tapped some of the snow off his shoes, removed his cap, strode purposefully up to the desk. The librarian looked up over the tops of her spectacles, kindly eyes below soft waves still much more blonde than grey. Forty, maybe? Ten years younger than him anyway. 'Good morning, Mister Wylie. We *are* bright and early today.'

He smiled in return. He was always bright and early. 'Morning, Mrs Wilson. Yes, I've a lot to get through.' She was wearing the obligatory twin-set; the pink one today. He placed his briefcase on the counter, took out a sheaf of papers. 'Now then, here's a tester for you: St. Nazaire. I need a list of citations and medals awarded to British Commandos after the raid on St. Nazaire in March of forty two. Can do?'

'Certainly. Please take a seat.' The conspiratorial look; 'The book goes well, I trust?'

'Yes indeed. At least, that's what I think.' He tried a self-deprecatory laugh. In reality the book was going nowhere: all research, little writing and what there was, more flawed each time he looked at it. He took off his coat and his scarf and his gloves, picked up a copy of The Times, sat down in his usual place in front of one of the computer terminals. He was the reference library's earliest, indeed its only visitor thus far. He wouldn't be on his own for long. When the men's hostel turned out its overnight guests one or two of them would be drifting in, poor devils. For the hundredth time he wondered what it would be like. He'd know soon enough. He shuddered at the very thought of the expected sequence, all the secret panic rising: ATM swallowing his credit card, bank blocking their joint current account, building society foreclosing. Then hello DSS, goodbye Melissa just as soon as she found out that no salary had hit their account this month, discovered how he'd been quietly fired on minimal severance all of three months since and him, her husband, the executive manager found guilty of sexual harassment as charged. Not guilty? Who would she and the world believe, World Chemicals Inc and that silly, lying little Debbie Field or himself, Gordon Wylie, dirty old man?

Hell, never mind! For all the comfort Melissa was or was likely to be he might as well be on his own. He blinked, turned over to the Times' page two but couldn't for any money have told anyone what he'd read on page one. Maybe Jenny? At least his daughter in Australia would believe him. She would cry for him, wouldn't she? Could they take the car? Would they take it? Of course they could, he told himself; and of course they would.

He found the Times sports section. Great news, the mighty Arsenal had won again. Then here came Mrs Wilson; 'It's on the terminal now, Mister Wylie. Copy of the London Gazette for April and May, nineteen forty two. Oh, and you'll find a full account of the battle itself, which was actually begun on 28th March. It includes all the consequential awards for Gallantry. It's in the military history section; D1692.'

He smiled his appreciation. 'That's very helpful. Thank you.'

'It's no trouble. That's what I'm here for. Besides, I feel I have almost as much interest in the Royal Marines as you do by now. After all I've been with you on your book ever since 1664 when they were formed, haven't I? You know, the Royal Marines?' From his seated position his eyes were on a level with her chest. He looked up. She was smiling. She said; 'It'll be Dieppe next, I expect. That's an easy one, Cockleshell Heroes and so on. Oh, the lovely young Trevor Howard!'

'Yes.' For the sake of the cover-up he switched on the terminal, made a series of meaningless notes from the jumble on the screen, suddenly realising almost all of these names would be those of dead men, many of their deaths pre-dating the citations in fact. All that pain, all the dulled metal and long since faded ribbonry. And now? Just dead words. He switched off the terminal and went to find D 1692, took it back to his seat.

'Mister Wylie?'

'Yes, Mrs Wilson?'

'It's best not to leave your case unattended.' She wore her confiding, I'm protecting my respectables against the riff-raff look.

He acknowledged her concern with a smile and a nod, turned to the book and began again to go through the motions, page turning, making notes. Someone had left an old lottery ticket sticking out as a book mark between the pages of the chapter covering the St Nazaire citations. The ticket bore five lines of numbers. He looked at the date. November twenty first last year. He sighed. Another loser. Idly he tapped up the opening screen of the Net, keyed in 'National Lottery,' scrolled through the lists of winning numbers until he found November twenty first: Two months back. It took him twenty seconds to compare the winning numbers with those on the ticket in his hand then to check again and re-check. No doubt about it, four numbers on one line on this ticket were correct. And another two of the lines with three correct numbers. Total due, one hundred and forty two pounds. Wow! Lady Luck had for once decided it was his turn for a smile. Definitely finder's keeper's! He put the ticket in his pocket and went to close the book, noticing that someone had underlined a name in red biro. Just as well Mrs Wilson hadn't caught them at it. Defacing a book was the cardinal sin in here. The underlined name: Lieutenant C.B.M. Boarder-Lacy. He read the citation. The man had received a posthumous Military Cross for exceptional bravery. He'd gone back in the face of overwhelming enemy fire in a vain attempt to rescue one of his wounded men. Twenty three years old and dead, leaving a Military Medal and someone who still grieved for him these sixty long years later. Put another way, dead and gone six years before he, Gordon Wylie himself, had first seen the light of day. He shook his head, got up, closed and replaced book D 1692. Maybe I should have died at twenty three, he thought. Cut out all the hassle.

He put on his scarf and coat, touched his cap to Mrs Wilson, hurried outside and down the hill to the Post office. It was trying to snow again. The lady on the lottery desk put the ticket into her computer, read the result; 'One hundred and forty two pounds.' She smiled at him in the way that people smile at a winner. 'That's an ancient ticket. Just remembered it, have we?' the counter lady asked.

'Yes, that's right.' He pocketed the money and turned around. Melissa was coming in, directly behind him. There was no escape. Beneath the fur hat the still pretty face, lined faintly by the years but flushed pink by cold, displayed a puzzlement rapidly hardening into suspicion.

'Gordon? What on earth are you doing here?'

'Can't stop now, dear,' he blurted; 'Had a bit of luck on the old lottery. Have to get back. 'Bye now, I'll see you later.' He went to move off.

'Wait. There's a man from the bank wants to get hold of you. He says it's urgent.' She grabbed at his arm; 'Where did you get the money from for the lottery anyway? It's not in our budget.'

The counter lady was taking an ill-concealed interest in their encounter. He whispered; 'A hundred and forty two quid! I have to go.'

'Gordon!'

'Let's talk tonight, OK?' He removed her restraining hand and hurried out. Snowflakes like small parachutes landed softly on his face and his coat. Bloody typical. You get lucky one minute and then the next you fall right in it, right up to here in the smelly stuff. He headed back uphill, looking to occupy a couple of hours until he could decently take his place in the Baker's Arms. At least he could afford more than his usual pint and pie today. Or could he? Melissa already knew of his 'winnings' and would soon be back at home entering it into her blasted computer budget. Well, to hell with her budget and to hell with all the upcoming tears. The snow-melt had entered through the hole in the sole of his shoe long before he re-found the shelter of the library.

Mrs Wilson said; 'Back again, Mister Wylie? We'll have to be charging you rent.' He wondered how she would look without clothes, cleared his constricted throat to chuckle his response and removed his cap. His curiosity - perhaps his conscience - had finally got the better of him. He found the local telephone directory, looked up the B's. Amazingly enough there was one 'Boarder-Lacy. C.D.' Address 'St Nazaire House, Church Hill Road, Alminster.' He slipped his hand into his pocket, felt the comfort of the fold of banknotes, shrugged, picked up the Times. The old man sitting close by had the vagrant's smell of wet, unwashed clothing, stale beer.

He couldn't concentrate on the financial pages, nor even on the sports reports. But, well, no harm in looking was there? Damn all else to do. He could walk up to Church Hill Road, buy some of those plastic overshoes in town on the way.

St. Nazaire house stood, semi obscured by a group of ancient yew trees behind the half circle of a snow-covered drive. Two large white vans were parked close up to the front door and a quartet of men were carrying out what seemed to be a well draped upright piano. Without quite knowing why, he scrunched up the drive, asked the baseball-capped man with the check-board for Mr Boarder-Lacy. The man said; 'It's Mrs, mate, not Mr. The old lady's in the drawing room, first right off the hall.' He turned to one of the carriers. 'Christ, George, watch that mirror will you? It's worth a small bloody fortune.'

Before going in he removed his snow-caked galoshes, wondering again why he did so; indeed, why he was here at all. The door to the drawing room was open, inside it a tiny, very old lady sitting up ramrod straight in front of an immense stone fireplace. Her chair was the only furniture left in the room. She was surrounded by packed tea chests and some boxes apparently of papers which she was intent on feeding into the blaze, a few at a time. He knocked, called out, 'Mrs Boarder-Lacy?' feeling more stupid than ever.

She turned to look up at him; 'Yes. Is it about my sister? Oh, that is a very silly question, Mr ...   I'm Catherine Boarder-Lacy. I'm afraid my sister Millicent is no longer with us.'

'Wylie. Gordon Wylie. Look, I'm – I'm very sorry.' He felt even more intrusive, realised he was doing the fiddling with the cap bit. He looked around, noticing the dust-marked rectangles on the walls where pictures had hung undisturbed for many years and the unmarked, unfaded shapes on the hardwood flooring where the carpet and pieces of furniture had once resided.

'Mister Wylie, please do come closer to the fire. Why don't you sit on that tea chest in the absence of a proper seat? You look half frozen. Forgive me for going on with these papers. It's a long job, I'm afraid. I can only put them on a few at a time if I'm not to burn the old place down before they take it away. That would never do.' She turned back to the fire, added a handful of what seemed to be old bills.

He coughed, began again. 'Mrs Boarder-Lacy …'

'Mr Wylie,' she interrupted, 'If it's about debts or money you want I am afraid you will really have to see the young man who is in charge of what they call our 'winding up.' He is Mister Tillock at Messrs Freckleton McGeough, the solicitors. They're down in the town, you know. They have all our bills and commercial papers.' She indicated the fire; 'These are just our personal things.' She looked at him again, smiling; 'Going the way of the two of us, I should say.'

He couldn't prevent himself; 'Look, Mrs Boarder-Lacy, I think this money may belong to you.' He held out the banknotes. And that, he told himself, is why you've never been and will never be what they call a winner. 'One hundred and forty two pounds less twelve pounds for my expenses in getting here.' The galoshes would come in useful if nothing else. 'I think you mislaid a lottery ticket in the reference library?'

She looked at the money without any response. He prompted her; 'The book it was in was about the Commando raid on St. Nazaire in 1942?'

'Oh.' She bent forward, used a long handled poker to stir the flaming papers. 'But please. Please do sit down, Mister Wylie; you're making me uncomfortable. Oh no, that lottery ticket would be my sister's, not mine. Millicent was the gambler of the house, silly old fool.' Her bright eyes reflected the leaping oranges and reds of the fire . Suddenly he realised she was close to tears; 'If she hadn't been so much of a gambler perhaps I could have been allowed to live out my life here in peace. But please do keep that money, will you? Call it your reward. For honesty being the best policy, you know? I'm told there will be sufficient 'proceeds' to pay my Nursing Home fees without recourse to the State. I don't need any of my sister's money.'

'Well, I won't argue with you, Mrs Boarder-Lacy. And thank you very much.' He put the bill-fold back in his pocket, sat down gingerly on the tea chest, coughed, changed the subject before the old lady might think better of it. 'I suppose your house name relates to the war-time action?'

'St Nazaire? Yes, of course. I'm afraid that particular raid was not one of our better military ideas, as it turned out. A lot of boys killed, my husband included.' She sighed deeply. 'We had been married only a little more than two months at the time.'

'I'm sorry.' It seemed such a facile thing to say sorry. 'Your husband was Lieutenant C.B.M. Boarder-Lacy, then?'

'Yes, Charles Bayley Michael Boarder-Lacy. Charlie was my darling, Mister Wylie.' She paused for a moment then laughed quietly, fire-light accentuating the lines and wrinkles around her eyes and her mouth. 'Look, I really don't know why I'm taxing a total stranger with this. I do hope not but perhaps I see a fellow sufferer? Anyway, with Millie now gone ... I can telly you that Charlie was also my sister's darling; Unbeknown to me at the time, naturally.' She dug deep into the next box, pulled out a handful of old lottery tickets, getting ready for the blaze to die down a bit. She turned to him again. He could see some remnant of what Charlie must have seen in her all those years ago. And in this lady's sister? Well, well. At least the young man must have died happy. She went on; 'I'd spend some of that money on a new pair of shoes if I were you, young man. It's not good to be walking around with wet feet in this weather.'

Young man? That was nice. He looked down at the pale saturation marks around the uppers of his otherwise shiny black shoes, knowing that but for the galoshes it would have been considerably worse. 'Why not indeed?' he said, 'And thank you again. It was very nice of you. Please excuse me but I couldn't help noticing … those lottery tickets. I suppose your sister did thoroughly check them through for winners?'

'Oh, I wouldn't know about that.' She threw the handful of tickets on to the flames, watching the flare-up. 'It became an illness, like any other. She had to gamble. It is very odd, isn't it, but I often wondered whether actually winning anything was an irrelevance. We must have kept the bookmaker's children at public schools and paid for his house and pension, of that I've no doubt whatsoever. Never mind, after all she didn't get much in the way of comfort from her sister, I'm afraid. No more than from her sister's husband.' She rummaged in the box, got out another handful of tickets.

He said; 'Would you mind if I checked those out for you before you burn any more of them?'

She shrugged, looked from the tickets to him and back again; 'Please do so if you really would like to.' She handed him the shoe-box. 'And you can keep all the proceeds if there are any, which I very much doubt. Millie was absent minded but she was not senile, you know.'

The removals man with the list looked in at the door. 'About half an hour, Mrs, then we'll need the chair. You want me to call someone to come for you?'

She smiled at him; 'Thank you, young man, but I've made my own arrangements. And I have a little something for you and your crew when you're all finished.' He touched the peak of his cap before retreating, shouting out his orders.

Gordon said, 'You know, you should have all these papers thoroughly checked before you dispose of them,

Mrs Boarder-Lacy. I mean, not just the lottery tickets. I would be happy to do it for you, if you like? Obviously I would totally respect your privacy.'

'That is most kind of you but really, I think it must all go with me. I mean, not actually *go* with me. There is no room in that place for such frippery as boxes of old letters, etcetera. I mean just go away up the chimney as I myself go away through the door. In any case, Mister Wylie, there's nothing of note in here. Nothing much happened after St Nazaire and the baby. Millie and I simply grew old together, hardly even speaking, specially after her lovely daughter had left home to have her own little girl.'

'You have no other relatives? Your niece's husband?'

'There was no husband, Mister Wylie. Like mother, like daughter, I'm afraid.' She smiled sadly; 'And my niece died last year, so the only one I have left now is my niece's daughter, dear, dear Charlotte.'

'Charlotte is coming for you?'

'No, Mister Wylie. She doesn't know about any of this. I haven't told her because if I did she would insist on my moving in with her. And she really does not deserve that.'

'Well,' he hesitated, 'Cannot I at least escort you to the Nursing Home?'

'Thank you, but I wouldn't dream of putting you out. As you can see I have lots of this inconsequential history left to burn. I shall be perfectly all right here until the taxi comes for me. And besides, I want to walk around the gardens this one last time. Sixty three years … '

'I do understand. But it's still snowing out there, Mrs Boarder-Lacy. I would keep by the fire if I were you.' He stood up to shake hands, to bid her goodbye, but on impulse leant down to kiss the wrinkled cheek. He put on his galoshes in the porch, scrunched away on the drive and down the hill, the shoe-box of old lottery tickets tucked under his arm, in that special silence produced only by thickly falling snow.

Safely inside the warmth and comfort of the Baker's Arms restaurant he ordered himself a sirloin steak and chips and a bottle of good Burgundy. Eat, drink and be merry, for tomorrow... etc. It was useless, merry he was not and could not be. He had to go to the place called home and face Melissa. Besides, he couldn't rid himself of the thought of that childless old lady, burning her papers in an empty house ... burning up all her memories.

He took the Park and Ride bus, found his car, drove carefully over snow packed roads. So, home again! Taking a deep breath he turned the key in the lock.

Melissa hit him like a gale of wind from the frozen north. 'Would you mind telling me just what you think is going on? Why aren't you at the office? I asked the man who calls himself the general manager and he wouldn't tell me a damned thing. What were you doing in Alminster today?' She stood in the hallway, blocking his way like a small spike of rock. There was a note of rising hysteria. The tears and the flouncing upstairs would not ordinarily be far away. But this was no ordinary Melissa thing . The woman was seriously concerned for herself, frightened even. She wouldn't be doing any flouncing until she knew what was happening. 'Gordon,' she insisted, 'I asked the silly man why no salary had been paid into our account this month. The idiot referred me to you again.'

Fuelled now by the good Burgundy Gordon, sighed, said, 'Shut up, please, Melissa, will you?' He took off his hat and coat and gloves and scarf, draped them over the stairs handrail. For a moment she was left speechless and gasping at such an unexpected display of insubordination. Before she could say anything more he took her arm, steered her into the kitchen, sat her down. 'Right. Are you ready for this? I've been fired. Months since. I was accused of putting my hand on a young girl's bum. Not guilty. If I did such a

215

thing it would have been accidental. You believe me? No, thought not. Anyway we're broke to the four winds. There isn't any more money. What else do you need to know? Melissa was sitting there open-mouthed. He found the newspaper, went to the living room, sat himself down. It took under a minute before she followed him like a wildcat tornado. He would always try hard to forget the next two hours. He hadn't really known what ranting and raving was all about until that afternoon. He thought he'd seen some crying, but nothing to compare with the floods of tears that came after all else had failed her. He supposed it didn't help that her husband was saying nothing, ignoring her behind the pages of the Daily Mail. But the storm died down as all storms do and then she'd disappeared upstairs and there was silence then some banging and crashing and after a while the sound of her dragging and bumping a heavy suitcase down. 'Goodbye, dear,' he called out. 'Shut the door behind you, please.' But the door opened right behind him and for one moment he expected it, wondered what a blunt instrument to the back of the head would feel like.

All controlled dignity now, she said; 'I am taking the car and my father will pay up the mortgage so the house will be mine. Oh, and when you sober up and go upstairs you will find I have attended to that model railway of yours. I've wanted to do that for years, for all the time you've spent on it. Never mind, diddums, don't cry.' Now, at last, she sounded pleased with herself. She slammed the living room door behind her. The front door, being so much heavier, slammed shut with an even more satisfactory bang.

He took a deep swallow of the whisky, poured himself another, grinning at his image in the mirror above the fireplace. He needed the distraction of the old lady's lottery tickets. Tipping them out on the floor he got down on hands and knees, sorted them all out. There seemed to be ten tickets of five lines each for each twice weekly lottery draw, random numbers. The dates must have gone back to when the thing started eight years ago. Many tickets in the long sequence were missing, presumably burned in the old lady's fireplace. He read on the back of a ticket that claims would be entertained up to a date one hundred and eighty days after the date of the draw. He replaced all the hundreds of outdated ones in the box, put the in-dated ones into a large envelope, the envelope into an inside pocket, called himself a taxi.

One of the Reference Library computer terminals was unoccupied. Half an hour to closing time. Just enough. He keyed himself into the National Lottery, began checking numbers. It took him twenty minutes to find there were no winners in the envelope. He sat back, disappointed not so much for himself as for lovely old Mrs Boarder-Lacey.

Even before she spoke, he knew Mrs Wilson was right behind him. It was the perfume. He turned towards her smile and the fullness of her figure, felt a ridiculous urge to bury his face in it. Softly, shyly she said; 'If you have time, Mister Wylie, I was wondering if you might join me for a drink after I close up here?'

It was all happening too fast. He must have seemed stupid, worse yet, must have appeared to be looking for an excuse to turn her down but, 'Too bloody right, I would,' he blurted out, then, 'I'm sorry, Mrs Wilson. Forgive my bad manners. I certainly would like to join with you for a drink. It's just that today has been one of those days. I was going to the Baker's Arms, anyway. I'm afraid I don't have my car with me though.'

'I have mine. Can I get rid of those for you?' She indicated the pile of lottery tickets, still smiling, 'They're no use. Great Grandma Millie gave me the good ones before she died. There were twenty three ten pounders, seven assorted four line winners including the one I left for you to find. Oh, and one ticket that won me one million four hundred thousand and seventy six pounds.' She laughed openly. 'My great auntie would have given you those,' she indicated the tickets, 'After you returned her money?'

He was absolutely stunned. 'One million four - hang on a minute. You're saying … Mrs Boarder-Lacy up at St Nazaire is your great aunt? My God; you're Charlotte?'

'Yes, come on then. I'll tell you all about it in the pub.'

'Won't your husband mind us, you know, taking a drink together?'

'I could ask you the same but no, I don't have a husband. My family's not strong on husbands. I call myself 'Mrs,' more easily to pick and choose my companions, Gordon.'

'Gordon? You know my name? I definitely need that drink.'

'Of course I know your name. I don't manage a reference library for nothing you know. And yes, I do realise you're a married man.'

He tried a light laugh. 'At least that's one thing you've got wrong, Charlotte.' Her name rolled so easily off his tongue. 'As of today I'm out of work and out of wife.' There, it wasn't hard to say. 'But your great aunt, is she going to be all right, you know, where they're taking her?'

Charlotte showed her surprise. 'Take her? Take her where, exactly? What on earth do you mean?'

It didn't take them long to get there. St Nazaire was all in darkness. Charlotte parked in the drive, switched off. It had stopped snowing. In silence they walked around the outside of the big old house, looking for lights, testing windows and doors, high-stepping through the pristine drifts. By the light of the full moon the old lady's footsteps were easily picked up. They led from the locked kitchen door, went off down the garden path. He took the lead, stumbling, trying to run. There were no returning tracks.

The old lady was sitting on a cane chair in the gazebo. Coatless, upright, small smile frozen, calm in death. Pinned to the front of her dress was a medal; a silver cross suspended from a white ribbon with purple down-stripe. Catherine Boarder-Lacey's very, very own ticket to St Nazaire.

The End

I know how it is to be made redundant, (although not for Gordon Wylie's reasons!) The loss of the corporate umberella is very keenly felt unless you have a wife as understanding, as confidence building as mine. And yes, many's the time we've found in library books improvised and forgotten bookmarks in the form of old cloakroom or Tesco receipts. But never an old lottery ticket - thus far.

49 years old ex-schoolteacher Annette Piper is confined to a nursing home. Her illness has blinded and almost completely paralysed her. However Annette is blessed with near total literary recall. It is this saving grace which illuminates and uplifts her life, and this story, as Annette and her daughter face up to the ultimate decision...

Speaking of Champions

She was having a good left arm day. Whenever this happened, for some reason she could smell everything better. The breakfasts for instance - other people's of course. They'd left the window open so she could also smell all kinds of flowers and flowering shrubs and cut grass and the earth itself, rich and warm and damp after the rain. And she could feel the soft air of summer moving across her face, even hear the responsive movement of the curtains. She could see all the rainbow colours, still marvellous. No shapes, not any more, just the wondrous, ever changing colours. And of course Annette Piper could turn to - could turn - all those wonderful pages of her memory.

Murmur of voices. Door opening: two people coming in, stopping in silence alongside the bed. Who? What might they be thinking, them so bright and tight; 'Hello, mother. It's me,' said one voice. Another pause. 'Matron, I suppose she is being lifted regularly? She doesn't look all that comfortable.'

Ginny! So clumsy. She hoped matron wouldn't be too upset. Matron; 'Of course she is, Mrs Constable, you've no need to worry now, so you have not.'

Annette Piper could feel the tucking in of the bedclothes, the tightening of them across her chest. Matron smelled of flowery deodorant, woman, liquorice, lipstick, antiseptic. She tried hard to say, 'Matron's right, darling, you've no need to worry. No need at all.' But trying to talk with a tongue and a mouth and a jaw that would barely move when you wanted them to … stupid She felt her daughter's finger touch down on her lips.

'Mother! Sometimes I really think she hears and understands and tries to say things. But this gibberish she's started … it's so awful.'

'Oh no, Ginny, it's not,' she tried to say. 'Not awful. Really. Not any more anyway…' But it was no use. Right. Who should I be? Yes, today I'll be Mister James Joyce being Molly Bloom thinking about the loss of her virginity. Yes. And so came the words, so sharp and clear on the page. She gathered herself together, marshalled her best possible attempt at an out-aloud voice, recited; '*O and the sea crimson sometimes like fire and the glorious sunsets and the figures in the Alameda gardens yes and …*' all the words that made her want to cry for herself as she had been, and for all young women. Ginny: 'Mother!' She read on, pausing as little as possible to take breath because James had excluded all the commas for maximum, unique effect: '*…and the rosegardens and the jessamine and geraniums and cactuses and Gibraltar as a girl where I was a flower of the mountain yes and …*' and they'd found each other down by the sea, hadn't they? She and Rafe Morajani, and had hiked together up to the Alhambra which was where it had happened for them, also. She paused, skipped some, went on… '*and I thought well as well him as another and then I asked him with my eyes to ask again yes and then he asked me would I yes to say yes my mountain flower and first I put my arms around him yes and drew him down to me so he could feel my breasts all perfume yes and his heart was going like mad and yes I said I will yes.* Mister Joyce, how wonderful. And for a man. But now this is me, this is Annie Piper being your Molly Bloom. Slow in-breath, thinking her way into it then, 'And I could hear him because he was making those lovely piteous noises into my hair yes and I could see the dark chocolatey sweaty shine on him yes and I could smell his maleness and I wanted to tell him shush baby shush it is all right yes oh yes it's all right now yes' Oh no, Ginnie! You're starting to cry. Just like you, Rafe. Oh, cry baby Rafe! In the beginning was your seed and your seed was made Virginia. Now she could feel the cold wet flannel on her forehead.

Matron, unarguable; 'Will you please just shush up now, Annette. Don't fret, Mrs Constable. It means nothing. Her condition. She will know who you are, I'm quite sure of that and there's nothing in her gabbling to worry yourself. It'll just be her way of talking to you, so it will.'

'But - my mother - she's only forty nine, matron. That's nothing, and ... and she was so lovely.' And there it was, there in her voice, the little girl catch, the appeal for help or for explanation, for someone to understand. And then the switch, typical of Ginny; 'David and the kids. They're outside in the car.'

Annette Piper tried again. 'Ginny, dear, you can't stop up the leakage of your mother's life. You cannot gather up what's been spilled. Nobody can, darling, nobody. It's gone, but it's all right, I'm all right. Oh yes. I am.'

'I can't stand this, her noises. God! I mean... Look, there's no way I'm bringing them in today. I'll just go and tell them to go on home, come back for me at twelve. I think, if we can open the French windows, wheel her bed outside on to the patio? It's such a lovely day.'

Matron hesitates, then, 'Yes? Well all right then.' Resignation at the thought of added work. 'I'll just be away for a couple of the girls.' Doors opening and closing, receding, one after the other.

Annette Piper senses the evacuation of her bladder. A fly has settled on her cheek. Interesting. Stay still. 'Still'? She has a choice? She'd like to laugh, now thinks she can feel the quick march and tickle of the fly's feet. How many feet? She doesn't want to frighten it but has to try out her good today arm. Slowly, very slowly. The fly's gone. She had definitely felt the spring of its legs, the downdraft from the initial whirring of wings. Her fingers touch her face in the place where the fly had been. That's good, Annette, very good. Put it back, now, your arm. That you can move it today, that's private isn't it? But OK who now? Who's next? She scans the hard drive, stops it at that one particular sixth form, the special one with Janine Stone. She looks now along the seven rows of faces. All different, all lovely with their looked after young lady hair stylings, some of them very pretty, some not, but each of them beautiful. And each one of them intent. Looking, watching, waiting for her, expecting the daily demonstration of their teacher's famous total recall. 'All right, ladies, this is Virginia Woolf being Clarissa, that's Mrs Dalloway. Clarissa is here thinking of her home city of London. Are you ready?' Without reference to any printed page she begins the lengthy quotation about the hush then Big Ben striking the hour, irrevocable, and about leaden circles dissolving in the air, about what was there *in people's eyes, the bellow and the uproar; the carriages, motor cars, omnibuses, vans, sandwich men shuffling and swinging; brass bands; barrel organs; in the triumph and the jingle…*She takes another breath, hears a small cough, 'Miss?' Janine, the little red head in the front row. 'Yes, Janine, you'd like to comment?' 'Well, Mrs Morajani, I think that was beautiful, but I think your writing's just as good.' The sudden pale-skin blush. You smile for the girl. 'Oh, I don't think you should compare my efforts with those of Virginia Woolf, Janine.' Giggles in the classroom. Vision of Miss Woolf walking into the river, pockets of her woollen, drape-styled coat weighed down with rocks in its side pockets, the darkening of the day as the waters of the Ouse close over her head. 'Girls. The wonderful thing is this: that we, all of us, *we know* what's wonderful! And do remember this, Janine, creative art is not some kind of a competition.'

But Janine again, challenging, questioning, impressing herself as usual on her teacher and the rest of her class;

'Yes, But when we did Hemingway, he wrote in one of his letters to William Faulkner that writing's like fighting, didn't he? He said there are losers and winners. He said, *'Dr Tolstoi and Mr Dostoevsky were both better than both of us'*. And he said Shakespeare was the all time champion, didn't he?'

She would never know, would she? About whether Janine might have been right about her teacher's writing. And Janine herself, pushy little Janine who would go on to fight for attention and have people listen to her and achieve most of the things her teacher had wanted for herself. Wanted, but evidently not wanted enough.

She'd like to blink back the satisfying tears of self pity but the blink has mostly gone, was one of the last things to go actually, in the same way that, bit by bit, nearly all of her other musculature had 'gone'. Oh, might still sometimes twitch as if in uncomfortable memoriam but gone for sure and forever and gone with them that thing called dignity. Gone, too, her vision and her voice control and such of physical beauty as had been allocated to Miss Annette Piper, ex-Mrs Annette Morajani. Oh yes, and by the by, he, her husband, he'd gone as well. But, she thought, you still have your hearing and most often your ability to smell things and that odd hypersensitivity in some parts of the surface of your useless lump of a body. Most and best of all, Annette Piper, you can think. Your mind, still intact, in toto, sharpened if anything, racing all the time, turning over the teeming contents of that famous memory of yours. You, Annette of Green Leas Nursing Home, you have the blessing of that mind with all things so sharp and so clear across so wide and so thrilling a country, far better travelled now than ever it has been.

How was it for him, Rafe, back now in Spain the last she knew? She recalled Janine talking about Hemingway's champion of champions, Will Shakespeare. White man Shakespeare being the negro general, Othello … *If I do prove her haggard - Though her jesses were my dear heart-strings - I'd whistle her off, and let her down the wind, ... She's gone, I am abused, and my relief - Must be to loathe her ...* Footsteps again. Ginny's voice, too loud, too close; 'Mother, whatever's the matter? Oh, matron, I think my mother's crying!'

Matron; 'No, I don't think so, Mrs Constable. She cannot blink properly, you see ...' Feeling of a tissue wiping away the wetness from around her eyes, down her cheeks, the dribbled corners of her lips. 'Your mother's been, always, such a brave, brave lady. We all agree - no-one here's ever seen her cry, you know. Not properly, so they haven't.' More people coming in now. Girls. Their chattering slows and stops.

Matron; 'Right, girls, one to each corner. I will myself be keeping control of her bag stand. Are we ready ... steady ... go.' Bumping. Unsprung castors not for comfort in transit. Giggles. Swinging round, onwards, burst of super-hurtful brilliance, flung over bedclothes, new darkness muffling matron's voice. 'Sorry, Oh, I didn't think ... Jesus, the sun was in her eyes, just. Why don't we push it over there, under the shade of the apple tree. Will that be suiting you best, now, Mrs Constable?'

More bumping, stop, covers off her face. Gorgeous now, all the colours. She can hear a car changing gears up the hill, and hear pop music. Yes, Neil Diamond: *Jonathan Livingstone Seagull.* And the creaking protest of a departing heron. Must have disturbed your fishing of the pond. Sorry Mr Heron. Up close there is the hum of bees or some other kinds of flying insects. She can smell the apples and she can remember the shape and the colours - the look of it, the apple tree. Russets, she remembers. She wants to break one away, one apple; take it in her hand with its stalk and two tiny, dark green leaves still attached and see it all gold and, well, russet! She can feel the rounded furriness in her hand and against her lips, smell its sweetness as she bites into it, crisp and hard, hear the crunch of it between her closing teeth and her mouth flooding with the taste of it and more, much more than that, she wants, without the slightest hope of doing so, to write down all the words.

Ginny, more cheerful; 'We'll be all right here, mother, won't we? Thank you matron. And Beth, Tiffany. Yes, we'll be OK now. I'll bring my chair out.'

So, Annette, here we go with the hard drive; whish, whirr, stop; '*At first thou gav'st me milk and sweetnesses; I had my wish and way - My days were strewn with flowers and happiness; there was no month but May - '* George Herbert; candle-lit, goose feather quill hovering over the sheet of parchment, corrections done, thinking now, nibbling at the tip of his feather, nib-dipping the ink, going back to the beginning, scripting the single word title, *'Affliction'*

'Mother. For God's sake stop that. Listen, listen to me. I'm going to tell you about David and Sean and Greta. They'll be bringing some tea and biscuits. I know - I know you can't have any but ... I hope you can understand. Anyway, David's been promoted First Captain. He's on the South America routes now. It means Sean can go to Stowe and we're thinking about moving. Oh, don't worry, not too far away ...' and on and on her daughter's voice, adding to the gigatrillion nothing words born to serve some purpose vague and then at once to die. OK, how about Thomas Carew. Died sixteen forty. *'On the Death of Donne.'* No voice attempt now, let Ginny just go on, no need to listen ... *The Muses' garden, with pedantic weeds* - *'Oerspread, was purged by thee; the lazy seeds* - *Of servile imitation thrown away; - And fresh invention planted. Thou did'st pay - The debts of our penurious bankrupt age.'*

'Mother! Are you getting any of this? I've something very important... Mother, please? I'm telling you about Sean. His birthday last week. Six, imagine that!' A hesitation then out it came, all in a rush. You'll never, never change, Virginia. 'Mother, you remember asking me all the time to get you that pill from work and I couldn't? Well, I wouldn't? Oh God, I have it here, mother. It's what you still want? Please say. Oh please.'

Out aloud now; '*...for their soft melting phrases. As in time - They had the start, so did they cull the prime - Buds of invention many a hundred year, - And left the rifled fields, besides the fear -*' Annette Piper felt her daughter's fingers alight once more upon her lips.

'Please, please, mother.'

'*Rifled fields*' ? How very wonderful of you to have thought of that one, Thomas Carew. I found some unrifled ones, too, didn't I? It's just, it's just that I didn't - couldn't - cultivate them. Very slowly she moved her left arm, bending it at the elbow, opening the hand, bringing it up. How dark her lovely daughter's face, imagined now against the light. Curve of forehead, fine arch of eyebrows, pillow lips, high African cheekbones pink on brown, so odd a match with the green of her eyes, her mother's eyes. Now the light slap and drag of rubber soled shoes, probably trainers approaching across the patio paving, her beautiful daughter's gasp, filled up with pointless guilt. The girl with the tray; 'You want me to pour? Ooh, your mum's moved her hand up, hasn't she? They told me...'

Shakily; 'No. Just leave it please. Thanks, Beth.'

'But the lady, she moved!'

'Yes, perhaps she did. Please?'

Annette Piper could almost hear it, almost see it in the clattered down tray, teaspoon tinkling on saucer - the shrug of the shoulders, the smart about turn, the quick retreat. Then the scrape of Ginny's chair legs, moving closer, the drone of an aeroplane high up, going where? going why? Ginny's two cool hands around her own left hand. 'Mother. Mother, did you hear me?'

'Yes, I heard you, darling,' she said. 'Oh yes, I did hear you. How many hundreds of days and nights staring into the many coloured darkness, thinking about it, that little thing you have, imagining it like a pebble in my mouth, waiting for it to break me loose from all these rotten chains.'

'Mother? Yes, I don't know what you're trying to say but you *do,* you do understand! I know you do. I know you know all about it. It'll just make you sleepy, mother. After a while you'll go to sleep and,' there it was, the catch in the voice; 'and then you, you'll dream lovely dreams and for ever. And you won't wake up. And there's no time in heaven, is there, so one day I'll be with you … '

'Yes. But now I don't know any more, Ginny. Pain? Of course, darling, but pain really is nothing, an irrelevance, just some illusory protection device for healthier bodies, you see. But … now, I don't know. I'm not sure if I can leave them, Ginny. All my friends, my champions, all their lovely words, all their places, all their things, all their real people. Nevermore? Truly I'm not afraid, darling girl, and I do know what it's costing you and I'm so very, very sorry. Me living. Me dying. You watching. Your pain. The pill? Well, what difference whether some unconsidered speck of a microbe or some silly little pill to find for me the way out? She needed to make a massive effort, willed the turn of her hand against her daughter's hold, felt the release, the long silence and the waiting, palm up and open. She didn't feel the placing of it there, just her daughter's fingers around her fingers, helping them to close. 'I do love you, Ginny,' she fought to say, and felt the tickle of her rolling tears. The left hand, closed all around its last small cargo, back by her side now. The once again wiping dry of her face.

'Mother?' Ginny's whisper. 'I did see you moving your hand up to your face. You *do* understand! I hope … wait 'til we've gone? Oh, don't worry, I won't be getting anyone into trouble. If they ask me I'll admit it was me gave it you - but only if they ask me, and they probably won't. And they won't do anything to me, anything bad, so don't worry about that.' Now the relieved lightening of her tone. 'I had a letter from Daddy. He said I'm to tell you he went back to the Alhambra but it didn't seem as beautiful as you'd know when, he told me to say. And you should just see Sean, he's getting really big for a six year old. Bigger than Greta already. The other day he …'

'Good girl, Ginny,' she thought. She didn't try actually to say it, didn't want to hinder her daughter's safe retreat. 'Talk on darling, it's not that I'm not interested and I do love to hear your voice but you should be with those you want to tell me about and I should be with my champions, listening to their words. Who knows, perhaps I can meet them now… *To die: to sleep: no more* … She could actually feel it, or imagine it, she didn't know which; the pill, a tiny egg held safe and warm in a nest made by the palm of her left hand. She felt strong, in control, felt for one brief moment the swollen triumph of her youth, the greatness that had lain like a ticking, living embryo within whatever Annette Piper was to be… 'Sean's poem won a school prize. It was about you, mother. He wants to read it you. When David brings them in…'

Annette Piper thought about those word fighters of Hemingway's, the ones who'd somehow got to understand about humanity or at least some parts of it, had understood so much about the cruelty and the beauty of the world in which it existed; those writers who had created and expressed the stuff that would prove stronger, so very much more lasting, infinitely more important than they themselves could ever be. She thought on about the collection of Books, Gospels and Psalms created by all kinds of Hebrew scholars and mystics, champions all, about the gathering together and the rendering of them into so sublime a form of language by a Scottish king and those appointed by him, making one book to out-shine, out-distance, out-champion everything and everyone…

John 1:1 … *In the beginning was the Word, And the Word was with God, And the Word was God.*

' ...They're back, mother. I can hear the car. Gosh, it must be twelve already!' In Ginny's voice a new kind of a desperate, die-cast brightness.

David; 'Hi, love. Hey, it's nice out here, isn't it? Everything OK?' More tentatively; 'Hello mother-in-law.' The dutiful forehead kiss.

Ginny; 'Hello. Sean, say hello to your Nanna. David, where's Greta?'

'Her friend Christine came round. They wanted to go off to play at her place. Hope that's OK?'

'Well ... yes. Sean, why don't you read your poem to your grandmother now? We can't stay long. Not with that great lump of lamb in the oven.'

Sean said, 'You've been crying, mummy. Can I tell it to Nanny on my own, please?'

'Crying? Oh, it's just ... Look, Daddy and I'll take a walk around the garden if that makes you happy. I don't really see why we need to, though. God knows you're not that shy. Anyway, do please hurry.' Chair legs scraping. 'Come on, David.' The catch had wormed itself back into Ginny's throat. Their retreating voices, the shuffling of Sean's piece of paper, Sean clearing his throat, readying himself..

She said; 'Sean, can you understand me? No?'

'What? I don't know what you're saying, Nanny.'

'Oh, it's nothing. Just read for me? Please?'

The boy had leaned in close to her face. She could feel his breath on her cheek, smell the toothpaste and the soap. He was whispering now; 'I've called it, *'My Grandmother Nanny.'* Cough, pause. *'My grandmother Annette is very brave - For God could not her eyesight save — He cannot make her move again - Although she does not cry with pain.'* He stopped. She recognised one of those anxious, small boy silences, giving himself time to assess reactions, think, re-group. *'Now she has to stay in bed all day - So each night I think of her and pray - So I shall write God a long long letter — and I think soon he'll make her better.'* Another stop. The end? Another clearing of the throat. No, not the end. *'She is white and Grandad Rafe is black – And mother says he will come back - My mum and me are brown and yet - We love our white Lady Annette.* That's the end, Nanny. Did you like it?'

'Thank you, Sean. That was wonderful.' She tried her very best. 'I - I much more than liked it. I want to hug you to me, Sean. Oh how I want to do that, to find ways to talk to you. Listen to me, I can help you get to be a champion. My own champion: *Sean Constable, Nobel winner, Poet Laureate.*' She opened the palm of her hand, turned it to let go of the egg. As if in agreement a nearby song thrush released a couple of his sleepy mid-day musical phrases. 'Right,' she said, 'That's decided, then. Give me a kiss now, Sean, dear. I've a lot to think about.'

She felt the hot little peck full on her lips. Had he understood? He couldn't have understood her, could he?

He said, 'Oh, you've dropped your sweetie, Nanny. Can I have it please?'

Annette Piper concentrated all that was left of herself into the forcing up of the left arm, right up, up to her mouth, index finger weak, bent, pointing.

Sean sounded surprised, slightly hurt. 'I didn't know you liked them. Well, it *is* yours. Can you open your mouth for me? Wider please, now, Nanny; they're coming back.'

The end

I have spent hundreds of hours sitting by wheelchairs and bedsides in nursing homes. The courage and resilience of the seriously disabled never ceased to move me, just as the professional detachment and simultaneous kindness of staff never ceased to impress. This final one of my Twenty Bites won a leading UK award for short stories back in 2004.

... and finally: this from whence the cherries came ...

Down in the Dordogne

The rainstorm when it overtakes is big, big,
but we walk on unbothered by the size
or the drum-intensity of its warm drops
and finally at the bottom of this valley, drip-dry
sunheat re-paints the colours of the day
and the outskirts of an old, still sleeping village.

Walking alongside an ivy covered wall
overhung with branches of a cherry tree,
swollen fruits droop, tempting, before our faces:
bunches of them shining, rain-globulated,
butter into high-lit blue-red into magenta, cerise,
framed by dark bouquets of such life-green.

Tight-smooth they are, to my fingers, those cherries:
I taste free rain, bite to the stone
and the eye-closing sweetness of that valley
spurt-sprays taste buds, floods over me,
penetrating every part and corner
and still today my memory.

Bryan Islip

Other works by Bryan Islip:

Non-fiction: *An Incomer's Views ON WESTER-ROSS in 24 paintings, poems and narratives.*   ISBN 978 -0-9555193-0-7

The novel: *More Deaths Than One*   ISBN 978-0-9555193-2-1

The novel: *Going With Gabriel*   ISBN 978-0-9555193-1-4

Original paintings, Prints, Greetings Cards, Calendars etc see http://www.picturesandpoems.co.uk

Bryan Islip: his story thus far …

At time of publication I'm seventy five years of age and resident in the north-west Highlands of Scotland.

I was born in a London suburb but as a boy moved extensively around England according to my father's position within the UK's civil service. An education at Abingdon School in Berkshire was terminated for parental reasons three months short of my fifteenth birthday, and first employment as apprentice pharmacist lasted until my National Service in the Royal Air Force.

At the age of twenty I was a civilian husband and father, wanting to write but needing to embark on a more secure (perhaps more available) career. By my mid thirties, by then proud father to my four children, I had become European marketing director of an American industrial packaging group.

In 1989 I formed my own packaging consultancy and, later on, my own manufacturing business based in Winchester, (England), Bahrain and Saudi Arabia. My first wife passed away after many years of serious disability and later on I married for the second time.

In 2001 I was finally able to 'retire', determined at last to write as I had planned those forty years before. In order best to do so second wife Delia and I decided to re-locate to our beloved Wester-Ross in the north-west Highlands of Scotland. Here, whilst writing what I intend to be high impact, high quality literary fiction I paint in a variety of media and compose associated verse, selling the results as original pictures or in the form of prints, cards etc under the trade name *Pictures & Poems*. See http://www.picturesandpoems.co.uk

Delia and I also run a Bed&Breakfast at our home here in Aultbea. See http://www.aultbeabedandbreakfast.co.uk

Bryan Islip / October 2010

So, that's it. Goodbye now.

Bryan Islip

monotone rendition of a self portrait in oil paint

Lightning Source UK Ltd.
Milton Keynes UK

176225UK00001B/2/P

'My brother never cared a rap who read him. I think he wrote to make things clear to himself. 'Why publish, then?' it might be asked. Well, the expression of our ideas and impressions, even when intended for ourselves, becomes clearer when addressed to others.'

Stanislaus Joyce
My Brother's Keeper

Author's note

I wrote my first short story in 1955 and my second in 2003. In between I gathered enough real life material to spark off many, many stories such as these *Twenty Bites*.

A short fiction is usually an episode in the life of the central character beginning with a dramatic problem. His or her attempts to resolve it only worsens the situation until comes the climactic effort, often unsuspected by the reader. Most of my stories conform; not all of them.

Of course, the way the writer puts together fragments of his or her experience, whether first, second or third hand, to create a satisfying story - that requires practice. I have had plenty of that over recent years in the writing and editing of my two novels, *More Deaths Than One* and *Going with Gabriel.* There's a third novel in the offing but I don't like to talk about it. According to Hemingway, to talk about a work in progress is to handle the dust off a butterfly's wings thereby condemning it a flightless death. A little story all by itself, perhaps. He also wrote …

> *'All good (fictional) stories are alike in that they are truer than if they had really happened and after you have finished reading one you will feel that all that happened to you and afterwards it all belongs to you; the good and the bad, the ecstacy, the remorse and sorrow, the people and the places and how the weather was.'*

One can but try! Enjoy the results.

Bryan Islip
www.bryan@bryanislip.com